WHEN THE SNOW FALLS

ST. JOHN'S SECRETS
BOOK 2

SELENA COLLINS

ENDLESS
ROMANCE PUBLISHING

ENDLESS ROMANCE PUBLISHING

Published by Endless Romance Publishing

First Edition May 2026

ISBN 978-1-963671-06-3 (paperback)

ISBN 978-1-963671-07-0 (ebook)

SelenaCollins.com

To Patrick, for telling everyone we meet that I'm an author and making me feel like a real one at last.

CONTENT WARNING

This is a romance book that explores dark themes. While I hope you enjoy the sizzling heat and happily ever after, there are subjects mentioned or depicted that may be disturbing to some. Please read responsibly.

- Violence
- Murder
- Explicit descriptions of death and injury
- Death of a child (off-page)
- Description of child murder (on-page)
- Mention of sexual assault of a minor
- Abduction and kidnapping
- Explicit sexual scenes, including BDSM
- Law enforcement

Please note that this list is as comprehensive as possible, but there may be some subjects you find personally triggering that are not on this list. Please use your own discretion when deciding if this book is for you.

Mental health matters.

If you or someone you know is struggling with mental health or a substance use disorder, confidential and free help is available.

988 Suicide & Crisis Lifeline: Call or text 988 anytime for 24/7, confidential support from a trained crisis counselor.

Crisis Text Line: Text HOME to 741741 to connect with a live, trained crisis counselor via text.

SAMHSA National Helpline: Call 1-800-662-HELP (4357) for referrals to local mental health and substance use treatment facilities.

Emergency: If the situation is life-threatening, call 911 or go to your nearest emergency room.

Updates to the content warnings for this book after publication can be found on the book listing page at SelenaCollins.com

CONTENTS

1

Never was there a room so cold as the one where love had died.

Alexis stared at the woman sitting on the other side of the table, wishing it wasn't true, but the signs were all there. In her mannerisms. In the way she looked back at Alexis. In the stiffness of her body.

Alexis knew, but knowing something and accepting it were entirely different. She didn't want to accept it. She didn't want to believe it was real, that this was it. Even as the words spilled from Amanda's lips, Alexis tried to convince herself it wasn't real. The sound was like someone speaking underwater, thick and wobbly, and she shook her head against it. This wasn't supposed to happen. This wasn't supposed to be the end.

She rubbed her sweaty palms against her jeans underneath the table, desperate to look anywhere but at the woman across from her. She forced back the tears that threatened as their whirlwind romance played through her mind. A reel of clips: the day they'd met over coffee at Sweet Bea's, their first kiss, the plans they'd daydreamed about as they lay stretched out alongside one another in bed. Their connection was instant, the forever kind. Or so she'd thought.

"I wanted it to be you." Amanda's voice was barely a whisper, and her hand stretched across the table, beckoning Alexis to grasp it. It was a gesture of comfort, but to Alexis, it was a slap in the face.

"It could've been," Alexis said. She lowered her eyes to the ground and took a shaky breath, pulling her arms around herself. She wasn't sure whether she was trying to comfort or hide within herself. Her eyes darted around the restaurant, and her skin flushed at the subtle glances sliding their way, adding a ruddy shine to her light brown cheeks. She tightened her arms around her body, hyper-aware of the feel of the fabric of her shirt, smooth and cool against skin that was only getting hotter and hotter.

"We want different things." Amanda withdrew her outstretched hand. "I want to settle down. I want a family."

"I want that, too. Just not right now."

"Or ever."

"You don't know that."

"You don't either. Lex, I know what I want, and I don't want to keep waiting for you to figure out... whatever it is you need to figure out," Amanda said, her eyes pleading. "It's over."

Alexis shook her head slowly. A tear slipped down her cheek, and she dashed it away with the back of her hand, sniffling and picking up a napkin to dab at her nose. Her throat burned, and her chest was tight as her heart splintered like so many shards of glass.

"I *am* sorry." Amanda stood and smoothed down the front of her white button-up shirt. Always so pressed and polished, Amanda wore minimal makeup and kept her black hair cropped short on one side with a sweep of bangs to the other. She flicked them out of her eyes without a thought. It was a small gesture, a force of habit Alexis loved. Had loved. Amanda looked at her with heavy-lidded eyes that were once dark and smoldering. Now they were cold and aloof. She held her mouth in a tight line, her slim jaw clenched tight.

"Okay," Alexis said.

What else could she say? She had too much pride to beg or to give false comfort and tell Amanda that of course she was fine. She was only tearing her heart out and smashing it under her heel. Alexis ran her hand through the mass of tight curls at her forehead, pushing the thick sweep of it away from her face. She grabbed hold of her glass and took a deep sip of wine as Amanda watched her.

Alexis swallowed. "What do you want me to say?"

"Nothing," Amanda said, but she looked disappointed. Amanda's eyes dropped to the floor, and she kicked her toe against the deep red carpet at their feet. Shoving her hands into the pockets of her pleated black pants, she raised her gaze again and shrugged. "I guess I'll see you."

Alexis raised her glass and cocked her head at that, and Amanda turned around and walked from the room, her pace slow and measured. Alexis couldn't help it. Her eyes followed every step until Amanda was out of sight. She swirled the dark wine in her glass, watching as the yellow lights from above slid across its swirling surface. She looked up when a server stepped up to the table.

"Are you ready to order?" the man asked.

Alexis shook her head. "It looks like I won't be eating after all. I'll take the check, please."

He nodded and backed away as quickly as he'd appeared, leaving Alexis to ponder whether she should finish her wine. She set the glass down on the slick lacquered wood and traced the lines of the grain as she waited to pay.

Could there be a worse way to be dumped than in a room

full of people who knew you? In a small town like St. John's, there was no way she wasn't about to be fodder for the gossips for the next several weeks at least. She couldn't wait to walk through town with her heart and her pride bruised with the hum of a hundred gossiping ninnies trailing behind her. She chuckled to herself, bitter at the thought.

Alexis drained the last of her glass of wine in a last gulp and took care of her bill with the server. She smacked her lips and stood, steeling her shoulders against the whispers already at her back. She smoothed down the front of her black dress and took hold of the crystal point of rose quartz that hung just below her breasts. Her hand wrapped around it tightly, the rounded point digging into her fingers. So much for being a symbol of love, she thought as she raised her chin high, clenched her jaw, and walked confidently from the restaurant. Even if she wasn't feeling confident, she was sure as hell going to look like it.

Let them talk, she thought.

Sliding into her car, Alexis threw her bag onto the passenger seat and started the engine. She gripped the steering wheel with every intention of leaving the parking lot, but a thousand moments flooded her mind and her vision blurred. The weight of the evening pressed in on her, and she leaned forward in her seat, letting her forehead drop to the wheel.

The tears that threatened felt like the force of a raging river behind a faltering dam, but she held them back as long as she could, and when they came, they came with heat and fury. The wave of sadness rolled over her, and because there was no one to see, she finally relinquished and let them. She cried until she was empty, then wiped the wet away from her cheeks and stared at herself in the rearview mirror.

Her eyes were puffy, and the whites around her golden-brown eyes were bloodshot and red. She pushed her hair behind one ear, fluffed the curls that framed her face, and rubbed her fingers under each of her lower lashes to wipe away the streaks of eyeliner and mascara. Sniffing, Alexis looked down at the bright numbers on the clock in her car. It was barely nine o'clock, and she was nowhere near ready to head home for the night. Anger bubbled just below the surface as she put her car in gear and pulled out of the parking lot.

She wasn't in denial that her relationship with Amanda was over—Amanda had made that quite clear inside—but it wasn't what she was focusing on. At the moment, all Alexis could think about was her anger over the way the situation played out. Who breaks up with someone they'd been seeing for that long in a public restaurant? Who does that?!

Unless it was to avoid an emotional outburst. Perhaps Amanda was scared that Alexis would get angry or cry or try to persuade her to stay. The rational part of her brain acknowledged the very real possibility that she probably would've done all three, but she wasn't ready to face that particular personality flaw just yet.

Alexis merged her car into the congested downtown streets. Summer had brought the annual flood of tourists to her little coastal town, and the square was busy compared to just a few weekends before. She put on her blinker and changed lanes as she headed away from the square and toward her little neighborhood a few blocks away. Suddenly, her chest tightened, and she inhaled sharply. Instead of the road before her, Alexis saw a blur of trees flashing past her.

Leaves crunched beneath her feet, and her chest heaved with every rasping breath. Her heart raced, terror flooding her veins with adrenaline. Rocks and sticks tore at the bottom of her bare feet, but she kept running. She could hear footsteps following behind her in the darkness, and they were steady and unhurried. She chanced a look behind her, but all she saw were shadows and the outlines of trees.

Just then her foot caught on a root, and she tumbled to the ground. Her hand connected with something sharp, and she felt the skin tear and blood well in her palm. She cradled the hand to her chest and scrambled on three limbs until a tree hid her. The bark scratched at the clothes on her back, and she pressed her uninjured hand to her mouth to smother the sound of her breathing. The footsteps were closer now—she could hear the distinct sounds of the heel and toe of the shoes coming down on the ground. In front of her, she saw a marshy area of green algae-covered water, a rotting wooden boat sitting at the end of the slimy pool. The footsteps slowed, and there was silence. No sound. Not animal or human. Just an eerie blanket of quiet and darkness all around her.

The flash of a headlight coming toward her and the blare of a horn snapped her out of the vision, and Alexis swerved. She narrowly avoided the car, over-corrected, and swerved again to avoid a tree that grew thick and proud over the edge of the sidewalk. With a yip, Alexis let off the gas and jerked her car to the side of the road. She slammed it into park and let out a loud groan.

She was back in her car, back in the present moment, a blur lingering on the edges of her vision. Alexis rubbed her face roughly, chastising herself for letting her guard down and allowing it to happen again. She could've killed someone! She could've hurt herself again, she thought as she looked down at the jagged scar on the inside of her left bicep.

With a forceful shake, she turned the ignition off and grabbed her purse, sliding back out of her car and heading down the sidewalk with long, purposeful strides. Her heels clicked against the concrete beneath her feet, and she looked around. She wasn't sure where she was headed or what she'd do when she got there, but she didn't trust herself to be in a car right now. The dinner (if you could call it that) with Amanda had shaken her up more than she'd been willing to admit, enough to allow another vision to eek into her consciousness. She couldn't let that happen.

The humid night air slid along her skin like hot silk, and the vigorous walking had her blood pumping hot around her body. It added a subtle glimmer of sweat to her skin. Alexis looked around at the bright lights and neon signs around her, breathing in the sweet ocean breeze that drifted in from the coast. A glance across the street made her realize she'd walked all the way to The Railway, a favorite hot spot for the locals and so named for the abandoned railroad tracks that ran behind it.

Alexis looked up and down the street, waiting for a gap in traffic. When the opportunity arose, she darted across the street and headed into the bar, thankful that it wasn't karaoke night. After the night she'd had thus far, she deserved more than a few cold drinks and the shoulder of her favorite bartender.

2

When she reached the door at The Raleway and yanked on the handle, a blast of cool air and the roar of music playing loudly over the speakers greeted Alexis. She stepped inside and breathed in deeply. It smelled of bodies, sweet liquor, and beer. She loved it. With a shake of her head, Alexis turned to the bar and walked over. She leaned on the cool surface and signaled the bartender.

"A glass of the house white, Ben."

"You got it." Ben grabbed a glass from a rack behind him and a cold bottle of white wine from the fridge beneath the bar. Pouring it in front of her, he asked, "What brings you in here tonight? Mia meeting you?"

Alexis shook her head. As close as she was with her best friend, Mia Clark, she needed to nurse her wounds alone. She still wasn't sure exactly what had happened or what to do about it. Where had they gone wrong? What had she done to Amanda that was so egregious? She couldn't think of a single argument or fight that could've triggered it. There wasn't an instance when she'd forgotten a holiday or birthday. They weren't living together yet, so there was no possibility that she'd missed some important chore. Amanda had simply gone from hot to cold in the span of a few weeks, and Alexis wasn't sure why. Sure, the electricity had calmed a bit for both of them, but that was to be expected. They couldn't live in the honeymoon phase forever.

"Here you go."

Ben set the half-full glass in front of her. He moved off to the other side of the bar with a smile and a nod. Alexis turned to survey the room. It was the end of the week, so friends in small groups filled the tables around a small dance floor, and singles lined the bar. Alexis brought the glass to her lips and drank a deep gulp of the golden liquid. Her eyes scanned the room, but her thoughts were elsewhere. She pictured the night she and Amanda had met—in this very bar, in fact—the dance they'd shared on that dance floor, and the night they'd spent together afterward. Their connection was instant, like setting fire to a pile of dry paper. Only apparently, they'd burned out just as quickly.

"Lex! Hey, how are you?"

Alexis turned to see Harper moving toward her from the other end of the bar. She smiled at the woman, an old classmate from high school, and said, "I'm doing good. You?"

"I'm just fine," Harper said.

"Market keeping you busy this summer? I've seen quite a few houses going up for sale downtown recently. Those yours?" Alexis took another sip from her glass, hoping Harper wouldn't notice how quickly her wine was disappearing from it.

Harper nodded but looked pained. "Yes, that and my cat."

"Your cat?" Alexis leaned in, tilting her ear toward the other woman to make sure she'd heard right.

"Yes. We just got moved in, and she decided to run off for a couple days when I wasn't paying attention to the door. She finally came back, but she'd already gone and gotten herself pregnant."

"Oh," Alexis said. "What are you going to do?"

"Have kittens, I guess." Harper lifted her glass and took a sip of her martini. She pulled out the toothpick and ate the olive, taking care that her ruby-red lips didn't touch either the olive or the stick. She looked back at Alexis. "I don't suppose you want a kitten in the next few months?"

Alexis laughed at the thought of it. "No, not me. How are you settling in?"

Harper's painted lips stretched into a toothy smile, and Alexis almost envied her those perfect pearly white teeth. While her top teeth were fairly straight, her bottom teeth were a jumble below them. "You mean other than becoming a grandma? Great, actually. Everyone is so welcoming. I am glad I know at least one person on the street, though. It's always nicer that way."

"I agree. You're welcome to drop by whenever you want. I'm usually around."

"I'll do that, thanks. By the way, is Amanda meeting you here tonight? I've got a quick question for her."

"No."

"Oh." Harper seemed taken aback, her face caught between confusion and curiosity.

Alexis didn't feel like explaining, but she didn't want to be rude either. Everyone would know soon enough anyway, she thought with a sigh. She might as well rip the band-aid off now. "We aren't seeing each other anymore."

"Oh, honey. I'm so sorry to hear that."

"It's fine."

"Are you okay?"

Alexis shrugged. "I'll be fine."

Harper nodded and touched a hand to her shoulder. Something caught her eye over Alexis' shoulder, and she raised a hand in a quick wave. "There's Brad and Sarah. I'm going to go say hello. Make my rounds. Wanna come?"

Alexis shook her head.

"You sure?"

"No, thanks. I'm going to drown my sorrows in alcohol and pretend all is right in the world."

Harper leaned in for a quick hug, the red lights from the bar washing over her fair skin. Alexis was reminded of the year her childhood dog, Copper, died. It had been their senior year. Harper had crocheted a little stuffed version of him and given it to her to hug whenever she found herself missing the smelly old thing. They'd lost touch somewhere between college and careers, only recently reconnecting when Harper moved closer to town and became Alexis' new neighbor.

But she still had that silly little stuffed animal.

It was funny what you held onto and the memories attached to those things. Alexis was like a wanderer with roots, and she wondered what she would still hold on to when she was old and gray.

Turning her back to the room, Alexis signaled to the bartender again, and Ben grabbed the wine bottle from under the counter and refilled her glass. When she drained it quickly and called him over again, he seemed to sense something was off and leaned his forearms on the bar in front of her.

"Are you going to drain me dry in silence or tell me what's going on?" Ben asked.

Alexis rolled her eyes, but her legs were already feeling a little unsteady, so she lifted herself onto a bar stool and leaned in. "Amanda called it quits tonight."

"Really? Like a full-on breakup?" he asked.

Alexis watched him refill her glass again. She counted in her head how many she'd had so far. One at the restaurant.

Two since she'd gotten here. This would be her fourth in all. Alexis nodded, more to herself and her own internal line of thought than to his question, but the effect was the same.

"Why are you here then?" Ben grabbed a tall glass in one hand and a plastic scoop with the other. He dug the scoop into the ice, the sound of the tiny cubes crashing together even louder than the music for a moment. He filled the glass with ice cubes and began preparing a Long Island Iced Tea.

"I didn't want to go home," Alexis said with an elegant shrug. The thin sleeve of her dress slipped to the edge of her shoulder. Her dress was not quite falling, but anyone attracted to her would be strongly tempted to imagine it slipping all the way down her arm. Alexis didn't notice. She was too busy blissfully floating on the increasing effects of the wine. She knew her problems would still be there when she came back down to Earth, but for now it was lovely to escape.

Turning to Ben with an incredulous look on her face, her brows drawn together in righteous anger, she said, "Do you know why she wanted to break up? Because I don't want to settle down right now. Did I say never? No, I only said right now. But that's not what matters. Apparently, it's now or never. I'm supposed to know what I want right this second or lose everything. Which I did. Because I don't."

Ben murmured in acknowledgment. He watched her with hazel eyes beneath lashes so short and thick that he was often accused of wearing eyeliner. Ben had been bartending here for a decade, had known Alexis for even longer, and he knew when to argue and when to shut his mouth and agree. He could also hear the slight slur slipping into her voice, and he quietly began preparing a glass of ice water with a hint of lemon. He couldn't reverse the accumulated effects of half a bottle of wine, but he could hydrate her so the hangover tomorrow wasn't as bad.

"Here," Ben said, pushing the glass of ice water toward her.

"I don't want this. More wine, please," Alexis said, but her words went to slush at the end.

"Now, darlin.' You know I'm not going to do that. You've still got a whole other glass in there that hasn't kicked in yet."

Alexis sighed and dropped her chin into her palm. "Do not," she grumbled. He raised a brow and opened his mouth, his tongue curled back against the roof of it in a look of disbelief. She rolled her eyes, but a wave of warmth swept over her, and she had to admit he was right. "Alright, alright, but call me a cab, will you? I don't want to make any more of an ass of myself."

"I'll do you one better." Ben turned to a man about two feet down the bar from her and asked, "Hey, Sid, do me a favor?"

"Only if you never call me that again," the man said, his body leaned against the bar.

Ben grinned at Alexis, propped an elbow on the bar, and looked back at the man. "Will you make sure Alexis gets home?"

"Sure, I'm headed out anyway." He straightened himself and moved closer to them.

Ben turned back to Alexis. "Lex, this is Sidney Neal, a detective over in Candler County. He'll get you home safe and sound, and he'll save you the cab fare," he said with a wink.

Alexis' head suddenly spun, and she smiled and nodded gratefully. Maybe she'd drunk a little too much in a little too short of time, she admitted, and on an empty stomach. Genius-level adult right here, she thought as she grimaced inwardly. Alexis moved to stand and looked up as Sidney grasped her elbow when she wobbled. He was taller than she was, but not by more than six or seven inches with her heels on, and she found she quite liked that. Not that it mattered, though.

"Alright there?" he asked.

Alexis nodded and waved to Ben. She looked up at Sidney. "So you're Officer Do-Good, huh?"

"Yes, ma'am. Alright if I take you home? I can still call you a cab if you want me to."

"No, you'll do."

His brows drew together at that, but Alexis ignored it. For now, all she wanted was to remove the dress that was suddenly so constraining and snuggle into the softness of her bed. Even now she imagined how lovely it would feel for her body, languid and relaxed from the wine, to sink into the mattress and curl into her thick blankets. She sighed at the thought of it... and of what it would be like for the yummy detective to wrap his arms around her.

If she were considering inviting him to join her, then that was her prerogative, too. Wasn't it?

3
_____

Sidney didn't imagine this was how his night would turn out, but he supposed there were worse things than pouring a beautiful woman into the passenger seat of his car and driving her home for the night. He walked Alexis through the bar and held the door for her as they left, his hand moving to the small of her back when she walked past him.

"This way," he said and steered her toward a dark sedan.

When they reached his car, he opened the passenger-side door and helped her sit, lifting her legs in and gently closing the door before walking around the hood and sliding in behind the wheel. He started the engine and glanced over. She was struggling with the latch of the seatbelt, so he took pity on her. He leaned over to help her with the belt. The metal clicked into place, and he straightened in his seat, but not before he caught her scent. He smelled the wine, of course, its sweet and tangy notes, but there was also a hint of something floral with a splash of citrus. He suspected it was her perfume or her soap. Not that it mattered. It was intoxicating either way.

He put the car in gear and pulled out into the street. It was still early for most, and people walked up and down the street as they passed. Music played over the car speakers and mingled with their occasional raised voices as they drove past. He glanced over at Alexis again and noticed that she'd leaned her head back and closed her eyes.

"I wouldn't do that," he said.

"Do what?"

"Close your eyes. It might make you sick."

She opened her eyes and looked at him with a raised brow. "Is that so?"

She didn't look like she believed him, but when she leaned back again, she kept her eyes open and forward. Sidney wondered what had sent her into the bar to drink. She didn't look like the type to let go completely or often. She was too put together, too polished to be the type who was regularly fall-down-drunk at the bar. Not that she was that drunk now. Inebriated and unable to drive, yes, but there was nothing sloppy about her.

"So, where am I headed?" he asked slowly.

"Down this street until you hit Maple. Then turn left and into Plantation Gate," she said, the fingers of her left hand tracing circular patterns on the leather of his center console. Her other hand rested over the curve of her belly, atop a black dress that hugged her curves.

"That's an unfortunate name."

"You're telling me. Amanda used to go on and on about the South and its obsession with history and heritage, particularly one side of it. Not that I didn't agree with her."

"Who's Amanda?"

Alexis waved a hand in the air. "My girlfriend."

Ah, so she wasn't single. He wondered why this Amanda

person wasn't at the bar with her. Did they have a fight? One thing that made him such a good cop—if he said so himself— was his natural nosiness, and he couldn't help but want to know more about this woman's story.

"Ex-girlfriend, really. I guess," Alexis said, her voice slurring on the last word. She leaned her head forward to look at something outside the window as they drove past. He heard her murmur something to herself, but he didn't quite catch what she said.

Not single then. That explained it, he thought to himself. He imagined the pair had only recently split, judging from her current state, but he wondered why. True, he didn't really know the woman in his car well, but she seemed like an attractive, reasonably sane person. What had caused the lovebirds to fly off in separate directions?

"What happened?" he asked. He watched her shrug her shoulders out of the corner of his eye.

"I don't know. Nothing. Everything," she said, blowing out a breath through her lips.

She fidgeted restlessly in her seat and leaned forward to turn up the radio. She fell back against the back of the seat with a cushioned thud, and Sidney's mouth cracked up in a close-mouthed smile as he watched. The effects of that last glass of wine were really kicking in, and he was both amused and grateful that he could lend a hand getting her home. Everyone should have a soft place to land after a breakup.

When Alexis began loudly humming along to whatever song was playing, he looked over and shook his head. He might as well have not even been in the car for all the attention she was paying him. He didn't know the song she hummed by heart, but he was familiar enough with the slow rhythm and heartbreaking message. Her voice, slurred from alcohol, soon replaced her hums, and he tried desperately to smother the grin as she belted out the lyrics off-key and out of rhythm.

"Because of you... I guess we'll never know... but isn't she lovely as she walks away..."

Light from the streetlamps they passed streaked across her face. Abruptly, she turned her body toward him, her hands gripping the console between them.

"Do you want to get married?" she demanded.

"I think it's a little soon for all that."

"Shut up. Not us," she said, settling back into her seat but keeping her body turned toward him.

The hem of her dress rode high on her thighs, and he dutifully dragged his eyes back to the road, but not before he got a glimpse of beautifully sculpted legs. Shaking his head, he pulled his thoughts from the gutter. It wasn't very gentlemanly to ogle the woman you were driving home, especially an inebriated one.

Focusing on her question, he said, "Marriage to someone ever? I suppose I'll want to. Eventually."

"Exactly! That's what I told her I wanted. I never said I didn't want to get married or settle down or have kids. I only said I wasn't ready now. Is that too much to ask for? A little time to figure out what I want? Isn't what I want important, too?" She was speaking passionately with her hands gesturing wildly as if to punctuate her words.

"You told that to Amanda? The ex?"

"Yes, who else?"

"Just trying to keep up," Sidney said, taking a turn from Maple Street into her neighborhood. The houses were older and quaint, built in the minimalist post-war style, but they were well-kept with small yards huddled close together. Most were small squares of red brick, but there were some that were slightly larger with long, thick panels of wood siding painted navy or gray or yellow. In the yards of some were tricycles and bikes, skateboards and soccer balls. Stone statues and flowering azaleas decorated others. Nearly every yard was home to an oak or a dogwood tree. The dogwoods were no longer in bloom since summer was in full swing, but they were still beautiful.

"It's this one," Alexis said, raising a hand to point at the house approaching on the left. It was one of the red brick-style homes with a proud old oak standing off to the side.

Sidney turned into the driveway and put the car into park, shifting his body to look at her. "You know, if you're not ready to settle down, then maybe it's better that things are over."

"You're not supposed to bring common sense into this. You're supposed to be on my side where we yell about the people who break our hearts even if we still love them."

"Do you still love her?"

"Yes. No. I don't know anymore." Alexis groaned and threw her arms out, the backs of her hands connecting with a thud against the window on one side and his chest on the other. She giggled and cupped her hands over her mouth, her eyes dancing as they met his. "Oops."

He grinned despite himself. "Do you have any roommates? Anyone who can keep an eye on you tonight?" he asked, rubbing his hand where his chest smarted.

Alexis reached out, leaning across the center console, and pressed her finger to his lips. She was only inches away from him when she shook her head, a gleam of mischief in her eyes. "No. It's just me."

Sidney wrapped a hand around her fingers, drawing them down from his face. Butterflies danced in his stomach, and he couldn't help the pull of attraction he felt. "I'll walk you up then."

He pushed open his car door and moved to open hers, holding out a hand for her. Alexis gripped it and slid out more gracefully than he expected from someone in her state, and they walked up the curving sidewalk from the driveway to her front door. Her house didn't have a porch but rather a small concrete patio. On it sat a bush of some sort (dying in a pot by the door), an old white chair, and a small barrel overturned to serve as an accent table.

With her fingers still twined with his, Alexis dug into the bag over her shoulder and drew out a ring of keys. She pushed one into the lock and turned it until the bolt clicked. Turning around, she sank back against the door and pulled Sidney against her, placing his hand on her hip and looking up at him from under her lashes. He could feel her curves pressing up against him, and his entire system revved. She wiggled her hips seductively against his, and the butterflies in his stomach turned to knots.

"Will you stay with me tonight? Keep an eye on me. You can scare the nightmares away," she said, twining her arms around his neck.

He was sorely tempted, his entire body hot with desire. He let the backs of his fingers trail down her cheek, finding it warm and soft against his skin.

Still, he shook his head. "Not tonight."

"And why's that?" She leaned up and nipped at his lower lip.

"I never sleep with someone for the first time if we've been drinking."

"Is that a personal rule?" she asked with a smile, nuzzling into his hand and pulling his face down until his lips were a breath away.

"You could call it that."

"It's kind of sexy."

"I like to think so."

"Mmmm," she murmured, reluctantly running her hands

over his shoulders and down his chest. He caught her hands in his, his skin tingling where they touched. His heart pounded in his chest, and it was everything he could do to keep himself in check, especially as the damned woman wiggled against him. God, but she was driving him crazy.

"Maybe I can drop by in a few days to check on you, and we'll see if you still want to make me that offer," he said, dropping her hands and taking a heavy step back. She pouted her lips, a playful gleam in her eyes, but she nodded and tucked a tight curl behind her ear.

"You do that then. 'Night, Officer Do-Good.'" Alexis twisted the knob and took a half-step backward into the doorway. Then she smiled and closed the door behind her.

Sidney watched the lights go on in her house, pushed his hands into his pockets, and sauntered back to his car. He started the engine and backed out onto the empty neighborhood road. Even though he had left the woman behind, it didn't seem like she was really gone. His lips were hot where her teeth had nipped, his skin hot where she'd touched. Even her perfume lingered in the car, its lightly citrus and floral scent dancing around his body.

The woman was alluring and drop-dead gorgeous; there was no doubt about that. Her skin was smooth, like silk to the touch. It was too dark to see the color of her eyes clearly, but he hadn't missed the thick sweep of lashes or the way they gleamed with playful energy. Despite his best efforts to keep his hands to himself, he knew enough about the curves of her body to be completely and thoroughly aroused. She also seemed to be headstrong and completely comfortable with her emotions, and he wondered what other fascinating facets of her personality awaited discovery.

But as intriguing as she was all around, she was trouble, the kind of trouble he needed to stay far away from. Sexy, confident, and just out of a relationship. One that he gathered hadn't ended on such wonderful terms. No, she was exactly the opposite type of woman he needed in his life right now.

Whether he would actually stay away from her, though, was still up for debate.

4

Alexis sat on her couch with papers spread across the coffee table in front of her. She was ferociously taking notes on the pad in her lap, leaning forward to jot more notes in the margins of the papers. Her pen flew across each page, moving so quickly that she knew she'd need to transcribe all of this to her computer before she forgot what she'd actually written. The author would receive their edits with changes tracked in a digital file, but she preferred to do at least one pass on paper.

It was technically a Sunday and therefore an off day, but her deadlines didn't seem to understand, and this manuscript needed to get back to its author soon. Everyone was on deadline.

At first, when her phone rang, Alexis didn't even hear it; she was so caught up in her work. When she did finally notice, she looked over to see who was calling and immediately considered letting it continue to ring. Unfortunately, it was her mother, and if anyone knew she was physically incapable of ignoring a call or text message, it was her mother. With a sigh, she grabbed the phone and slid her finger across the screen to answer.

"Hey, Momma," she said, bringing the phone up to her ear.

"Alexis, dear, how are you?" Genevieve answered.

"I'm fine. How are you and Dad?"

"Oh, he's doing fine. Out mowing the yard and spraying for weeds. The man is happy as a clam as long as there's something needs doing."

Alexis nodded into the phone. "Sounds like Dad."

"He'll outlive us all. Are you coming over for dinner tonight?" Genevieve asked.

Alexis shifted the phone and propped it to her ear with her shoulder, her eyes scanning the pages in front of her. She quickly filed through her mental notes as she multitasked, wondering if she'd even agreed to dinner with her parents that night. "No, I don't think so. I'm slammed at work and on deadline this week. I had to bring some work home this weekend."

"You know I don't like when you do that."

"Yeah, I know."

"What does Amanda think about you working all the time, hmm?"

Alexis took a breath and pinched the bridge of her nose with her fingers. She took a deep breath and let it out in a sigh, the air slipping slowly through pursed lips. "We broke up last week."

There was a pause.

"I'm sorry to hear that, honey."

Wait for it, Alexis thought.

"But don't you take too long getting back on that horse. I want some grandbabies." There it was. Her mother's attempt at humor or comfort, she supposed.

Despite that, Alexis knew there was an underlying impatience, as if the closer to thirty she got, the more entitled to grandchildren her mother was.

"One day," she said. Rolling her eyes, she gave up trying to work and have this conversation at the same time. She dropped her pen on the coffee table and leaned against the back cushion of the couch.

"Mmm," Genevieve murmured into the phone. "You know, Viola was telling me just the other day that her son was single. He'd be a perfect match for you. Maybe I'll give her a call."

"Momma, isn't he being deployed soon?"

"He just got back, I'll have you know."

"Please don't call Viola. I have no interest in dating at the moment, thank you, especially not a Navy boy."

"I'm surprised at you, Alexis. There's nothing wrong with a man who serves his country."

"I'd think the family he leaves behind probably feels differently," Alexis said, immediately regretting her words.

"You'd better count your lucky stars that your father isn't in the room to hear that."

"Momma," Alexis said with a sigh, a headache already beginning to pound behind her eyes. "I wasn't insulting Dad. I'm just tired from working all day and a little raw from the breakup. Give me some time, please. I'm not ready to get back on the horse."

"I understand, but dating is a lot like having babies. You're never really ready. Now I've got going, but you call me if you change your mind and want me to set something up with Viola."

"I will. Love you, Momma."

"I love you, too. Bye now."

"Bye." Alexis clicked to end the call and threw her phone to the floor. It landed on her dark green rug with a dull thud.

With a long groan, Alexis rubbed her hands over her face. Every conversation with her mother ended the same way. They'd start catching up all casual and polite, and then at some point the conversation would devolve, and Alexis would endure her mother's subtle guilt-tripping. At which point Alexis would apologize, make up some kind of excuse, and the call would end. Her mother was simply incapable of empathizing with anyone outside of her own mind. Even this time, her mother's entitlement to grandchildren was more important than the health and happiness of her daughter, her only daughter, in fact.

"Well, I'm not getting any more done right now."

Alexis stood, bringing her glass of ice water with her. The cup was cold in her hand, and the condensation on the outside of the cup beaded around her fingers. She walked out onto her front patio, enjoying how the summer heat wrapped her like a blanket outside. Not everyone loved the sweltering summers of the Georgia coast, but she lived for them. She lowered herself into the chair and set her glass on the overturned barrel beside her. Crossing her legs, she leaned back and breathed deeply.

Her little street was busy at this time of day, and she loved it. Kids played across the street and next door, kicking balls and running after one another. A stray cat streaked across the driveway opposite her, taking refuge from their screams beneath a rusty old pickup truck. This was what she loved: the hustle and bustle of small-town life. She imagined there were some who thought it boring and slow, but there was so much life here. You just had to know where to look for it.

Next door, Alexis watched a car pull into the driveway. Harper stepped out, looking as polished and pristine as always. She waved at her, reminding herself to invite her over for dinner and wine some night soon. Usually she'd give Mia, her best friend of who knew how many years, a call, but Mia had a lot on her plate at the moment. Plus, Harper needed a proper welcome to the neighborhood, and it had already been a few weeks since she'd moved in.

Alexis hadn't finished the thought before Harper was running across her lawn in heels chasing her now infamous cat. A beautiful gray, the long white fur of its belly dragged against the grass as it crouched low and scampered across the yard. She imagined the cat was busy searching for her long-lost love, the fly-by-night tomcat who'd seduced her, knocked her up, and then disappeared. It would make a great story. Apparently, males were trash no matter the species.

So says the bisexual woman who trashes men and then still sleeps with them, she chided herself with an inward smile. The irony was rich.

Finally, Harper caught up to the cat and lifted it into her arms, leaning her face close to its ears and murmuring to it in harsh tones. Alexis couldn't quite hear what she was saying, but from the sound and the look on her face, she'd call it kitty discipline.

Alexis watched Harper stomp inside and shook her head. That was why she didn't have any pets, she thought as she brought her glass to her lips. She was just taking a sip when a dark car pulled into her driveway. The driver's side door opened, and the man she remembered as the cop from the other night slid out from behind the wheel. The sunglasses on his face hid his eyes, but still she could see that he was more attractive than she recalled. He walked up to the patio with fair skin just barely touched by the golden glow of a summer tan, his dark brown hair tousled and a touch overgrown.

"Officer Do-Good," Alexis said with a smile. This was a welcome surprise.

"I did promise I'd come check in on you." He grinned back at her, and she noticed he had a slightly crooked eyetooth. Could he get more adorable?

"So you did."

"Well, I'm checking on you now. How are you?"

"I've been better, but I think we can all agree that's the typical emotion after getting off the phone with your mother as an adult."

"I'd agree with that. Do you see yours often?" he asked, pulling his sunglasses off and clipping them to his heather-blue t-shirt.

She shrugged. "About as often as anyone," she answered evasively. She changed the subject. "I didn't try to talk you into bed, did I?"

He shoved one hand in his pocket, propping the other up on a wooden column. "As a matter of fact, you did."

"Interesting," she said. She didn't see the point in being embarrassed. Sex was natural, as was the need for someone when the heart was hurting.

"You're not going to apologize?"

"And why should I? I've nothing to be sorry for."

"Of course not."

"And I'll have you know—" she paused, blinking. "Wait, what?"

"Of course you don't need to apologize. I was only curious that you didn't. I liked it," he said simply. He tilted his head and looked up at her with a flirtatious twinkle in his eye, his grin showing that crooked eyetooth.

"You confuse me." Her brows furrowed, and she let her shoulders fall against the back of the chair with a quiet thud.

"What confuses you?" He crossed one leg over the other as he stood.

"You drove me home without complaint. You didn't take

advantage of an offer of sex because I'd been drinking, and you're a cop."

"What's confusing about that?"

"In my world, those rarely exist together."

Catching on, he said, "Ah, I see. Maybe I think it should be a better world."

"Maybe." Alexis slapped her hands on her knees and stood. "Well, you might as well come inside then before the sun melts us both."

"Is this a repeat invitation?" Sidney asked, following her inside.

She glanced at him over her shoulder and grinned back at him. "Not yet."

She led him through her chaotic living room, waving her hand and telling him not to mind the mess, and into her little eat-in kitchen. It was small but quaint, and she loved how intimate it was. A memory of her and Amanda cooking together and eating at that little table flashed through her mind, and she violently shoved it away. She was not about to pine for an ex, a woman who'd made it very clear she didn't want her, while a perfectly sexy man sat at her kitchen table.

"Want a glass of something? I've got water, sweet tea, coke, and beer," she said.

"I'll take a beer." He dropped into a chair, looking around the room with curiosity and budding appreciation. He liked her style. Cozy with touches of vintage and modern. His eyes settled on her collection of framed postcards on the wall behind the table. "There's so many. Have you been to all those places?"

Alexis shook her head and walked back to the table, her jean shorts making a rough sweeping sound with every step. She handed him the beer bottle and sat down, setting her cup of ice water on the table in front of her.

"Some of them my mom collected for me when I was little. My dad was still in the navy then, so we moved around a lot. Friends or coworkers gave me others when they traveled. I like to collect them, dream about all the things people do when they're off adventuring."

"Do you want to travel?"

She moved one shoulder and tilted her head. "I did it so much when I didn't want to growing up that I'm not sure I want to now. Sometimes I feel itchy, and some days I enjoy having my roots here. What about you? Have you traveled much?"

Sidney cracked off the top of the bottle and dropped it on the table. He took a quick sip, looking from Alexis back to the postcards. "I did some traveling when I was younger, but I found out that I'm a roots kind of guy, too. I came home pretty quick."

"How long have you lived in St. John's?"

With a grin, he replied, "You keep asking questions, and I'm going to have to consider this a date."

"Oh, really now? Since when does getting to know someone mean it's a date?"

"Since that person already tried to talk them into bed."

She laughed at that. He seemed to enjoy the sound because he smiled at her, the skin at the corners of his eyes crinkling. "Fair enough. So, where does that leave us now?"

"I suppose it's only fitting that I ask you out."

"On an actual date?" she asked, trying to maintain the playful atmosphere. She wasn't sure a date was what she had in mind. Maybe some rebound sex, sure, but dating someone? Even casually, it seemed like a terrible idea.

"You know, two people going out together, maybe grabbing a bite to eat and walking down to the beach. Pretty standard stuff around here, I hear," he teased, his blue-gray eyes dancing with humor.

She leaned forward onto her elbow, running her hand over her head where she'd pulled her hair back into a puff. "I don't know about that. I'm kind of..." she said, thinking about the last date night out she'd had, the one where her girlfriend had essentially told her she wasn't worth waiting for, "In a weird place."

"Fair enough," he said, echoing her words from a moment before. "I'll leave you my number instead. Call me if you change your mind."

He pulled a card out of his wallet and slid it across the table. Alexis picked it up, looking over his name and department information. Sidney Neal, she read. She wondered how he'd come by his first name. It wasn't one you heard given to boys often, like Ashley or Kelsey. Though, to be fair, she quite liked when men had such names. Maybe it was the inner rebel in her. She flipped it over and saw his personal cell phone number scrawled across the back in blue ink, each number carefully written out.

"Do you always come prepared?"

"It's a character defect."

"How did you know I'd want your number?" she asked with a raised brow.

Sidney stood and walked his empty bottle over to the trash can, dropping it inside with a clank. "I had a feeling you might, is all."

She made a noise in her throat and looked back at the card. It said he was an investigator. Still a cop, though. She thought about her father, an overly strict, stiff, impersonal, authoritative man. Sidney was likely similar, she imagined. She didn't have many positive experiences with the "man in uniform" types. Never mind that so far this man didn't seem so rigid, but that was admittedly just so far. In truth, she really didn't know him well enough to judge. More, she wasn't in a place to want to date. A quick, rousing round of sex to soothe her hurts after the worst date of her life? Sure. An actual date with someone new? Not so much.

Still, her mouth went dry when he turned and walked toward her.

He had broad shoulders and muscled arms above a tummy that appeared a little soft beneath his shirt, and Alexis imagined it was likely to do with time divided between field and desk work. She wondered if he had any hobbies. Was he a little outdoorsy like herself? Or was he the "let's order in and chill" kind of guy? Did he like to read as much as she did? Or was he the type who always thought the movie was better? Shaking her head, she pushed the thoughts from her mind. It didn't matter because she wasn't meeting up with him. No matter how yummy he looked.

"Well?" he asked.

"What?" He had an expectant look on his face that had Alexis shaking her head, as if she'd missed something.

"Was my feeling right?"

Alexis replayed their conversation in her mind, fast-forwarding through the bits of inner dialogue where she was nearly drooling over him in her kitchen. Grasping what she was pretty sure was his last sentence, she replied, "Maybe, but that doesn't mean I'll be calling you for that date."

"But you might," he said with a grin. Her stomach knotted at the sight of it. That lopsided thing was a dangerous, albeit adorable, weapon. "Thanks for the drink. I'll see you around, Alexis."

He leaned down and kissed her cheek before showing himself out, leaving Alexis baffled and bothered at her kitchen table. How had he reduced her to a virtual puddle by doing nothing at all? Was she that desperate for a bedmate? She considered that. No, she reasoned, she wasn't desperate for it.

She just couldn't deny that a nice little rebound might be just the thing to give her heart a reset. Maybe a one-night stand... or two. Her intoxicated mind had conceived the notion before. Why deny herself such comfort now that she was sober?

Perhaps she'd give Sidney a call after all.

5

The humidity slapped at Alexis the moment she stepped outside her door. It was the kind that made her instantly want to retreat inside and close herself off in her air-conditioned home. As much as she loved the summer weather of the south, the air was so thick and moist today that breathing was like drowning.

However, neither retreat nor surrender was an option today because today was the grand opening of her best friend's book-shop. Loyalty demanded that Alexis be there for champagne!

Or damage control.

It really depended on how the day went. Though hopefully it would be the former. While she was fiercely supportive, she had to admit that her patience was wearing thin. Since Mia's late husband died, their relationship had changed. It wasn't bad, really, or at least not to toxic levels yet, but she felt this chasm widening between them.

Mia was often preoccupied or absent, and Alexis felt like she gave and gave and gave without getting much back. So far, she'd been content to wait it out, to allow her friend to grieve in her own way and in her own time. She'd even nudged her about getting away or making a change. Relationships weren't a transaction to her, but a little more reciprocation wasn't too much to ask.

At least that's what she'd hoped for. She hadn't expected Mia to, instead, up and buy a house, quit her job, and open a bookstore. Still, despite being drastic, those were all steps in the right direction. And maybe it meant that the Mia she knew and loved was finally finding herself again. She missed her.

So despite the summer heat and the humidity, Alexis stepped out of her house, determined to brave the wilds of tourist season and retail customers. Everyone's two favorite things.

She slid into the driver's side of her car, started the engine, and cranked up the air conditioner. While she waited for the air to cool, she rolled down the windows, hoping to clear out some of the overheated air inside the car.

"I swear you could cook an egg in this heat," she said, reaching out to test the temperature of her dash. It singed her fingers, and she yanked them back. Gingerly, she tapped on the steering wheel, grateful that while it was hot, it wasn't skin-melting hot. The air blowing out of the vents cooled finally, and she rolled up the windows and backed out of the driveway.

The drive downtown to St. John's downtown square wasn't long, and Alexis was glad of it. After all the preparations (of which she'd been a part, of course), she was insanely curious to see it all come together. She'd known no one who had opened their own business before. It was all very exciting.

Pulling onto the street, Alexis maneuvered into the first parking spot she could find, noting with pleasure that there were many people milling about on the sidewalks. That had to be good for business.

She got out of her car and walked down the sidewalk. On

her left was a small park area with benches and trees lining the concrete. To her right were the buildings where Mia had located her bookshop. The bricks looked freshly pressure-washed; the signs painted, and the landscaping updated. It gave the street a vibrant aliveness, and Alexis appreciated the care put into her little community. People needed self-care, but so did cities, however big or small.

"You came!" Mia peeked her head out from behind a book-shelf and squealed as Alexis walked into the bookshop.

"Of course I came!" Alexis said. She walked to Mia and wrapped her arms around her in a hug. She drew back and looked around, adjusting the shoulder strap of her small brown backpack more out of habit than discomfort.

The bookshop was exactly how Mia had envisioned it, a blend of modern and whimsical with an undertone of comfort and warmth. Where Alexis stood, there was a conversation-style seating area, and on the other side of it, brown wooden shelves stood in tidy rows facing the front of the shop. Each bookcase was labeled according to the genre it held on its shelves, and there were fantastical creatures and characters carved into the top.

From where she stood, she could see the sides of end caps stocked with books, and more bookshelves facing longways lined an area further back. In front of that, on the side closest to the door, was an area designated as a children's area. Shorter shelves surrounded a small area ideal for children's storytime.

"Mia, it's so beautiful."

"Thank you! I've barely opened, and I must have already rung up five people. I think I need to stop drinking coffee."

"Do you want me to make you some herbal tea? Do you have any here?" Alexis asked, gesturing to the drink bar set up behind and to the side of the checkout counter.

"That would be lovely, thank you. How long will you be staying?"

"Oh, I'm here for the long haul, baby. Who's going to stop people from stealing all these books when you have to take a bathroom break?"

"I don't think that'll be a problem," Mia said. At Alexis' bland look, she laughed awkwardly. "You were joking. Right. Sorry, ha, I'm a little tightly wound."

Alexis held out her fingers and spaced them just a few millimeters apart. "Just a little." She brought a piping hot mug of chamomile tea to the sitting area and set it on a table, gesturing for Mia to join her.

Reluctantly, Mia sat and brought the mug to her lips, blowing on the steam that wafted from its surface. It wouldn't be ready to drink for some time while it steeped and cooled, but Alexis expected it gave Mia something to do with her hands.

The day progressed much the same. Mia moved from task to task like a little hummingbird. Alexis reminded her to stop and rest every so often. Then they repeated the process.

She talked to people who came for the books, laughed with friends as they dropped in just to say hello, and, most importantly, rang up sale after sale. Content to be a part of the hustle and bustle of it all, Alexis explored the shelves when foot traffic lessened. She pulled some to read and others to browse, and she made conversation with those who came to do the same. It was the most exciting—and also the most exhausting—day she'd had in a long time.

"I can't believe how many people were in here today," Alexis said as she leaned onto the counter in front of Mia and handed her a bottle of water. She'd continued to impose her caffeine ban on Mia the entire day.

"I was just thinking the same thing. I must have sold two

hundred books," Mia said with a smile. She looked around, and Alexis happily followed her gaze around the store. There were so many obvious gaps on the shelves and empty displays that Alexis was sure Mia would be busy for hours the following day just restocking.

"I believe it! Sarah and her book club bought up the entire romance display, and your children's section is almost completely cleaned out."

"I know," Mia said with a laugh. "I can't believe it. Thank you so much for being here. I don't know what I would do without you."

Me neither, she thought to herself with a bit more snark than she should, but the feeling was temporary. It was nice to be thanked after all.

"You'll have to—" Alexis stopped mid-sentence and turned at the sound of the doorbell jingling as it was opened. She raised her eyebrows and turned back to Mia when none other than Nick Robinson walked in, big as life.

Nick Robinson was like oil to Mia Clark's vinegar nowadays, though Alexis remembered when they'd been like three peas in a pod: Mia, Nick, and Ewan, Mia's late husband. Despite Mia being, well, Mia, Nick seemed interested in her in a new way. The sexy, spicy kind of way. It was amusing just how off balance he made her, and Alexis couldn't say she wasn't enjoying it immensely. It was about time Mia had someone sweep her off her feet, even if she was kicking and screaming the entire time.

Nick didn't even spare Alexis a glance, gesturing to something on the floor and saying to Mia, "I see you got my present."

Alexis looked from Mia to Nick and back again, both of them having completely forgotten her presence. The air crackled with sexual tension, and Alexis had to fight with every fiber of her not to grin and giggle like a schoolgirl.

"And that's my cue," she said, finally catching Mia's attention with a grin.

Alexis leaned down, grabbed her bag off the floor, and walked backward toward the door. She pointed at Nick, his back still turned to her, and fanned herself with her hands, teasing Mia and only encouraged by the flush that appeared on her cheeks. She even brought the back of her hand to her forehead and leaned back with a theatrical sigh. Nick hadn't taken his eyes off Mia, which only confirmed Alexis' suspicions that she was about to be swept off her feet.

She pushed out the door, smiling happily to herself. As the door slapped closed behind her, Alexis turned to walk down the sidewalk and noticed an older gentleman sweeping the stoop of the next shop over. He had his back to her and was humming along to some piano music playing over the speakers of an old silver radio set on a wooden bench.

"Excuse me," Alexis said politely as she skirted around him.

The man turned toward her; the broom handle extended, and she tripped right over it. She gasped and fell forward, catching herself on the awning support pole. Despite his age, Alexis found that the old man could move. He threw down the broom and was at her side within seconds.

"Are you alright, darlin'? I'm so sorry!" His voice was unexpectedly loud. He grabbed her forearm with surprising strength, bracing his other hand against her back as he helped her straighten.

"It's okay. I'm fine," she said, pushing her hair out of her face.

"Hold on," he said loudly again. He reached behind his ear, and his fingers fidgeted with something. Alexis belatedly realized it was a hearing aid. "Sorry. What?"

"I said, it's okay. I'm fine."

"Ah, that's what I thought you said. I'm glad to hear it, I am. My goodness, I'm sorry about that, dear."

Alexis shook her head and waved her hands. "It's nothing, really. I promise I'm fine. Out of curiosity, though, how were you humming along with your hearing aids turned down?"

"Oh, that. The car noise hurts my ears. I turn them down when it's busy, but I know the songs by heart, so it doesn't bother me not to hear the words. As long as I can hear the music."

Interested now, Alexis said, "You know these songs by heart?" She could barely remember the lyrics to her favorite modern-day songs and was fascinated that he could hum right away with a song he could barely even hear.

"I wrote it."

"You wrote this?"

"Yes, ma'am. Back in my piano teaching days. In fact, I still have the piano I taught on back in the shop. Can't bear to part with it."

"I can imagine," she said, taking a moment to look more closely over his shoulder at his shop. She couldn't see too well inside, maybe some furniture and a few bookshelves. A large sign on the door proclaimed it to be an antique shop.

"I'm Alan," he said, holding out a hand.

Alexis took it and shook his hand. She noticed he held her hand firm, but his handshake was gentle. It was an interesting combination. "Alexis Donnely. Are you the Baker who owns that place?"

Alexis pointed at the sign over his shop that read, "Baker's Antiques."

"The very same," he said.

"Well, it was lovely to meet you, Alan Baker."

"Same to you, Miss Alexis...?"

"Donnely. Alexis Donnely."

"A pleasure to meet you, Miss Alexis Donnely. You don't be a stranger now."

"I won't. Have a good day."

Alexis walked down the street and wondered what she'd do with the rest of her day. She'd expected to go out for celebratory drinks with Mia later, or maybe grab some dinner together. That clearly wasn't happening—which was for the best! She was not mad that her unspoken plans had changed. She hoped her friend was getting laid at this very moment, she thought with a laugh.

But it left her with a void of time to fill. She supposed she could go home and read. It might be nice to pick up a book for pleasure, for a change. As much reading as she did as a book editor, it wasn't for pleasure. She was always on, so to speak, marking edits, jotting down feedback, that kind of thing. It was rarely a relaxing event.

After being surrounded by books all day, falling into one for no one else but herself didn't seem half bad. She could grab some wine on her way home and choose a book from the handful she'd ended up buying for herself at the bookstore today. There was even one, *The Company Courtesan*, that seemed interesting.

She'd just reached her car when her phone rang. She dug it out of her bag and looked down at the name. With a barely contained groan, she realized it was her mother, and there was only one thing her mother would call her about at this time on a Saturday night.

A damn blind date.

6

Alexis braced herself and answered the phone. "Hi mom," she said as politely as possible. She didn't quite succeed at keeping her voice natural, but it was the best she could do without more preparation.

"Good evening, dear. I only have a moment, but I have the best news," Genevieve said, and Alexis could hear her smile through the phone.

Alexis closed her eyes and pinched her nose, inhaling deeply. She could predict her mother's next words, could feel the headache already brewing behind her eyes. "What's that?"

"I just got off the phone with Viola, and her son is free tonight. Isn't that lovely news?"

"The military guy I told you I wasn't interested in?"

"Oh, hush up. You can't keep taking your sweet time about all this. I'm giving you a nudge, that's all. All you have to do is pretty yourself up and go to Mary's tonight. Hunter will meet you at seven sharp."

"He has a name now. I was worried we'd just be referring to

him as my stud," Alexis snapped, taking a sharp, shallow breath and leaning her head against the glass window. She picked at the stitching on the steering wheel in front of her, wondering why she'd even answered the phone, why she always answered the phone.

"Don't be crude," Genevieve snapped back. "And don't you go lollygagging around. He's a sweet boy, and I didn't raise you to keep a man waiting."

"No, you didn't," she murmured, pulling at the string she'd loosened. She thought of all the times they'd marched along to her father's hurried but precise tune, all the stories she heard of her mother's girlhood aspirations ground to a halt the day she'd walked down that aisle. Alexis didn't want to wish herself unborn, but she wondered what her life would've been like if her mother hadn't chosen to march to someone else's drum. What would their relationship be like without her father at the helm? Would she have even been born at all?

"I certainly did not," Genevieve was saying. More words followed, but Alexis stopped listening. Nothing good would come out of it anyway, and the best she could do now was wait until her mother ran out of steam. Alexis could tolerate a lot, and she felt duty-bound to exit the conversation. Respectfully, of course. But her patience was wearing thin.

It seemed every time she spoke with her mother, she was being pushed in a direction she didn't want to go. How long before she couldn't stand to be pushed any longer?

She sighed deeply, keeping her voice flat and calm. "Momma, I have no intention of meeting Hunter or going on a blind date with him or any other friends' sons you fix me up with. Now or ever."

"That's nonsense. Of course, you'll go out with Hunter. The two of you will get along like peas and carrots. I know it."

"No. I'm not going, Momma. I mean it."

"What am I supposed to say to Viola then? I told her you'd be there." Her mother's voice sharpened as she laid on the guilt like someone spreading jam on biscuits.

"I don't know. That I'm not interested, maybe?"

"That's enough, Alexis Marie. How are you going to meet someone if you don't put yourself out there? How am I supposed to have grandbabies if you don't stop fooling around and marry yourself a man?"

And there it was. There was the unspoken thing always hovering at the edges of these conversations with her mother.

When she'd mentioned being attracted to women as well as men as a teenager, her mother's response had been, "Now, Alexis, is that really information you want everyone to know about you?"

She'd left the room as quickly as she could and cried herself to sleep that night. Never had her sexuality been anything more than tolerated, her mother always hoping the phase would pass. That she'd settle down with a man and make babies like a good little wife. Not that Alexis was against marriage to men as a rule. She considered herself an equal-opportunity lover. But tolerance wasn't acceptance, and it stung that her parents' love was conditional.

"I don't exist as a breeder for your grandchildren, and I don't even know if I want them at all. I might go childless just to spite you. Who knows?" Alexis said, throwing her hands up.

She shifted her grip on the phone in her hand, looking out across the park outside her window. A bird flew across the sky, followed by two, three, five more. They danced with each other in the air, twirling and spinning freely around one another. Never had Alexis wanted anything more than to fly like that. She didn't need to soar away or leave her home for far-off adventures. She wanted only to dance through the sky.

"Don't you talk like that, young lady. Now I've dealt with a lot from you, and I've done my best to be patient while you dragged your feet, but you're an adult now, and you've got to start acting like one."

"Which means becoming a broodmare and finding a good sperm donor. Thanks, Momma. Let's do this again soon."

And with that, Alexis hung up the phone, then switched it off completely.

She'd turn it back on in a few hours to an endless string of angry text messages and voicemails, and she'd dutifully respond to them and apologize to her mother for being rude. But not right now. For right now, she simply leaned forward and laid her forehead on the steering wheel.

It was no use trying to convince her mother of anything that didn't strictly fall within her defined view of the world and everyone's duties within it. Her parents were well matched in that way, both walking around carrying a bucket with a top dotted with round holes. And she was the square peg.

It was why she'd never really fit in or been accepted for who she was in her own family. Rather than carve a new hole for her, their solution was to shave down her sides. To make her fit.

Without thinking, Alexis took a deep breath and drove out of town. She took the scenic route, giving herself ample time to choose another direction or find a new destination, but she didn't know anyone else who would understand, and before long, she was pulling into Amanda's driveway. She didn't know whether she was relieved or terrified that Amanda's car was also in the driveway.

"At least she doesn't have company," Alexis muttered aloud.

She stepped out of the car and shoved her hands into her pockets, walking up the hill to the house atop it. The garage door was open, and Alexis could see cardboard boxes stacked on top of one another. Dozens of them.

Her brow furrowed, but she kept walking to the front door, pressing the doorbell and kicking the toe of her sandals against the wooden boards of the porch as she waited. She was only standing there a few moments before Amanda opened the door. She looked surprised, as if she'd opened it without looking at who was on the other side. Inside, Alexis saw more cardboard boxes stacked behind her.

Amanda stayed behind the screen door and asked, "What are you doing here?"

Alexis wanted to spill it all, every emotion she'd had during the conversation with her mother, every word they'd spoken. Once upon a time, she would've. She would've unloaded all of that baggage and then wrapped herself up in love and let Amanda soothe away the hurt. Now, she wasn't sure what to do. She wasn't even sure why she'd come here.

"I wanted to talk to you," Alexis heard herself say.

"We don't have anything left to talk about. I have a box of your stuff, though. I was going to call you and see when I could drop it off, but I can give it to you now."

Alexis nodded. "Thanks."

"You can come inside while I go grab it." Amanda hesitated. "Or stay out there. Whatever you're comfortable with."

Alexis thought staying outside was silly, but more than that, she felt vulnerable here, exposed to the world. She pulled open the screen door and stepped inside as Amanda moved away. Looking around, she saw there were more boxes along the far side of the room and on the kitchen counters, almost as many in here as there were stacked in the garage.

"What's with all the boxes?" Alexis called out.

From down the hallway, she heard Amanda's voice answer back, "I'm moving."

Alexis' stomach dropped. Her mouth went dry. "Where to?"

"Atlanta." Amanda appeared from the hallway stairs to Alexis' left with a medium-sized cardboard box. It was neatly taped with her name in block letters on the side. She imagined it was also labeled on the top. Amanda was nothing if not highly organized and precise. Like Alexis' father, she supposed.

"What's in Atlanta?" she asked as she took hold of the box.

"A new job. Um, I already sealed up the box, but you can cut it open and look through it to make sure it's all there if you need to." Amanda shuffled where she stood, wiping her hands on the sides of her jeans.

"So, you've been planning this for a while then?" Alexis asked, shifting the conversation back to the move and the new job. What she said was technically a question, but there was a thick undercurrent of accusation in her tone.

"A few months, yeah."

"Months," Alexis repeated, as if that would take the sting out of it. They'd only broken up recently, but clearly, Amanda had taken a job and planned a move months before.

"Lex, don't do this."

"Don't call me that," she said slowly. She shifted the weight of the box from her chest to her waist to get a better look at Amanda. Despite her plea, it was clear she was wildly uncomfortable. Everything from her slouched stance, the way her fingers fidgeted, the anxious way she bit her lip, gave her away. Well, she should be! It was one thing to break up with Alexis with no warning. That could be expected. People fell out of love, they moved on, they wanted different things. She wasn't owed a warning, didn't expect a notice. But it was another to completely betray her. "How long were you planning this while you were still fucking me?"

"It wasn't like that."

"Then tell me what it was like. Tell me how you got a new

job and planned a move to a city three hundred miles away and had the nerve to go on acting like everything between us was fine."

"Everything wasn't fine. The signs were all there, Alexis. You didn't want to see."

Alexis scoffed, jerking her head back. "So, what? You were just waiting for me to figure it out?"

"I was waiting for you to grow up!"

"There it is! Take away all your pretty words, and that's what you really think. I'm a child, and you're better than that."

"No, I want more than that. I want a family. I want to stop dreaming and making plans and build a home with someone who knows what they want. I want kids. We couldn't even talk about it."

"I'm not ready. Why can't I not be ready? How can you tell someone you love them and not be okay with that?"

"Wake up, Lex. You're never going to be ready. You're so terrified of ending up like your mom that you won't even have a discussion about how different it could be."

"Don't," Alexis warned, her eyes filling with tears. Her voice was tight, and her throat burned.

"Don't what? Talk about it? As if you would." Amanda swiped away tears of her own—hot, angry tears that betrayed emotions she'd suppressed for far too long. "You should go."

Without another word, Alexis turned and fled. She jammed the box into the passenger seat of her car, clicking her seat belt into place so forcefully that she pinched the tender skin between her thumb and index finger. Blood welled, and the skin there turned red and angry. Alexis gasped and held her hand to her mouth, blinking her tears away. She refused to let them fall. She refused to cry. She wouldn't shed another tear over a woman who'd said she loved her even as she planned her getaway behind her back. It was over. Completely and finally. Apparently, it had been over for quite some time. Alexis just hadn't realized it.

It didn't matter. She was young. She was healthy. She was successful. She didn't need a partner to feel worthwhile. She was worth it. She was worth waiting for, no matter what Amanda had to say about it. But as she backed carefully down the steep drive, Amanda's words played on repeat in her head, and doubt niggled at her.

Was she being childish? Was she refusing to grow up because she wasn't ready to settle down? What if she never wanted to settle down? What if she never wanted children? Was she somehow missing out on some key step into adulthood?

As much as her questions begged to be answered, she couldn't bring herself to do it. In that respect, Amanda was right. She could very well be wrong about everything else— Alexis could believe that, all things considered—but Amanda was right. She didn't want to end up like her mother, didn't want to bow to the wishes of a partner who cared nothing for her own dreams or ambitions. It would be death to become a bird whose wings had been clipped so long that she no longer wanted to fly. But she couldn't even talk about it, not even to herself. She couldn't get past the fear of that future long enough to figure out what she actually wanted.

What did Alexis want?

She didn't know. What she wanted from this life was a mystery. She knew only that she needed to fly. She needed to be free to spread her wings and frolic through the sky, then come home to a cozy nest and all the familiar things she loved. And right now, that's especially what she needed.

Unlike the other night, this time her broken heart needed solace and solitude, and she'd give herself that. She'd give herself the time she needed to nurse her wounds and bandage her bruised pride. Maybe she'd even take a few days off work to pamper herself. It had been some months since she'd taken any real time off at work, and it could be good for her.

By the time Alexis pulled her car into her driveway, she was already planning how to spend her impromptu vacation, and she was going to start enjoying it right now.

At home, Alexis considered sitting in her backyard and enjoying the sunset with a cold glass of wine and a book, but it was summer, and that meant one thing worse than the hottest, most humid weather: mosquitoes.

Frankly, she didn't want to sit in a cloud of mosquito spray.

That was one thing she felt Hollywood always got wrong about movies set in the South. There were never enough bugs. Well, there were never enough of those annoying bugs. Directors loved their singing cicadas and chirping crickets, the whimsical lightning bugs, or fireflies. Rarely did their characters have to experience critters like mosquitoes... and giant wolf spiders. Or water bugs.

Because her home was an older, box-like brick building built in the years after World War II, she didn't have a garage or a porch. Instead, she had two concrete patios, one out front and one out back, and neither was screened in against the tiny invaders.

Realizing she hadn't checked the mail in several days, Alexis changed course and walked across her postage stamp of a lawn to her mailbox. She pulled open the flap and hefted a stack of letters, advertisements, and postcards, all nestled between a folded local magazine. She flipped through the letters with quick fingers. Nothing but bills. Skipping a stack of ads, she stopped on the cover of the local magazine. It sported a photo of a dental office's staff, all smiling back at her in their blue scrubs. She recognized the woman standing front and center in the photo, Meredith Elkins.

"Well, well. Dr. Elkins celebrates the grand opening of Heritage Family Dental," she read out loud.

Pushing the stack of junk mail under one arm, Alexis opened the magazine and flipped to the feature article. The last she'd heard, Meredith was working as a dentist one county over. Not that it had anything to do with anything right now, but it was interesting.

She walked back across the lawn, already dreaming of takeout and a candlelit bath, a better alternative to a sunset date with the summer bugs. There was also a new face mask sitting on her bathroom counter that she'd been dying to try out. It would be the perfect recipe for soothing both her mind and body. Typically so self-assured, she felt bruised and vulnerable, and in consensual, enthusiastic denial about it. Her slouched posture as she trudged slowly over her lawn betrayed how emotionally drained she was.

Like lightning, white flashed across her vision, and Alexis no longer saw her front door in front of her. She stared down at her hand, her tiny fingers wrapped around the yellow wood of an ice pop stick. Sticky red liquid dripped from the frozen rectangle and flowed over her fingers.

Beside her, a girl giggled. She looked toward the sound, but everything beyond her hand was blurry and out of focus. A girl and a boy appeared from around the corner of a house to her right, shooting water guns at her. A happy squeal erupted from her mouth, and the girl to her right took off running after the kids who quickly screamed and retreated behind the side of the building.

She wanted to run after them, but she worried she'd drop her ice pop. There was a noise behind her, and she turned. There was a scream. Was it her own? Then pain cracked across the side of her skull, and the world went black.

Alexis came to on her knees in the grass. She hunched over mail scattered over the surrounding grass. Stars danced across her vision. Her world spun, and she struggled to keep the nausea at bay. She leaned forward onto her forearms, her knees folded beneath her, and let her face rest against the cool grass. Deep breaths in and out. From somewhere to the side of her, she heard a strangled cry, and then Harper was at her side. A hand stroked her back gently.

"Are you okay?" Harper asked. "What happened?"

Alexis shook her head, her hair making a soft, raspy noise as it moved against the sharp blades of grass. "I'm fine. Dizzy, that's all."

"You don't look fine. Here, let me help you inside." Harper pulled Alexis to her feet, but when she tried to gather up the fallen mail, Harper said, "Leave it. I'll come back and get that for you."

Alexis let herself be led into the house, grateful when the spinning stopped. Pain still blasted across her skull, and she prayed Harper would leave her alone quickly. Not that she wasn't thankful for the help. She was. If Harper hadn't seen her, she would've had to drag herself across the grass to get inside.

But Harper was a friend, and she might ask questions. The last thing Alexis wanted to do was even acknowledge that she'd let another nightmarish vision pull her away from reality—she couldn't afford to be so careless—let alone talk about them with another person. Better to lock it away.

Harper lowered Alexis onto the couch. It was a second-hand lump of questionable wood and dark green fabric, ugly as sin but the most comfortable couch she'd ever sat on. The moment she sat on it in the thrift store, she had to have it.

One day she'd show it how much she loved it by re-covering it with the beautiful fabric it deserved. For now, she let herself sink into its embrace, leaned her head back, and closed her eyes.

In the kitchen, the sink ran, and moments later a cool, damp cloth lay across her forehead. Harper pressed a glass of ice water into her hands. She sat down beside her, her straight blonde hair falling over her fair shoulder in a golden waterfall. Alexis looked at her with one eye open, her dark gaze meeting Harper's icy blue one. Her eyes were filled with concern, and she watched her with a worried frown, chewing on her bottom lip. Alexis noticed her typical red lipstick was missing today.

"Feeling better?" Harper asked.

Alexis nodded. "Yes, thank you. I don't know what came over me."

"Maybe the heat?"

"Yeah, that's probably it." Forget that she hadn't been in the sun but a moment and had certainly not been doing anything strenuous. If it was an easier explanation for Harper to believe, it was a good option for her.

"Is there anything I can get for you?" When Alexis shook her head, Harper gave a quick nod, stood, and walked toward the open door. "I'll go grab your mail then."

Alexis pushed the cool cloth further up her hair and scooted her back up the couch. She sipped the water, sighing when the cool liquid soothed the last of her upset stomach. She couldn't keep letting it happen. She needed to be better at keeping it under control. Taking another sip, she watched the doorway until Harper walked back inside, setting the stack of mail on the thin table just inside the door.

"I'll just—oh no!" Something caught Harper's eye outside, and her body tensed like a spring being loaded. She stopped herself and glanced at Alexis. "Will you be alright if I leave you now?"

"Yes, of course. I really am fine."

Harper looked to be only half-listening, her gaze glued to whatever she was watching outside. "Good. Wait. Are you sure?"

"Yes, go. What's got your panties in a bind?"

"I've got to go get my cat again."

And then Harper was racing out the door and across the yard. Alexis gingerly pushed herself to stand. She walked to the door, careful in her movements. She looked out and saw Harper cursing in a low voice and creeping over to where the gray cat sat at the far side of the yard. It was looking very satisfied with itself and curled up like a fluffy loaf of bread. It swept its tail back and forth as it smugly watched its owner approach.

Chuckling to herself, Alexis closed the door, snapped the deadbolt into place, and turned back to the room with a deep breath. It looked as it always did, a jumble of new and old things she'd collected in her ten years of living on her own.

On the thin table to her left sat the pile of mail Harper had gathered up for her. There was a collection of photos arranged on the wall above it. She'd lived in this house for several years and had no intention of leaving. She was a landlord's dream, really, and every inch of the space screamed Alexis Donnely.

Grounded earth tones mixed with the deep burgundy reds she loved so much in the textures of the room and its decor. Pops of bright green and gold kept it bright and fun. The walls were still the same creamy beige they'd been when she moved in, but Alexis liked to think of it more as a solid base than plain walls.

On the other side of the living room was the eat-in kitchen with a table and chairs arranged in the recess of a small bay window. On the ceiling between the rooms, there was a thick chunk where the popcorn ceiling had been patched. Alexis imagined that at some point long ago these rooms had been divided. She moved through her house quietly, taking in everything that made her space unique. It may be small and a little dated here and there, but it was her home, a comforting nest close to everything and everyone she loved.

The thought of love brought a flash of pain in her heart, and she shook her head against it. Today was for her, and she wasn't about to give any more of her precious time to the one who'd hurt her. She was moving on. Onward and upward, as they said.

Determined, she walked down the short hallway to the two bedrooms. The first was officially her office, but really it was for storage more than anything else. She rarely actually worked in there, often preferring the couch or her bed. Passing it, she moved into her bedroom and opened her closet. She lifted a thick, luxurious bathrobe from a hook on the door. Leaving the bedroom, she walked back across the hall to the only bathroom in the house, hanging a robe on another hook.

She bent down and ran the water in the tub hot, then moved to the counter where an arrangement of thick pillar candles stood. Alexis pulled a box of matches from a drawer, striking one on the side of it with a sharp crack. She lit each candle one by one until all of their flames burned high and straight. Steam rose from the tub behind her, and she watched it curl over her shoulders in the mirror. Twisting open the new face mask, she slathered the minty green cream over her skin, smiling at her own reflection.

Yes, this was exactly what she needed.

8

What Sidney needed was a good night's sleep and a solid lead, but it didn't look like he'd be getting either. He stood in his bathroom, his entire body revolting against being out of bed after a weekend as the on-call detective. His vision was still blurry from sleep, but he propelled himself through the morning motions as quickly as possible.

Trying to sleep the night after a child disappeared was never a simple thing, but the logical side of his brain knew he was no good to her asleep on his feet. He'd gotten the bare minimum and was up with the sun today, blinking against the morning light but awake all the same. Brushing his teeth and washing his face with cold water helped, but he knew nothing would truly wake him like that first hit of coffee.

Moments from the weekend cases flashed in his mind as he dressed, but the most vivid ones were those from the child abduction case. He pulled socks over his feet, adjusting his pant legs back down over them. He padded across the thick carpet of his apartment to the closet and chose a gray button-up shirt and steel-blue tie. His fingers fumbled at the buttons as he mentally counted down until the automatic coffee maker finished its cycle. He really should set the timer for thirty minutes earlier. Wrapping the tie around his neck, he stepped back into his bathroom, watching himself in the mirror as he worked the long silk fabric into a knot at his throat.

Satisfied, Sidney carried his belt and holstered gun into the kitchen just as the switch for the coffee maker clicked off, the quiet signal that his savior was ready for consumption. Like a devotee taking hold of a spiritual vessel, he gripped the travel mug with both hands, inhaling deeply, letting the scent slowly awaken all his senses.

As he drank, he thought about his schedule for the day. He knew he would spend most of his early morning on paperwork, updating his case notes, and making calls. However, he had an interview with a witness scheduled for later that morning, and he hoped it would prove beneficial.

Finally, feeling awake enough to operate a car, he grabbed his belt from the counter and pulled it through the loops of his pants and the holster for his sidearm, securing it at the front. He adjusted his gun so that it sat comfortably behind the crest of his hip, checked that it was secure, and turned to grab his travel mug of coffee. Snapping the lid on it, he grabbed his wallet and keys from a glass bowl on the counter and left.

When he arrived at the station, he was pleased to see it already bustling with activity. This was what motivated him, the hustle of it all. There was a lot about the job that was draining, but this kept his pulse moving. He nodded to a few coworkers on his way to his desk and avoided others he didn't get on well with.

The first thing he did once he was sitting down was to check his messages. He listened to each other, diligently taking down notes as he did so. They were all from the family of the abducted child. They were calling for updates—and who could blame them—but they also thought they might have some additional evidence that could be helpful in finding their daughter.

Picking up the phone, he dialed the home number he had on file for them. "Hi, may I speak with Beau Smith?" Sidney asked. He waited a moment and heard the phone changing hands. Another man's voice came on the line. "Hi, Mr. Smith. I'm Detective Sidney Neal calling you back about your daughter's case."

"Do you have any new information?" the man asked desperately.

"I'm afraid not yet. We're working as fast as we can to try and get her back safe and sound, okay? I'm calling to get some more details on something you mentioned when we spoke. Could you tell me a little more about what you remember seeing on the ground?"

"Sure. Uh, it was just a tissue on the sidewalk when the police were walking around. I didn't think of it at first, but you said any little thing might be important. Was it?"

"I'm not sure yet, but I'll be looking into it," Sidney said, making a note to take a closer look at the box of evidence as soon as possible.

"Good, good," the man's voice trailed off.

"Can you tell me more about this friend you mentioned on your voicemail?"

"Yes, of course. Right." He could hear the anxiety through the phone, the rapid breathing. Sidney doubted the man had slept much at all the night before.

"Mr. Smith, why don't you take a deep breath for me? I know you're worried about Ella. Any father would be. That's normal. But we're going to get through this, okay? Let's start with Ella's friend's name?" He propped the phone on his shoulder and waited, his pen hovering over his notepad.

"Thank you. Okay. Her name is Birdie. Davis is the last name, I think. They play together a lot, and we're friendly with the parents. All the neighborhood kids run around together, you know?"

"I do," he said, nodding against the phone. "Were Birdie and Ella playing when she disappeared?"

"I'm not sure. Her mom came by this morning and said Birdie was having nightmares about a man coming for her. Maybe she saw something."

"Maybe. What's Birdie's mother's name?"

"Danielle. Danielle Davis. Let me get her number out."

Sidney waited on the line, tapping his pen against his notepad as he logged this piece of the puzzle in his mind. He was a visual thinker. He likened every part of an investigation, every person, every piece of evidence, to a piece of the puzzle. Sometimes you were missing pieces or there were extras from an unrelated puzzle mixed in, but if you worked at it, you could still put them all together in the end. That was his goal.

"Here it is..."

Sidney listened and jotted down the number. Outside of the myriad of random details he'd noted during their initial conversation, this felt like the first solid lead they'd gotten. And there hadn't been many.

"Thank you for calling me, Mr. Smith. Let me give you my personal number so you can reach me directly if you think of anything else."

"Thank you, Detective Neal."

"We're going to do everything we can to get her back safe and sound."

When Sidney dropped the phone on the receiver, he finally

let his shoulders slump and relaxed against the back of his chair. He scrubbed his hands over his face. He had no evidence and no leads. None of the witnesses had seen anything definitive, but this new information from the missing girl's father seemed promising.

If the girls regularly played together, there was a chance they'd been together around the time she was taken. He picked up the phone again and dialed the playmate's mother. They spoke only for a moment, but he arranged an interview with the child and her mother within the hour. Other officers were with the family, canvassing the neighborhood, anything they could. Everyone wanted to find this little girl.

Pleased with the recent developments, he updated his case files, followed up with the lab about the tissue Mr. Smith mentioned seeing, and began combing through the records of anyone connected to the family or the child specifically. An Amber Alert had been issued almost immediately the day before, of course. Search teams had gone out and come back empty-handed. All officers were on high alert. Additional teams would be assembled to canvas larger areas of interest, but the best he could do right now was sort through the mountain of information he'd gathered the day before and start narrowing down his potential pool of suspects.

As of now, it looked to be a stranger abduction—he didn't consider the parents suspects at this time—but without a witness a struggle and with Ella kidnapped in the middle of the day, he suspected the kidnapper was at least familiar to her. Enough that she hadn't made a fuss. It was also possible that the kidnapper had incapacitated her, leaving evidence behind.

Grabbing his notebook, pen, and cell phone from his desk, Sidney stood and prepared to follow-up with a few people on the way to interview her friend. People like Ella's teachers who knew her well and might have something, anything, useful to help him find her.

He had to keep pushing, keep turning over every rock, asking every question. A little girl's life hung in the balance.

9

———

The best part of a staycation was the stay part. After days of rest and self-care, Alexis was feeling phenomenal. Knots of tension she didn't even know existed were suddenly unwinding in her shoulders, and she was more at peace.

It wasn't the total absence of stress she'd imagined, but that was to be expected. Life continued on as it must. It was strange for someone like her, a social butterfly to be sure, to spend nearly a week alone, but she'd enjoyed the time with herself. Plus, she hadn't been completely alone. She'd gone on brief trips out and eaten at the cafe by herself.

In fact, she was driving now to visit Mia under the guise of checking on her. Really, though, she was going a little stir-crazy. Peace and self-care were lovely, but she desperately needed her friend. She stopped at Sweet Bea's on the way and grabbed an iced coffee, cursing the old building and its lack of a drive-through for no other reason than that it made her go inside to order. Even a stir-crazy Alexis liked her drive-through.

Walking up to Mia's front door, she belatedly wondered if

Mia was even in the mood for company. Too late now. She shrugged to herself and rang the doorbell anyway. Besides, if Mia didn't want her to come check up on her, she should have answered her text messages.

"Hey, stranger!" Alexis crowed when the door finally opened. She gave Mia a hard hug, letting her chin drop to the little valley that formed between Mia's neck and shoulders. Releasing her and stepping through the doorway, she watched Mia smile bashfully, a tinge of pink flushing her cheeks. "I heard someone has been a grand success! Maybe that's why you haven't answered any of my texts."

"Yeah, sorry about that. We've been slammed every day this week. I almost felt bad closing today and tomorrow."

Alexis walked to the couch, dropping her brown bag onto Mia's favorite chair. "Well, you look exhausted, but you also look really happy. It's been a long time since you looked happy."

She was pleased when Mia sat down on the couch next to her and relaxed into the cushions. "It's been a long time since I felt happy, but I think I'm getting there. So, how are you? What brings you over here?"

Alexis rolled her eyes with a grin. "Well, for one, I had to make sure you were alive."

"Still here," Mia remarked with a small wave. Alexis wondered if waves could be sarcastic.

She decided they could.

"That's a relief."

Alexis looked around the room, taking in the subtle decorations and the way Mia had arranged her bookshelves. She hadn't been to her new home often, and it was still jarring to see her building a life outside of that drab apartment. It wasn't always drab, not when she and Ewan had called it home, but the life had died in it just as it had in him.

As she looked around, though, she noticed there were stacks of books haphazardly piled on top of one another, their spines cracked and covers bent. That was unlike Mia. More came into focus, and she noticed pictures hanging out of their frames and others that appeared broken.

"Did something happen?" she asked Mia abruptly.

"Oh, that," Mia said with a sad laugh. "Apparently, I had a break-in, so I repainted. You know, to reclaim my space and all that."

She held up a hand, closing her eyes and tilting her head to the side. "Hold on." She took a breath. "The color looks great... But someone broke in? Why? Are you okay? Did they take anything? Why didn't you call me?"

Her tone moved rapidly from concern to irritation, and she mentally reined her anger in, drawing a slow breath in through her nose and out her mouth.

"It just happened. I was going to call you. I was!" Mia said, her eyes wide. She grabbed a glass of water as if it were a lifeline, clinging to it with both hands as she gulped down a mouthful of cold water, the droplets of condensation falling onto her lap. Alexis snorted, watching as the water sat on the fabric, its rounded shape preserved before it was sucked down and spread into the fibers.

She took a moment to ensure her voice was softer. She could tell Mia was upset, and she didn't want to make it any worse.

"Are you okay? I worry about you."

It was true. She was worried about Mia. They'd been friends for more years than she could count, but she'd been different ever since her husband died. Withdrawn. Not like Mia at all. Things were improving, but from the outside looking in, it was more like she'd gone from laid out on the couch under a blanket of depression to running marathons with no training in between. Alexis didn't want to see her friend burned out and hurt at the end of the race.

Mia shook her head. "You don't have to worry about me, Lex. I'm fine. A little shaken up, but fine. Nothing was taken, and the police don't seem too concerned about it. A crime of opportunity is all. Nothing to worry about. Really." She paused. "How's work?"

"I see what you're trying to do," Alexis said with a raised brow. "But it sucks so much right now I'll let you change the subject so I can vent."

Mia laughed, relieved.

"They've laid off a few people—you left just in time to avoid that drama—but instead of hiring any new editors, they've just shifted their workload to the rest of us. So we're all drowning in emails, agents are getting upset that it's taking us longer than normal, and of course, Cathy is acting like it's all on us to fix it."

"Maybe you could come work for me," Mia joked.

"Now there's a thought."

"No, really. Think about it. If it stays this busy, and I have every intention of doing everything I can to make that happen, I'll need someone to help me, likely sooner rather than later, and there's no one else I'd rather spend all day with. It wouldn't be New York editor money, but it would be decent."

Alexis thought about her latest paycheck and snorted. "I don't make New York editor money now."

"Come by the shop the next day you have some time off, and we'll talk more about it."

"Sure! Right now anything sounds better than spending all day in the office with *that* woman and every waking moment out of it reading manuscripts. My eyeballs are going to revolt and run away in my sleep," Alexis said. "Now, in other news, you have to tell me everything that's happening with the delicious Nicholas."

Mia shifted uncomfortably. "Would you believe me if I said we're still just friends?"

Alexis snorted and shook her head. "Nay, nay, my dear. Spill it." She watched Mia at war with her thoughts, and it dawned on her. She clapped her hands together and cackled. "You've already slept with him!"

"No!" Mia cried, sitting forward. Then, with a grin, she fell back on the couch. "Okay, yes."

Alexis couldn't help the squeal that escaped her mouth. She pointed a finger at Mia. "I knew it! Tell me everything! Is he the slow and steamy type or rough and ready?"

"Both? The first time he picked me up and carried me all the way to the bedroom."

Alexis sighed and fanned herself dramatically. "I love it when they do that. Does he also do the... you know?" Alexis mimed pushing a man's head down between her legs. She'd never understand why so many men were resistant to it.

Mia laughed and nodded enthusiastically. "Oh, yeah."

"Hallelujah! So on a scale of one to ten, how is he?"

"Is it bragging to say that he breaks the scale?"

"Yes! Oh my, you have been busy. So are you two officially a couple?" Alexis asked.

"We're keeping it casual. I get the feeling he wants more, but we're just enjoying each other right now, no strings attached."

"Well, I'll be rooting for you because I'm loyal, but if rumors are true, he's quite the charmer. You'll be lucky if you can hold out against him. What I really want to know is how did all of this happen without a whisper to me?"

"I'm really sorry about that. I've been so busy with the house and the store and, I don't know, ghosts. It's just got me all out of whack."

The nightmares again. Mia had been having nightmares

about a little ghost boy for years now. Alexis wasn't exactly sure when they'd started, and Mia wasn't always generous with the details, but Alexis knew they terrified her.

They'd also led to something of a real-life murder mystery. Mia might not fear what could happen, but Alexis did. She didn't think her friend should stop looking for answers—she of all people certainly believed in ghosts—but she wished Mia would be more careful. These were real people who'd gone through real horrors, and the people responsible for it were just as real.

"You know, I ran into this cop recently who works over in Candler County. Please don't ask how we met. It's mortifying. But I'm supposed to be seeing him again soon. Maybe I can pick his brain and see what he has to say about all of this," Alexis said.

Technically, she wasn't supposed to be seeing him, but he *had* left her his number with the offer of a date. Maybe she would take him up on that. Or maybe they could skip the date and go right to dessert.

"That'd be great. Maybe go easy on the ghost talk, though."

"I'll keep it vague," Alexis assured her, already thinking of when she'd drop Sidney a call.

"In the meantime, I'll keep digging through the diary and see if I can learn anything else. Maybe I'll find another clue. Now, tell me more about this cop. Is he a dating kind of friend?"

"Not exactly."

The question sent flashes of her last date through her mind, and she was filled with visions of Amanda saying goodbye, of the boxes stacked around them, of feeling abandoned by one of the few people in this world who understood her.

Or at least that's what she'd thought.

Alexis shifted uncomfortably. A dusky red flush crept up her cheeks, dusting her brown cheeks with deep red and making the skin shine. She blew out a breath and hid her face in her hands. When her chin quivered, she silently ordered herself not to cry.

"So... the cop isn't exactly a dating kind of friend, and you're not really dating Amanda anymore? I'm confused."

"I don't want to talk about it," she said from behind her fingers, her voice tight from holding back tears.

"Honey, what happened?" Mia scooted closer, and her hand rubbed circles on Alexis' back. It was what broke the last of her defenses, and she couldn't hold back the tears any longer.

"I don't even know," Alexis said miserably.

Mia patted her hand on her back and stood. "I'll get the wine."

In the kitchen, Alexis listened as Mia rattled plates, opened the fridge, and uncorked a bottle of wine. She heard the faint tapping as crackers dropped onto a glass plate and looked up in time to see Mia walking out of the kitchen with snacks and two glasses of red wine balanced in her hands.

"Reinforcements?" Alexis asked, sitting up and wiping the last of her tears from her cheeks. She ran her fingers under her eyes, drying them and doing her best to remove the smudged eye makeup.

"Of course," Mia said. She set the plate down on the coffee table and handed Alexis a wineglass. "Now, are you going to tell me what actually happened, or do I have to ply you with more alcohol? Because I'll remind you I'm not above getting you trashed so you'll spill it."

"I really don't know. Or at least I don't know what went wrong. One second we were together, and everything was fine. Then the next she wants to break up and move to Atlanta."

"It can't be as simple as that."

"I'm telling you it is," Alexis grumbled into her glass, taking a sip of the tart red liquid. It slid over her tongue with a zing.

"And I'm telling you I don't believe that for a second. When did all of this happen?" Mia grabbed a cracker, topped it with a thin square of salty Parmesan cheese, and slid it into her mouth in one bite.

"Not too long ago, but the worst part was after we broke up. About a week later, I went by just to talk to her, you know, maybe grab a few of my things. Granted, it was a little unannounced—"

"And therefore you shouldn't be mad about anything you saw you weren't supposed to," Mia pointed out, gesturing with her wineglass as she raised a brow.

"Not the point."

"I would say that is exactly the point."

"And you would know that how?" Alexis asked, folding her arms one on top of the other across her chest, as grumpy a position as she could manage while holding her wineglass.

"Because you're clearly more upset by whatever you saw at her house than you were about the breakup. Otherwise, that would be the focus of your anger right now."

"I hate when you're right."

"But I usually am. So what happened at her house?"

"Well, now I don't know if I want to tell you." Mia gave her an arch look, and Alexis sighed. She knew she was cutting off her nose to spite her face here. It was childish. "Okay, okay, okay. Her place was full of boxes. It turns out she'd been planning a move to Atlanta for a while. Took a new job already, and everything."

"And that upset you?" Mia asked, her tone genuine, absent of any judgment.

"Of course it did! Wouldn't it bother you if someone were still sleeping with you, making plans with you, going out like nothing was wrong? But behind your back, they're already planning to leave you behind?" Alexis pushed back her amber hair, the tight curls bouncing back against the movement as soon as she dropped her hand.

"It would. How did it make you feel?" Mia asked.

"Now you sound like a therapist."

"But the question still stands."

Alexis blew out a frustrated breath and stood, her body itching to move. She paced back and forth along the long end of the living room, moving between the front door and the kitchen.

Truthfully, she felt stupid. Her pride was nicked, her ego bruised. How could she have missed all the signs? It should be pretty obvious when someone is falling out of love with you. Or planning to leave you behind.

"Humiliated," she finally answered, leaning down to set her half-empty glass of wine next to the plate of crackers, meats, and cheeses. She grabbed an olive and popped it into her mouth to fill the silence.

Mia said nothing, simply stared at her, waiting for her to say more. But she couldn't make the words come out. She didn't know what else to say.

"Did Amanda say why she didn't tell you about the job or the move?"

"Not really." Alexis avoided eye-contact with Mia, trying her best to pretend she was busy selecting the perfect cracker and cheese. But she didn't fool Mia. She knew Alexis too well and let silence wring the truth from her. "Okay, yes. Kind of."

"And?"

"She said it was because I wasn't ready to settle down, have kids, do all that big stuff. She all but accused me of not even knowing what I want," Alexis said, sounding almost like a child stomping its foot.

"But do you, Lex? Weren't you just telling me you were feeling itchy?"

"That's not the same thing."

"Lex..." Mia said with a sigh.

"Never mind. It's alright. I've got it all figured out anyway."

"What's that?" Mia asked, her brows drawn together.

"I'm going on the rebound. I'll get her out of my system once and for all, my ego will be restored, and life will move forward again as it should," Alexis said, talking with her hands in a precise, matter-of-fact way that betrayed her more free and fanciful nature.

"Is that really going to help you? Maybe Amanda has a point. Not about the breakup or moving without telling you. What a bitch," Mia said loyally. "But about figuring out what you really want. Should you think more about that?"

"I'll figure it out eventually. I don't see why anyone needs to rush it."

"Everyone else is rushing it? Or you're avoiding it?"

"Neither." Alexis dropped back down on the couch next to Mia, her eyes looking down at the floor beneath her feet and her hands landing limply in her lap. Mia made a noise in the back of her throat, and Alexis turned to look at her. "It'll be fine. Really. I've got a plan."

"I have a feeling it won't be as easy as you think."

"Of course it will. Just a quick wham-bam-thank-you-ma'am kind of deal. What could go wrong?"

10

The abrupt sound of his phone ringing on his nightstand was a far cry from the subtler alarm Sidney typically set during the weekday, and it had him scrambling to silence the damn thing. He slapped at it in the dark until his fingers found the button on the side. He pried open his eyelids. The room was dark, and the screen was out of focus, but he could make out the name of another detective he frequently worked with. With a sharp breath, Sidney hiked himself up, propping himself on his elbow. He answered the phone in a voice thick and groggy from sleep.

"Neal," he muttered, regretting the few extra drinks he'd let Ben talk him into at The Railway the night before.

"Hey, Sid. I've got something for you," said a voice on the other side. God, he hated that nickname.

"Connor, what is it? I'm not due in for..." Sidney said, pulling the phone away from his ear to glance at the time. It was close to nine in the morning. "Another two hours," he finished.

"Uh, I think you're going to want to back that up, boss," Connor said.

"And why's that?" Sidney scrubbed a hand over his face.

"Because we found the body of a girl, and she's got a note with the name of your victim on it."

By the time Sidney arrived, the scene was already secure, with various uniformed personnel working to document it and collect evidence. Mist snaked through the shaded trees, and morning dew covered the grass in the small clearing where Sidney stood. Ducking under a yellow line of police tape, Sidney walked over to a corner where Detective Connor stood. He was out of the way, his pen moving across his notepad methodically. Likely, he was taking notes and making quick sketches of the scene to revisit later.

"What happened?" Sidney asked.

Connor raised his chin toward a small body covered by a white sheet. "Birdie Davis, seven years old. Morning jogger found her earlier. Says he was running across the bridge and happened to look down and see her lying here. Fall seems to have broken her neck. Jogger's down at the station now for questioning."

"Think he's telling the truth?"

Connor shrugged. "I don't know enough to say one way or another yet, but so far, there's nothing suspicious about it. No signs of assault. No ripped clothing or marks on her other than from the fall. The medical examiner might find more, but we'll have to wait for that. Kid could've just as easily fallen from that thing as been pushed, I guess."

Sidney looked up at the large stone bridge arching above them. There weren't many natural hills this close to the coast, but this was one of the few man-made structures. It was always fascinating to him when man changed the landscape around him, like this marshy, wooded area. It was possible for a child to be playing above and fall.

"What did you find for me?" he asked, looking back at Connor.

Connor held out a sealed evidence bag with a piece of notebook paper inside. On one side of the paper, written on a square surrounded by creases where it was folded, were the names Ella Smith and Birdie Davis, surrounded by pencil drawings of tiny, lopsided hearts.

To: Ella Smith
From: Birdie Davis

The handwriting was large and chunky, exactly how you'd expect a young child's handwriting to look. If he was remembering correctly, Ella Smith was 7 years old and in the third grade, as was Birdie Davis. He looked over at the body as someone wrapped and removed it from its bed of leaves and debris. So small. So young. He'd sat with that little girl and her mother not three weeks ago.

"Have the parents been notified?" Sidney asked.

"They reported her missing this morning when the school sent out one of those automatic absent emails. Jogger found her shortly after. The parents are meeting with the medical examiner to formally identify her, but it's her. This town's not exactly two million strong."

Sidney nodded, his eyes scanning the ground and his mind already far away in thought. While the incident itself didn't appear suspicious, the note in her pocket, the connection to a still missing girl, was. Something else was off, and it nagged at him. His victim, Ella Smith, disappeared. Less than a month after that, her close friend turned up at the bottom of a runoff ditch. Something didn't add up. Scratching his chin, Sidney nodded to Connor and turned the note over to read the other side.

I miss you, Ella. If you're lost, will you please come home now? Please. If you can't find your house, go to Live Oak Lane. You live right next to me. Well, I hope I see you soon. Come back. I miss you times one hundred.

"Anything else I should know?" he asked, clearing his throat to fight back the tears that threatened and handing the bagged note back to Connor. The sadness in the words, the block-lettered handwriting, the not quite right sentences.

Connor took the bag and shook his head. He flipped back a few pages in his notepad, his eyes scanning the notes and drawings he'd made. He stopped. "Oh, we also found one of her shoes up top."

"Up there?" Sidney asked, gesturing to the bridge above.

"Yup."

"And that doesn't seem strange to you?"

"It does. That's why we're here. But like I said, Sid, I don't have enough yet. We'll see what the M.E. has to say, huh?"

He blew out a breath. Connor was a good cop, a thorough one. Sidney respected him, and he liked him, two things that rarely went together. But he couldn't say he always liked Connor's aversion to any form of speculation. Not that he didn't want all the facts, too. It was just that to Sidney's thinking, there were always an abundance of details, often too many. Not everything you found or learned meant something. That was probably one of his earliest lessons as a detective. Humans were weird, complicated creatures who just kind of did things.

The difficulty—and the challenge he enjoyed most—was figuring out what was relevant and what simply was. For Sidney, he needed to think through every scenario to know. He needed to see all the pieces of the puzzle to know which fit into the picture and which belonged to a different puzzle altogether.

"Got it. I'll go talk to the parents. See if there is any overlap with Ella Smith's case. You'll call me if anything changes here?" Sidney asked.

Connor nodded. "You know I will." He went back to his notebook, effectively shutting Sidney out of his mind.

Satisfied he knew everything he could for now, Sidney ducked under the police line. He trudged up the incline as best he could, the tops of his shoes damp from the dew on the ground and the bottoms slicked with mud. He looked down on the drainage ditch below as he neared the top and played out the possibilities in his mind.

If someone landed at just the right (or wrong) angle, it could cause a fatal fall. He wasn't discounting the possibility of an accident. Still, when the child at the other end of that fall was the best friend of the victim of an open abduction case, one who had been the last person to see said victim, it changed things.

A lot.

Putting the image of the tiny child's body out of his mind, a child who he'd seen sad but alive not long ago, Sidney turned his attention to the rest of his day. As distraught as the parents would be, he'd want to interview them as soon as possible before details got fuzzy. He needed to know how Birdie got from her home, half a mile away, to the bridge. Why was she there? Had she ever wandered off that way before? He had so many questions.

Back in his car, Sidney pulled out his notepad and scrawled across several pages. He'd head into the office now and get the paperwork portion of his day over and done with while he waited to coordinate with Birdie Davis' parents. As he slid into the driver's seat, he felt his phone buzz in the back pocket of his pants. He pulled it out and saw that his phone didn't have the number on the screen saved. He shifted the phone to his shoulder and stored the pad and pen in his center console.

"Neal," he answered.

"Sidney? It's Alexis Donnely. Do you remember me?"

"Oh, yeah. Of course I do."

"You sound like a cop."

"I am a cop," he said through clenched teeth.

Ugh, he *did* sound like a cop. Taking a breath, he shook his head and tried to pull his head out of his ass. He hadn't been expecting this, but, come to think of it, it wasn't exactly an unwelcome interruption given the scene he'd just left. "Sorry. Let's start over. How are you?"

"Good, thanks. Listen, um, I know this is random, but I've got a question."

Sidney settled back into his seat, preparing himself for a little flirtation and a welcome distraction. He'd been hoping she'd get around to calling him. It would save him the trouble of making a not-so-casual drive-by her house, hoping to catch her walking outside. You know, a completely normal, innocent, casual kind of thing to do.

God, he was an ass, he thought to himself. That would be completely inappropriate and borderline creepy. Which was why he hadn't done it yet, he reminded himself. Not that he hadn't thought about it.

Or her.

"Sure. What's up?"

"I've got a friend with a minor problem. I was hoping I could ask you a few cop questions?"

"Oh, uh..." Sidney paused. Whatever he'd been expecting,

this wasn't it. "I can't promise anything, but sure, I'll try to help however I can." Then he grinned and added, "If you do something for me."

"What?" she asked.

"Nothing huge. Just a fun little tit for tat."

"Ooookkaaaayyy...."

"Go out to dinner with me," he said. He hadn't meant to ask her out so soon. In fact, he'd really meant to leave the ball completely in her court, but the words sort of just tumbled out of his mouth.

"Dinner with you? And if I promise to do that, you'll answer my questions right now?"

"Yes."

"How do you know I won't get the answers and stand you up?"

He could hear her grin through the phone, and he allowed himself to be swept into the fun of it. He needed it today, of all days. "Because you're the curious sort, and you're curious where this will go."

"Mmmm. Pretty sure of yourself, aren't you?"

"Is that a yes?"

He could've sworn he heard her eye roll. He prepared for the let down, but she surprised him when she said, "Yes. I'll go out with you. Is tonight too soon? Because I've got plans later this week."

His first instinct was to say no. As much as he was enjoying the fun of the moment, today wasn't looking like it was going to be any less heavy. It wasn't exactly easy to let go of his work that completely after a hard day, and a beer alone in his living room seemed more fitting. Still, she pulled at him, and he reminded himself that while he was a cop (and a damn good one) he was still a man. He didn't have to be "the job."

"Tonight's perfect. I'll pick you up at seven?"

"Seven's great. Now, are you ready for me to pick your brain?"

"You got it."

He spent the next few minutes fielding her questions. He gave her the best answers he could under the circumstances; however vague her situation was. It seemed a friend of hers might have some evidence about a closed case previously ruled a murder-suicide. There wasn't much that could be done outside of contacting the police or trying to get in touch with the investigator on the case. He wasn't really sure what kind of evidence this friend had, but it didn't sound like much that was concrete. Sidney didn't hold out hope that anything of note could be done, but that the conversation won him dinner with Alexis pleased him.

Considering he was about to talk to the parents of a young girl gone far too soon, it was also nice to have something good to look forward to on the other side of that.

"Is that all you've got?" he asked finally.

"Yup. Thanks for your time, officer."

"Always happy to protect and serve."

"Is that so?" Alexis teased. "I suppose we'll find out."

Sidney's mouth went dry, and his stomach tightened. He couldn't remember the last time he'd been so tempted by a woman.

"I suppose we will."

He hung up the phone and took a deep breath, allowing himself to daydream about the woman for a moment longer before closing the box on his personal life and putting it out of his mind.

Now it was time to switch gears and continue with the less savory parts of his day.

11

___

"Thank you again for taking the time to meet with me. Again, I'm sorry it's under these circumstances," Sidney said.

It hadn't been long since he'd sat in this very room talking to a very alive Birdie and her parents about her missing friend. He laced his fingers together and leaned forward, resting his elbows on his knees.

He sat in the family living room on a small chair positioned at an angle across from the couch where the Davis' sat. There was a new stiffness about them, and they sat distinctly apart from one another. Sidney suspected that blame and resentment filled the space between. He'd seen it before. Many times, in fact. Most couples would move through their emotions, sometimes with the help of counselors, and reconcile their grief. Others would live with that wedge driven between them. And it would tear them apart.

He hoped it wouldn't be the latter.

"Of course," Danielle whispered.

"I know nothing we do will bring your daughter back, but I

am going to try my best to find out what happened to her. Is it alright if we start with a few questions about this morning?"

The mother nodded. The father, Lance, looked at his wife, but she stared resolutely forward.

"Alright. Tell me about her morning. What time did she get up?"

"Around six thirty. She likes to have time to play before school, so she always gets up early," Danielle said.

"I made pancakes today. She had a test. We always have pancakes on test days. It helps with the nerves. Makes it something to look forward to," Lance said. His voice was tight, and he twisted his hands into each other in his lap.

Sidney took notes as they spoke, his pen moving quickly over the pages of his pad in his own bastardized shorthand.

"Did Birdie know about Ella Smith's disappearance?"

"Yes. She was worried. I think she felt guilty, too," Lance said. His nervous movements seemed that much more disruptive compared to the stiff stillness of his wife.

"I told her to write her feelings down before school, so she did, and then she wrote a letter to Ella. Birdie said it was to help her find her way back home," Danielle added, her voice beginning to shake. She covered her mouth with her hand as her resolve crumbled. Abruptly, she stood. "I can't do this right now."

Sidney watched as she fled from the room. Lance raised an arm and looked for a moment as if he was going to go after her. Then he sighed, and his hand dropped to his lap. He looked up at Sidney with eyes full of sadness and confusion.

"She just needs some time."

"I understand, Mr. Davis. I know this isn't easy," Sidney said. "Was there anything different this morning? Anything not quite routine?"

Lance shook his head. "No, not really. I'm sorry if that

doesn't help. Birdie finished her breakfast, sat at the table writing with her mom, and then went outside to play before school."

"When did you notice she wasn't outside?"

"When it was time to go to the bus stop. That'd be a little before eight. Dani went to get her, but Birdie wasn't out front. I heard her yell for her a few times. Then she started screaming. I came running outside. When we couldn't find her, I called 9-1-1. I just—I should've checked on her. I was sitting right here. Right here." Lance fought back tears, clearing his throat and rubbing his hands roughly over his face.

"So, before you knew she was missing, you were in here?" he asked.

Lance shook his head. "The kitchen. I was washing the dishes. The dishwasher's broken."

Sidney nodded in understanding. "And where was Danielle?"

"Upstairs getting ready for work. She's been going in early and picking up extra shifts since I got laid off."

"That must be hard on you."

Sidney watched as he shrugged and looked away. Lance stared for a long moment, his eyes looking at something farther away than just the world outside his window. He turned to Sidney suddenly. "You know, she wanted to put Ella's note in a bottle and float it out to sea. She thought maybe Ella got lost in the ocean and needed someone to come rescue her."

Sidney sat with him in silence as Lance dropped his gaze to the floor. He wondered, as he often did on these types of cases, what he would do if he had a child go missing... or worse.

Would he try to be helpful and stoic like the father? Would he be distant and resentful like the mother? He'd like to think he was solution-focused, optimistic but realistic. But everyone had their breaking point. Would he crumble? Or would he possess a single-minded obsession with finding the truth?

Given his current line of work and how it consumed his life despite his best efforts—okay, maybe not his *best* efforts to be completely honest—he suspected he'd lean into the obsessive kind. Not his best quality, but it made him a damn good cop.

At least, that's what he told himself when he was sitting in his apartment later, surrounded by crime scene photos and files.

Alone.

Again.

Not for long, it seemed, if Alexis had anything to say about it. He was surprised she'd actually called him. Part of him didn't believe she would. He was just some guy, and she was just the woman he'd driven home from a bar after a nasty breakup. Nothing spectacular about their meeting, though serendipitous certainly.

But she was interesting, and she made him feel interesting. He liked how she was unapologetic about her feelings, how she carried herself confidently. He liked a strong woman, especially one who was drop-dead gorgeous to boot.

Glancing down at his pad, he pulled his thoughts back to the present moment. As much as he was looking forward to the evening, he had a job to do until then. One little girl was still missing, and he was losing hope he'd ever find her alive. Another was dead under mysterious circumstances. He couldn't afford to allow himself to be distracted.

12

"Nope, nope, nope," Alexis said to herself. She set her phone on the bathroom counter with a satisfying snap. The phone vibrated against the laminate, its ring mocking her with every chime. Amanda's name and face stared back at her from the screen, but Alexis refused to answer.

She looked back at herself in the mirror and drew a deep breath. She was getting ready for a date with Mr. Sexy, and she wasn't about to let a conversation with her ex ruin her good mood. Amanda could save her pity for someone else.

Alexis was quite content with her life the way it was. She had a job she loved, a roof over her head, and all the freedom in the world to live each day to its fullest. She didn't need someone dangling expectations over her head like a carrot. Or desperately trying to plan every second of the day.

When the phone was finally silent, she slid her finger over the screen until the sultry voice of her newest audiobook's narrator echoed into the bathroom. It was a story of love and loss and imperfect people finding love in one another again after royally fucking it up the first time.

Maybe not the best choice for her life at this moment—she certainly wasn't looking to rekindle a past relationship—but it was sweet and made her believe in second chances, and that was nice. Not everything she read needed to apply to her life. Thinking about the other books she'd read and their lists of trigger warnings only confirmed that.

With her mind drifting into another world, Alexis picked up a bottle of golden oil, poured a few drops into her palm, and smoothed it through her damp hair, finger curling the strands as she went. When she was happy, she spritzed a fine mist over her hair and turned on the hair dryer, pressing the wide, pronged diffuser attachment up through her curls and to her scalp. She held it there for a moment and then moved on to the next section. It was all part of her self-care ritual—a slow, often painstaking routine she'd once resented but now felt grounded by.

When she was satisfied with her hair, Alexis clipped it out of her face and moved on to makeup. She smudged black eyeliner over her lids and slicked mascara over her lashes. Always aware of the infamous southern humidity, she never wore much foundation and instead opted for a quick swipe of highlighter across the tops of her cheekbones. The shimmer made her skin glow and her eyes brighten.

Moving from the small bathroom into her bedroom, Alexis padded to her dresser and slid into a lacy set of black underwear and matching bra. She grabbed a slinky red dress from her closet, unzipped it at the side, and wiggled her body into it. The wine-colored fabric hugged her in all the right places, giving her curving hips, tummy, breasts, and thighs the round and regal look of a Greek goddess. It was one of her favorite dresses for that very reason. She felt modern and timeless all at once.

When her phone buzzed again, Alexis sighed and walked back into the bathroom. Fortunately, it was not Amanda's name that stared up at her from the screen but Ben's. She wondered if he was bartending at The Railway tonight.

She picked up the phone and held it to her ear. The smooth screen was slightly cold against the warmth of her cheek. "Hello?"

"Hey, Lex. What are you up to?"

"Getting ready for a hot date," Alexis said. She glanced at her reflection in the mirror and noticed the forgotten clips still in her hair. Propping the phone between her cheek and shoulder, she popped each clip out, dropping them in a haphazard pile on the counter.

"Ah, nice. Are y'all going to stop in at the bar?"

"I'm not sure. We didn't really plan out what we'd be doing."

"Sounds like your dream date. Who's the lucky someone?"

"Sidney Neal."

"Really?"

"You sound surprised."

"I am. I didn't think you two would hit it off, but good for you."

"We'll see. So, what's up?" she asked, her hands busy dispensing a lightly scented cream into her palm. She rubbed it on her hands, arms, and elbows, working it into her skin as the delicate scent enveloped her body.

"I have a favor to ask."

"Why?" she teased.

"You don't have to say yes."

"You're scaring me now." She ran tap water over her tooth-brush, phone still propped against her shoulder, and squirted a dollop of toothpaste onto the bristles. "What is it?" she asked from behind the toothbrush.

Ben hesitated again, and Alexis thought she might have to murder him. It was not in her nature to be especially patient. After what felt like hours, he finally said, "I've got a friend moving into town, and I want to introduce him around. I'm hoping you can help with that."

"Me?"

"You may not be the patron saint of strangers, but you know everyone, and despite your best efforts, you like most of them," he said. She could almost hear the shrug through the phone.

"Debatable, but I'll bite. So why the hesitation?"

"He's... a little standoffish at first."

"So, he's an ass."

"I wouldn't go that far, but you could say he's rough around the edges."

"Okay..." Alexis said again, slowly.

"Look, he's had it rough, and I really think moving out this way will be good for him. If someone besides me, especially someone with a pretty face, shows him around, maybe he'll believe me."

"You know, that's almost a little sexist, but you called me pretty."

"Did it work?"

Alexis sighed. "Yes, I'll meet your mystery friend and show him around. When will he be here?"

"We're still figuring it out. I'll keep you in the loop. And thank you. I mean it."

"For you, my love, anything. Now, I've got a date to finish getting ready for." At the sound of her doorbell, she said, "Shit, there he is. Gotta run!"

"Knock him dead."

"I always do."

She walked out of the bathroom and down the hall, grabbing her shoes by the back straps. She slid her feet into the heels as she half-walked, half-hopped to the door, throwing it open as she wiggled her second foot in. Sidney stood on the other side of the door and grinned at her hunched form.

"Well, hello there," he said. When she straightened, she watched as his eyes slid appreciatively over her body. "You look stunning."

She smiled back at him. "Thank you. I feel amazing."

"It shows," he said, pulling open the screen door.

"Oh, yeah?" she asked playfully, stepping back and gesturing for him to come inside.

"Uh huh. My momma always said that a woman looks even more beautiful when she feels beautiful."

"She sounds like a wise woman."

"Yes, well, she also said you can't trust a woman with two first names, so let's not give her too much credit."

Alexis chuckled and moved to the table where she kept her purse and keys and things. She liked the sound of his laugh as much as she liked the look of him. He wore a black button-down shirt with the sleeves rolled up just above the forearm, grey washed jeans, and black leather work boots. The effect was a comfortable balance between casual and dressed-up.

"Is she from here?" she asked.

"Southern woman, born and raised," he said with a nod, pushing his hands into the pockets of his jeans and rocking back on his heels.

"Must've been hard with all those Mary-Beths and Anne Maries running around."

"Well, I think it was probably more my daddy running around *with* them."

"That'll do it. Are you close with your family?"

Sidney shrugged. "My mom, yes. My dad... well, you can guess what kind of man he was."

"I suppose I can."

He looked as if he wanted to say something else, maybe even change the subject completely, and then his face changed. It was as if a mask came down, and there was the grinning man with the mischievous glint in his gray eyes again. Her heart did a little flip in her chest, and butterflies danced in her stomach. Oh, he was going to be the death of her tonight.

Unfortunately for him, she was determined to kill him first.

"Well, shall we be off then?"

Alexis nodded and followed him out the door. She pulled it closed behind her and turned to lock it. Over her shoulder, she asked, "Where are we headed?"

"I thought we'd try that new seafood place near The Calhoun House. What do you think?"

"As long as it's not *at* The Calhoun House, I'm game."

"Not a fan of the food?"

"Not a fan of the former plantation."

"Agreed."

"Really?" she asked as she turned. She didn't bother to hide the mild (and skeptical) surprise on her face.

"As a general philosophy, yes, actually. Plus, I've got more sense than to be a white man taking a black woman on a date to a place that's essentially a landmark to 'the south will rise again,'" he said the last with his voice taking on the accent and cadence of a crotchety old man waving his tattered confederate flag. "I'm not a completely ignorant ass."

"But still a cop?"

"Can't be perfect, I guess," he shrugged with a grin. "Are you ready?"

"Sure," she said, pushing away from the door.

She found him contradictory to say the least, and the

butterflies danced again. She wasn't sure if his contradictions attracted her or repelled her, but she felt drawn to him anyway. Like metal to a magnet, powerful and inevitable.

"Before we go, let's get this out of the way…" her voice trailed off, and she pressed her body against his.

She wrapped her arms around his neck before she could second-guess the impulse. She had set out to kill him after all. Her eyes locked with his, and she leaned in, stopping when her lips were a breath away from his, as if waiting for him to complete the circuit. Her entire system buzzed with anticipation. It roared in her ears.

"You mind if we just do this for a moment?" she whispered.

And then he was groaning and putting his arms around her. His lips pressed against hers, his eyes sliding closed as he relaxed into her. She pressed her hips into his, grinding up into him and intentionally letting a breathy moan escape from her mouth as his tongue slid along hers. His hands moved down the lines of her back and over her ass. He groaned when his hands filled with her. She pushed her hips into his again, changing the angle of the kiss and moving her hands until they were beneath his jaw. She felt him harden against her, and knowing that only denim and a bit of cotton were between them made her insides clench.

With a reluctant sigh, she eased away, grinning when he groaned at the space between them. His eyes crinkled at the sides as his lips broke into a delightfully confused smile.

"What was that?" he asked.

"Just an impulse," she said, dancing away from his hands.

"Are you trying to drive me crazy?"

"Is it working?" She grinned, inching off the porch.

"Let's skip dinner and find out." His eyes flashed with heat, and he stepped toward her dangerously.

"And ruin my chance to wear this killer outfit out? I don't think so."

"I'm not thinking about the outfit right now."

"Only what's underneath?"

"Something like that."

Alexis leaned toward him, tucking a curl behind her ear. "It's black lace," she whispered.

"Lord help me," he said and cast his eyes toward the sky.

When they sat down to dinner, Sidney was still thinking about the kiss. If he closed his eyes, he could feel her, feel the curve of her body pressed against his. Even sitting across the table, every movement she made sent his senses into overdrive. He smelled her citrusy sweet perfume and the subtle earthiness of whatever was in her hair. Even the way the fabric of her dress shifted across her body as she moved was tantalizing. In short, the woman was driving him as crazy as she'd promised. More so even.

And she knew it.

She smiled up at him from under sooty dark lashes, and he felt the breath whoosh out of his mouth. With a firm internal shake, he forced himself to focus on the present. He cleared his throat and grabbed his cup of water like a parched man in a desert.

"Are you okay?" Alexis asked with a grin.

"Mmm," he replied, taking another sip and clearing his throat again.

"Good. I wouldn't want you to go dying on me before we've even finished our drinks."

"Wasn't that the point?" he asked, trying to relax into the back of his chair.

"Death before dinner? Not quite."

"Just close apparently. Got it." She opened her smiling

mouth, and Sidney watched her tongue slide along her teeth. He wondered aloud, "Are you always this cheeky?"

"Only on dates with sexy men I'm considering sleeping with."

"Oh? And I fall into that category?"

His mouth was bone-dry.

She nodded.

"Obviously," she said, taking a sip of the shimmering red wine in her glass.

"Good to know."

"I like to think so. Everything's more fun with a little antici—"

"If you do a Rocky Horror Picture Show joke, I swear—"

"—pation," she finished with a laugh.

"Marry me now. Server, bring me a glass of champagne! I've found the perfect woman," he said and jokingly looked around the room.

"You're barking up the wrong tree there," she laughed again.

"You don't want to get married?" he asked, genuinely interested in her answer. As far as he knew, marriage was on the mind of every woman eventually.

Alexis shrugged, the movement somehow both elegant and detached. "Maybe not. Maybe. One day. Who knows?"

The server stopped by their table then, and they took turns ordering dinner. For himself, he chose a garlic and lemon Mahi Mahi dish, and Alexis ordered a similar meal with shrimp. It seemed they both shared an appreciation for coastal living and eating. One more tick in her favor. Not that she needed any help at all. The woman was already approaching goddess status for Sidney. Gorgeous, of course, but she was also unashamed of her emotions, confident in her sexuality, and quick as a whip.

The more time he spent with her, the more he wanted to.

A warning bell went off in his head as he thought about her

recent breakup. He was setting himself up for heartbreak if he invested too much in what was a rebound for her. He should remember that.

Luckily, he wasn't looking for anything serious either. They were simply two adults with a mutual attraction enjoying each other for however long that may be. He couldn't have created a more perfect arrangement if he'd wanted to.

Now if he could just survive this goddamn dinner.

13

Sidney led Alexis up the short walk to her door, his hand firmly at the small of her back, and the night air wrapped their bodies like a damp blanket. A breeze that stirred the hot air around them and whispered in their ear like a seductive mistress.

Alexis reveled in the way Sidney watched her move, not like a hyena waiting for a meal. No, Sidney watched her as a painter studies a scene before turning it into a masterpiece. He took in and appreciated every detail, how each feature made the whole that much more special. It was thrilling to be on the other end of that, and she had to admit she had shamelessly enjoyed tempting and teasing him for the last few hours.

She'd already decided that he wouldn't be leaving before dawn, but she wasn't done driving him crazy. He kept a cool demeanor, but his movements were a little less smooth, his body a little more stiff. She smiled to herself as she walked past him and unlocked the door.

"Such a gentleman to walk me up. Does this mean I get a

goodnight kiss?" she asked with a smirk, stepping backward into the open doorway.

Without a word, he closed what little distance there was between them and slid his hand over her hip to rest at the side of her waist. Pulses raced and breaths came out as tiny sighs on the summer air as their lips touched. People described these passionate kisses as electric, but Alexis likened his kisses to slipping into a bath, the kind that enveloped your skin in heat and filled your lungs with steam. Her head was spinning, her legs growing weak, and then she was pulling away before she got carried away.

She noted that rather than confusion on his face, there was simply appreciation. He would take only what she offered, demand only what she freely gave. Clearly, he hoped to take her to bed—his eyes were as hungry with desire as hers—but by his reaction, he would feel satisfied with wherever she drew the line. If she wanted to stop here and go to her bed alone, there was no question in her mind that he would happily kiss her senseless, then saunter off to his car with that confident swagger he had.

Luckily for both of them, she had no intention of going to bed alone.

Leaning forward again, she brushed her lips gently over his, their eyes meeting with an intensity that sent a ripple of antici-pation through her belly. "Will you stay?"

He captured her mouth once again and nodded as he devoured her. His hands gripped her hips as he maneuvered them through the door, kicking it shut behind him.

"I'm so glad you asked that again," he muttered against her mouth as her hands busied themselves with the buttons of his shirt.

She steered their bodies through the living room and into

her bedroom, stopping when the back of her legs bumped against the bed. "I'm so glad you said yes this time."

"Yeah, well, I happen to think consent is sexy, and I rather like to get that when you're still sober."

"Mmm, my hero."

"Is there anything I should know before this happens?" he asked. "Because, my god, this *is* happening."

His mouth moved down her cheek to nuzzle into the sensitive bend of her neck, his teeth grazing the skin there and setting off a shiver that raced down her spine and had her back arching involuntarily. Her fingers finished with his shirt buttons and began to work at his jeans just as he slipped her dress down her body, his hands moving to the clasp of her bra at her back, all the while his mouth teasing at her neck.

She could barely think. She didn't want to think. She wanted to be irrational and impulsive, to throw caution to the wind and let the consequences be damned. "Um, I'm not on birth control, I hate hickeys, and I haven't had sex with a man in years," she said. It was all she could manage.

"Okay. We'll take it slow then," he replied, moving away from her long enough to shrug out of his shirt. It fell softly to the floor atop her dark dress.

Alexis shook her head, turning their bodies so that his back was to the bed. She pushed his jeans down over his hips, and his snug boxer briefs followed. She wrapped a hand around his cock, already hard and throbbing, and stroked him as she whispered in his ear, "No. I don't want it slow, and I don't want it easy."

Her teeth sank into the soft lobe, and then she was kneeling on the floor before him. He groaned above her, his hands coming around to rest on the back of her head as she took the length of him in her mouth. She might be a little out of practice with a man's body, but she wasn't completely inexperienced.

Alexis stroked him with her hands and mouth, adjusting the position of her tongue, the pressure of her hands around him, noting what he enjoyed most by the sounds and movements he made. She moaned with his hands fisted in her hair and knew she was pushing him to the edge. She looked up at him, moving up his shaft until just the head of him rested on her lips.

"Condom?" she asked.

"Wallet. Back pocket," he gasped.

Then she went back to work on his cock, her mouth greedy for flesh that pulsed for her while her hands dug through denim. She let him fill her mouth, wrapping her lips around him from tip to base and enjoying the feel of him throbbing against the back of her throat. She looked up at him from under her lashes, locking eyes with him as she watched him dance closer and closer to the edge.

"My god woman," he said, and he pulled her to stand before him by fistfuls of hair. His lips found hers once more, and he devoured her as if she were his last meal.

Alexis pushed him back onto the bed, unwrapping the condom and rolling it down over his cock before climbing over his prone body. She straddled him with greedy excitement, positioning him at the opening of her.

Her eyes glazed over with desire as she felt the thick head of him pushing apart the folds of her sex. Now was not the time for patient seduction. She had played with him long enough to drive herself just as mad. With a powerful rock of her hips, she drove herself down onto him, taking the full length of his cock into her throbbing pussy in one powerful stroke. She threw her head back with a groan. She swore she'd never felt so full, and yet there was no time to revel in the sensation before his arms clasped around her hips, and he was driving into her from underneath. The room filled with the sounds of their moans and the feral, rhythmic slap of bodies pushing themselves toward ultimate pleasure.

Alexis' nails dug into his chest, and she matched his pace beneath her. The fingers of his left hand dug into her hips while his right hand moved up her belly. His fingers wrapped around her neck. He didn't squeeze hard nor aim to take her breath away, but instead put pressure on the sides until she saw stars. A floating sensation rolled over her entire body, and her head rocked to the side.

"Oh, fuck," she said breathlessly, the sound forcing its way out of her constricted throat. She leaned into the delicious sensation, reveling in the way her body was being used, at the mix of the pain and pleasure. She'd never imagined this would be what sent her over the edge.

"Come for me, baby," he urged her. Again and again he said it until it was like a mantra between them, her body responding to the instructions of his body and his voice as if his permission was the only way she would find pleasure.

A low, throaty moan escaped her mouth as the wave of her release swept over her. She arched, and her body shook and pulsed around his cock. Wet heat spread over him, and he growled at the sudden possessiveness of it, finally finding release of his own and emptying himself into her.

Breathless pants replaced their moans of pleasure, and Alexis slumped down over him. Their bodies were slick with sweat despite the cool air around them. They lay together, a tangle of bodies and limbs atop one another, until Alexis felt him grow soft inside her and decided it was probably a good time to stretch and clean up.

She slid from his body and made to roll from the bed, but before she could move far, he was already up and walking into the bathroom. He came back moments later with his own body cleaned and a warm, damp washcloth in his hand. She watched as he gently placed the cloth between her legs, the lips of her pussy swollen and aching. He stretched his body next to hers.

Alexis watched him appreciatively.

"You said it had been a while," he said.

"So it has," she replied. "You keep surprising me."

He shrugged, the motion so effortless that she would go to her grave believing he must practice it in the mirror daily. "I like surprising you."

"So you'll stay?" she asked.

He leaned forward, nodding, and said, "There is far too much left to do to leave now."

She bit her lip, her stomach already fluttering and her pussy clenching with desire. He cradled her face in his hand and rubbed her cheek with his thumb. His lips found hers in a kiss so tender she couldn't believe it came from the man who'd just given her the roughest quickie of her life—not that she was complaining. She wiggled against him and felt him grow hard again against her thigh. He deepened the kiss, his tongue sweeping across hers as their bodies melted into one another.

Pulling back with a grin, he asked, "Are you feeling adventurous?"

Alexis' hand went to her neck, and she remembered the feel of his hand there, the way it felt to be completely at his mercy, how her body had responded to... well, everything.

He noticed her hesitation, though he wasn't sure where it was coming from, and shook his head. "Another time."

She breathed a sigh of relief. Calling herself a free spirit didn't mean she never needed time to adjust. Best to take this one mildly chaotic step at a time, at least for now.

~

THERE WAS no other sound Sidney would rather fall asleep to than the soft sighing breaths of a beautiful woman in his bed. Or being in the beautiful woman's bed, as it was tonight.

Crickets, frogs, and cicadas vied for dominance in the evening air, each seeming to shout above the others to spread its song the furthest. If he closed his eyes, he could imagine he heard the lapping crash of ocean waves, but he knew that was only in his imagination. They were too far from the beach for that.

Still, it wasn't such a jaunt. Perhaps he'd invite Alexis out for a day in the sun and salt. He wasn't sure if she was a beach person—to be honest, he wasn't altogether sure what kind of person she was at all, yet—but if she lived in a coastal town like St. John's, there was a good chance she at least wouldn't be opposed to it.

Speak of the devil, she stirred against him, her head nestling deeper into his chest, and the scent from her hair and body wafted up. It was utterly intoxicating. She moaned in her sleep, shifting her body against his. He drew in a sharp breath and felt his cock stir once more. Arm wrapped around her body, he drew his fingers over her shoulders in lazy circles. Her skin was warm and soft beneath his fingertips. He calculated at least three ways he could wake her, each more licentious than the last.

She murmured and shifted again, though her movements seemed restless now, and her brows drew together. He adjusted his body on the pillows at his back so he could get a better look at her. She twitched again, and what was an inaudible murmur became more coherent, agitated even.

"Hey," he said, his hand gripping her shoulder and giving it a few firm rubs. "Wake up, baby."

As if in answer, she thrashed in her sleep, her words still incoherent but growing in volume. Her flailing dragged the covers away from Sidney and twisted them around her torso. He pushed himself up in the bed, one hand coming to support her neck and the other grabbing her shoulder.

Still, she stayed sleeping as if trapped in whatever nightmare world her mind created. When words became screams, Sidney decided he'd seen enough. Keeping one hand on her neck, he tapped her cheek with the other, yelling her name over and over.

Finally, Alexis jerked awake, eyes wide and cheeks flushed from more than Sidney's attempts to rouse her. She scampered back until her body collided with the headboard, her gaze bouncing around the room but never settling on anything long enough to focus.

With careful movements, Sidney scooted toward her, making soft shushing noises and muttering reassurances. "Hey, hey. It's okay, baby. You're awake now. Nothing's gonna hurt you."

In the moonlit darkness, Alexis came to like a figure appearing out of the fog. Pushing a hand through her hair, she took several steadying breaths, the air audibly shaking as it made its way into her heaving lungs.

"Oh my god," she said at last.

Sidney eyed her with a mix of curiosity and concern. "Are you alright?"

Alexis nodded, her attention focused on the bed. She pulled at the blankets, unwinding and adjusting them rather than meet his gaze. Her avoidance didn't go unnoticed.

"Are you sure?"

"Yeah, yes. I'm fine. I mean, I'm not now, but I'll be fine," she said as she picked at the sheets. Her voice had a faraway quality to it, as if she were already itching to move on to another topic of conversation.

"Mmhmm. Do you often have nightmares like that?"

She sighed. "No. Well, sometimes. It's really nothing. Really. Thank you for waking me, but I'm okay now. Really."

On the last word, she finally met his gaze, and he was tempted to let it go. He really was. But the same personality trait that made him a damn fine detective was the one niggling at him right now. Once he had the scent of something off, he couldn't get it out of his mind.

"Is there something you're not telling me?"

She seemed to feel more herself again, because her cheeks flushed with temper, and she pursed her lips. "Honey, right now you're still just the guy I met in a bar. What makes you think I'm going to trust you with the wild and weird of my mind?"

He liked her sass, and he considered it a good sign that she was fully out of nightmare territory. More than that, though, it did the trick, and the atmosphere felt lighter.

"What if I'm good with weird?" he asked.

She shook her head.

"It was worth a shot."

He shrugged his shoulders and motioned for her to snuggle back in. She eyed him for a moment, and he imagined she was contemplating how much of a pain in the ass to be. For what reason? Who knew? It seemed to be a hobby of hers, not that he was complaining. He liked a challenge.

But it wasn't long before she huffed out a breath and scooted toward him. He breathed a sigh of relief when she allowed him to wrap an arm around her, and she settled against him. That status quo was restored. He stroked her hair away from her forehead, enjoying the feel of her head on his chest, and closed his eyes.

It was only a nightmare after all.

What more could there be to it?

A storm raged outside her windows, gusts of rain blowing in thick sheets across the space between the trees. Wind shook the shutters of the house, and every now and again some yard decor or piece of trash would blow down the street. Alexis watched it all from the safety of her living room, the dim lights from the lamps around her casting a warm glow.

The weekend stretched out before her, beckoning her to do with it whatever she wanted. In theory, it was welcome: a seemingly endless amount of time tucked away in her mind, the storm keeping the rest of the world at arm's length.

Yet, despite having the time to do anything she wanted, the desire was nowhere to be found. A warm drink steamed away on the end table next to a half-finished book, a bookmark sticking out from its pages. Ingredients littered her kitchen counters, an abandoned attempt at baking bread. A small tool bag sat on the floor in the hall for a home renovation project she didn't remember starting.

With a groan, Alexis scrubbed her hands over her face.

Standing in the living room, she turned aimlessly in circles. Thunder rolled overhead and lightning streaked across the sky. The warm lights in the room flickered as if threatening to go out completely if the storm worsened.

Alexis sighed and padded over to the junk drawer where she kept the matches. She fingered the sliding drawer of the box open with a satisfying hiss, struck a match on the side of the box, she lit the candles on her desk one by one until half a dozen flames flickered to life. She dropped the box of matches onto its surface, her gaze dropping to the laptop sitting so still and quiet.

She ran her fingers over the cold metal, and an idea exploded into her brain like a thousand fireworks. Her eyes flicked over to the book sitting next to her chair. Why read when she could write?! Hadn't she pushed the thought from her mind so many times over the years? So many times she had edited stories and felt tempted to write her own.

Sure, she'd certainly written stories over the years. One didn't simply fall into the publishing industry without some love of writing. Not everyone had the desire (or frankly, the talent) to live a life as an author, and she certainly wasn't claiming she did either.

But she didn't have to do anything with it.

It wasn't like she was planning book tours or wishing for fan groups to form on the internet. It could just be a hobby, a personal brand of honor to have accomplished writing a book.

"Do I really want to do this?" she asked the empty room. Did she? Did she really want to write a book? Was that what she was proposing to herself?

Alexis took a deep breath, realizing how much of a walking cliché she was. An editor turned bookstore clerk who started writing a book. Somewhere there was an author having themselves a good laugh writing a story just like that. Still, the thought didn't dampen her enthusiasm.

She sat at the desk and pushed open the laptop. The screen lit up as it came to life, and she paused, staring at the blank screen of her word processor. Her brain whirred with possibilities. It would be easy to overthink it and shut herself down. There were so many stories to tell, so much that she'd read that had inspired her over the years. In the end, she set her fingers to work writing what she knew. While she contemplated writing a story inspired by her visions, that was a little too close to home.

Alluring? Yes.

Too vulnerable? Also yes.

Alexis smiled to herself as she wove a story about heartbreak and finding love again. It felt real and relatable, especially considering she was at a similar crossroads as her new heroine. That and she knew plenty of people who'd been through the worst of it and found themselves afterwards. Hell, that's what she was hoping for herself. Wasn't everyone always looking for their own happy ending? It could be healing to create her own, to see it play out across the pages of a book she wrote. Maybe it wouldn't come true in real life, but it couldn't hurt to daydream.

Besides, she reminded herself, this book was only for her. No one else had to see it or even know of its existence if she didn't want them to.

In that case, she thought wryly, it couldn't hurt to include some very specific inspiration from a certain rebound she was currently enjoying. Nobody would know except for her. Surely there was no harm in sprinkling a little spice into an otherwise inspiring romance. All her favorite romances had at least a little; some leaned even darker, teasing her curiosity about a world with which she was unfamiliar.

When she thought about it, that was the excitement Sidney brought to her bedroom. A little spice, yes, but something darker, too. She remembered when he asked her if she was feeling adventurous, and a flush crept up her neck at the thought of it. Adventurous? What had he meant? The most adventurous thing she'd ever done in the bedroom was some rough fucking and light dirty talk. She knew there was an entire world of kink that people enjoyed—she was neither ignorant nor naïve—but it simply hadn't appealed to her in the past. She wasn't sure whether her own disinterest or her partner's influenced her.

Amanda was vanilla as they came with regards to intimacy, and Alexis had loved her. They had a good connection, a shared history, and a friendship that people envied. Or had, at least. The few times something a little more outside of the norm had come up in conversation, Amanda had been very vocal about her opinions and lack of interest. So Alexis had really just put many curiosities out of her mind. What good was it to consider something that was off the table with the person you'd want to do it with?

Alexis sat back in her chair, her fingers taking a break from the keys as she thought about that. Had she ignored a desire to explore parts of her sexuality because a partner refused to engage in even a conversation about it? Had she been worried about being judged or shamed for those interests? Because now that Sidney wanted to know if she was adventurous, she couldn't stop thinking about what that could mean. She couldn't stop wondering about it.

What *did* Sidney mean? What was adventurous to him? Was there something specific he had in mind? So many questions, so many possibilities. They weren't dating exactly. Seeing each other was a better label for whatever it was they were doing, and so far they seemed to have good chemistry and enjoyed their interactions thus far. She wouldn't bet on having to wait too long to get all the answers she desired.

And then some, probably.

She placed her hands back on the keys and pulled herself back into the now. Biting her lip, she told herself that the rambling thoughts about her sex life could wait. She had a story to write.

Minutes turned into hours, and with the storm keeping the sun's light hidden, nothing but the soft ticking of the clock marked the passage of time. Twice Alexis moved away from her computer to use the bathroom or retrieve and reheat her mug of tea. Each time she shuffled back to the desk with zombie-like movements. She singularly focused on the words as they flew from her fingertips, sure they weren't her best but determined to get them out. Maybe they weren't even very good, but they were hers. This story was hers.

Finally, the feverish rush of inspiration ebbed, and she could no longer ignore the stiffness of her neck or the burning in her back. Thousands of words filled her screen, and she smiled when she stretched out her arms and saw how many hours had passed. Hours of bliss.

It wouldn't always be like this, she knew. She'd worked with enough authors on deadline to know how often they had to push through without inspiration or motivation. If she were actually going to accomplish writing a book, there were going to be times when that wouldn't be there for her, either, and she'd have to write anyway. But for today, the muse had been with her, and she was grateful for it.

Leaning back in the chair, she extended her legs, flexing and pointing her toes until they felt less like shoes of concrete. She rotated her wrists and felt the circulation return to her body like a computer booting up. She glanced down at her phone and saw several texts waiting for her. Funny, she hadn't even heard it go off.

There was a text from her mother which was certainly going to ruin her mood—skip.

She'd missed a call from Mia—she could return that later.

Last, there was a text from Sidney.

Alexis looked at the clock. It was early evening now. She could drum up the energy to go out, maybe even invite a certain someone over tonight.

SIDNEY

Wyd?

ALEXIS

Really? That's the opening text you're going with?

SIDNEY

There you are

And yeah, apparently

So... what are you doing?

Alexis rolled her eyes and pursed her mouth. She found herself amused and intrigued, despite her best efforts. Leave it to this man to be so shamelessly direct that it turned her into a grinning fool over nothing.

ALEXIS

Writing. Enjoying the storm.

I'm deciding between hunkering down or braving the rain and going out.

What are you up to?

SIDNEY

Working

Thinking of you, of course

ALEXIS

Oh yeah? Why are you thinking of me over there?

SIDNEY

Maybe I'm just hoping to see you again soon
is all

ALEXIS

Ah, well, that would explain it. Maybe I'm hoping you'll see me again soon, too.

SIDNEY

Great minds think alike.

Alexis thought for a moment. She could continue to tease him, to play coy and dance around the subject she really wanted to talk about. Or she could come right out and say it. She stared at her phone, willing her brain to make a choice until she muttered to herself in frustration and let her fingers type what she'd been dying to ask all day.

ALEXIS

The other night when you asked if I was feeling adventurous... What did you mean?

The seconds turned into minutes, and Alexis swore that her entire body prickled with anxiety. So focused was she on her phone that if there had still been a storm loudly announcing itself outside, she wouldn't have heard it.

SIDNEY

So much

Do you want to talk about it now?

ALEXIS

Yes

SIDNEY

Good

Alexis waited a moment, wondering what he would say next, but her phone remained quiet. She scooted her chair back from her desk and stood. Staring down at her phone—like a psycho, she chastised herself—she paced the room. The phrase "waiting on pins and needles" had never felt more of an accurate description of this anxiety than right now.

Well, that wasn't quite true, she admitted. There were certainly times in her life when she'd had more anxiety while waiting.

But this was just violently shoved into the top ten.

A knock on her door pulled her from her fixating and had her grumbling in frustration. She looked down at her phone forlornly as her hand grabbed the knob. No new messages. She groaned and opened the door, tearing her eyes away from the screen.

"Oh."

Sidney stood before her, hands tucked nonchalantly into his pockets, an adorable half-smile on his face. "You said now was a good time to talk."

"I did." She was so stunned it was a surprise she even got those words out.

He stepped toward her, his eyes glinting with mischief and heat. "Can I come in then?" he asked.

Alexis nodded, but when she stepped back to let him in, he didn't just follow her into the house. He closed the door behind him, his eyes zeroed in on hers. He moved so close to her that their breaths mixed between them. She sucked in a sharp breath when his arm came around her waist, and his lips closed the distance.

He parted her lips in a way that wasn't quite rough but was

far from gentle. Demanding, you could say. She moaned at the taste of him, the way his other hand slipped up the back of her neck, how he coaxed her mouth open and stroked his tongue along hers.

Abruptly, she pulled back and stared at him. "This isn't talking."

He nipped at her lower lip with a grin. "Well, I was getting there."

"Hmm," she said, but she couldn't help but grin right back. Her entire system revved, a mixture of tingling awareness and fluttering butterflies dancing through her body. She was at war with herself. Part of her wanted nothing more than to keep this going until her lust was sated. Another part was curious and eager to continue their conversation.

Luckily for her, Sidney intended to satisfy both parts.

His eyes stayed locked on hers as he maneuvered them to the couch, sitting down and pulling her into a straddled position in his lap. The feel of her thighs draped around him would have been enough to have his cock straining against his jeans if he wasn't already hard as a rock. He ran his hands up her legs, his fingers digging into her hips, and he pulled her roughly against the length of him. Her gasp turned into a moan, and he grinned at the fact that he was having the same effect on her as she was on him.

"Now, to the talking part," he said as he leaned forward, his teeth scraping across her collarbone.

"Hmm?" she said, her eyes covered in a dazed, unfocused film.

"You wanted to talk, remember?"

"Mmhmm..."

His breath was hot on her neck now, and he nipped at the skin that throbbed with every beat of her pounding heart. "You asked about adventure. Do you want to be adventurous?"

She could only nod. Her arms wound limply around his shoulders, her head held to the side as he seduced her neck. Her eyes were closed, and her mouth was open as he pulled her hips and ground her against his erection. He relished how quickly he could make her moan, how rapid her breaths were now.

He slid his lips across her skin to her shoulder, drawing a hand up her body until his fingers rested around her neck. "Do you like it when I put my hand here?"

She nodded.

"What if I do this?" He wrapped his fingers around her neck and squeezed. "I want to make you see stars."

Her breath was raspy as she moaned and nodded feverishly. Sidney was careful to press on the sides of her throat, to cut the blood not the breath, and he held her tightly just like that until he felt her body slacken. He buried his own growl into the curve of her shoulder as she ground her body against him. He wanted nothing more than to tear the clothes from her body and bury himself inside her, but there was so much more to discuss.

"Hmm... I wonder what other adventurous things you might like to try," he mused.

Sidney leaned back and let his hands trail over her body, giving them both time to catch their breath. He wanted her—more than he'd realized—and he was thrilled that she was interested in his more niche bedroom pursuits. Not everyone did. But he was keenly aware of her lack of experience.

He dragged his hands over her torso and cupped her breasts through the fabric of her shirt, grateful she hadn't bothered with a bra. He pinched her nipples between his thumb and finger, squeezing lightly and pulling.

"Do you like that?"

Some of the haze faded from Alexis' eyes, and she nodded.

He pulled harder, twisting experimentally. She gasped, but she didn't pull away. Instead, she arched toward him.

"You like that." It wasn't a question, but nor was it a comment. It was a command. He increased the pressure of his fingers and asked if she liked that, too. This time she flinched and shook her head. "Good girl."

He pushed her t-shirt up and captured her breast in his mouth. He pressed his tongue flat against her nipple, using pressure and friction to lap at the silky skin there. His fingers traced and cupped the curves of her breasts as he alternately nipped and sucked at her nipples until she was panting against him.

"Do you want to know how to tell me when you like something or when you want to stop?" Sidney asked, his eyes watching her carefully, taking in her state of being, measuring her ability to listen and consent.

"Yes," she whispered.

"Green, yellow, and red. Just like a stoplight. Green is good, yellow means pause and check in with you. Red means stop. Immediately. No matter what we do, we can always stop." He slid a hand up her sternum, splaying his fingers across her chest, enjoying the way she was moving her hands over him now, too. "Do you understand?"

"Yes."

"You're so beautiful. So fucking beautiful."

"Tell me what you want me to do to you," Alexis said, her hands pushing up his shirt then sliding down to the button of his jeans. Her hands were restless, her breathing rapid.

"Oh, you want to know what I want you to do?" he teased. "I want your lips wrapped around my cock. I want to feel it deep in your throat, feel it throb in your mouth. Would you like that, too?"

Alexis murmured her enthusiasm and finally freed his cock.

It sprang forth, ready and waiting, and he groaned at the feeling. She wiggled her body down to the floor in front of the couch, wedging herself between his open legs. Her lips parted and slid over his cock, and he arched against her. She took him from tip to base.

"Put it in your cheek," he ordered. She obeyed, and he stroked the fullness of her face with the tips of his fingers. Her eyes met his. "I want to slap that pretty little face of yours."

He felt her tongue sliding around his cock, her hand working the length of him not in her mouth. She seemed to weigh his words carefully, her ministrations slowing in contemplation, and then she nodded once.

Sidney rubbed her cheek and tapped it lightly with his fingertips, a sound of satisfaction rumbling in his throat as a flush danced across Alexis' cheeks. She nodded and moaned. He drew his hand back and slapped her harder this time, hard enough that he felt the impact on his cock inside her mouth. She nodded again, and he was pleased that she explored new desires and communicated her likes and dislikes, what gave her pleasure and where her limits were.

"Green or yellow?" he asked.

"Green."

"What are all your colors?"

She took his cock deep into her throat, gagging quietly as she swallowed all of him. Raising her eyes to his again, she locked her gaze with his as she drew back up the length of him, the head of him popping out of her mouth with the same sound as a lollipop.

Sitting up on her knees, she smiled and answered, "Green, yellow, and red."

"Good girl," he crooned. "Now, come here and give me that pussy."

HE'D STAYED. Despite telling himself he was only stopping by, he'd wound them both up so much that a little kink 101, some dirty talk, and a fuck on the couch wasn't enough to satisfy either of them. So, when she asked him to stay the night, there was only one answer he could give.

Now the morning sun was peeking through the window, casting a dreamy white haze over everything in the room, including their bodies. Alexis lay snuggled at his side, her head on his chest. His arm wrapped around her, and he stroked his fingers from bicep to shoulder and back again.

"Feeling good, love?" he asked, adjusting his face so that his cheek rested on the top of her head. The scent of her hair wafted up and filled his nostrils, a relaxing and intoxicating mixture that would never cease to mesmerize him.

"Mmhmm," she purred with a grin, stretching her arms and legs out like a cat who'd just filled her belly with cream. "Do you often find yourself in adventurous moods?"

He shrugged and smiled, his eyes twinkling, though she couldn't see it. "It comes and goes. When I have the time and energy, I enjoy indulging myself."

"What other types of adventures do you enjoy?"

"If you mean what kinks I'm into, I like what we've done, of course, but restraints and sensory deprivation are a favorite of mine."

Alexis was silent. Whether she was processing or simply considering what he said, he wasn't sure. Then she finally said, "Because you're a cop?"

It was blunt.

It was direct.

It was probably true.

Sidney took a deep breath, considering how best to

respond. "Maybe. Possibly. I'm sure there's some fancy social scientist somewhere who has a better idea of why we like what we like. I try not to worry about it too much."

"I'm interested. In being adventurous with you, I mean. Though I have little experience with it."

He looked down at her, noting the way her tone changed when she spoke of her inexperience. "It irritates you," he remarked.

"What do you mean?" she asked.

"Not having much experience. That irritates you."

She opened her mouth as if to argue, then closed it with an inaudible snap. "A little."

He understood what she meant even if she wasn't saying it. Alexis was a strong, brilliant, and confident woman. She was used to walking through the world sure-footed. Exploring something new, especially when it involved any level of submission, sexual or not, wasn't always easy. Easing her into it safely, though, and being a part of another human's journey toward self-expression and sexuality? He'd love every second.

"Would you like to fix that?"

Alexis licked her lips, nodding, and his gaze dropped to them. The way her tongue flicked over them so quickly, how it slicked the soft skin with wet. He was instantly hard. He twisted his body so that she was suddenly and completely pressed beneath him, their mouths so close that their hot breaths mingled in anticipation.

She tipped her face up, and her eyes caught his. He met her gaze, desire tugging at his stomach. Neither of them was looking for permanence. Excitement and adventure with the random connection from a bar, though? Absolutely.

"Good," he said, and the world faded around them until there was only this moment, this heat, and nothing else mattered.

15

lexis slammed her car into park faster than she ever had in her life. Her cheeks flushed, her breathing was heavy, and her underwear was, perhaps predictably, wet between her thighs.

This man was going to be the death of her.

Staring at her phone, she huffed and pushed the hair from her face. Flustered, aroused, completely hot and bothered... all words that could describe the current state of her mind and body. All because the man had sent a few texts.

Okay, they were good texts. Like, really, really good texts. Who would've thought a man like that could write such delicious filth? And get her, of all people, excited about it. It wasn't as if men were the primary gender on her menu.

SIDNEY

Cat got your tongue?

ALEXIS

Yes, and now you owe me a new pair of underwear.

SIDNEY

Done

Think about what I said, though. Seriously. Get online and dive into the rabbit hole of debauchery. Then tell me what catches your eye and what your limits are.

ALEXIS

I can do that. I've got to go now, though. Your flirting will have to wait until I'm done being a responsible adult.

SIDNEY

Don't be too responsible now, doll. All work and no play is bad for the soul… and the bedroom.

ALEXIS

Is your mind always in the gutter?

SIDNEY

Only when I'm talking to you.

See you later

Alexis rolled her eyes. It had been some time since she'd had a friend with benefits, and while the benefits were lovely so far, the emphasis on building some kind of friendship was nice for a change. Too often people said they wanted a friend with benefits but really wanted a hookup, which was fine, but it wasn't always what she was looking for.

Conversations with Sidney thus far felt easy, comfortable. They chatted and flirted—he knew how to get her all riled up, though it was clear she had the same effect on him—but there was more to it than the physical. She liked that he'd taken to calling her while he was driving sometimes or asking how her day went. She felt like he was actually interested in her as a person, not just a fantasy human on the other end of a midnight text asking, "Wyd?" Sure, it might be a casual, superficial interest, but it was there. She wasn't about to look a gift horse in the mouth.

She opened the car door into a wall of heat. It was almost enough to take the breath out of her, but while she often complained about it, she really loved it. Like anything painful, she thought, if you just relaxed into the sensations of it, it was actually quite enjoyable.

Alexis crossed the street and walked toward Mia's bookshop. "Hey!" she said as she saw Mia approaching.

"Hey yourself," Mia said. The keys jingled as she turned them in the lock, and the bells sang overhead when she pushed the door open.

Alexis followed her inside, looking around with a smile. The place was truly beautiful, and her friend's accomplishment filled her with pride. The bravery it took to go after her dreams... well, it wasn't easy for a normal person, much less someone in Mia's position.

She couldn't imagine the strength it took to lose her husband and all the future they'd planned together in an instant and still try to make something wonderful out of her life. That Alexis was getting a front-row seat on this journey with Mia was just icing on the friendship cake.

"It's even more beautiful than when I last saw it." Alexis pointed to the children's section. "I see you finished making the lighted clouds. I didn't know you could make those yourself. They look amazing."

"Thank you! The kids love them, too."

"I'll bet." Her chest heaved with a deep breath, and Alexis smacked her hands on the sides of her jean-clad thighs. "So, where should I start, boss?"

"Here. Let's sit and chat first." Mia led Alexis to a small seating area furnished with pillowy couches, chairs, and ottomans. Mia sat in one of the oversized chairs and folded her legs under herself as Alexis took a seat across from her and leaned forward. "I'm hoping you coming on to help will mean I'll be a little less exhausted at the end of the day. Ideally, I can also stay open six to seven days a week instead of five. I know there's a million reasons not to work with friends, but I think we could make it work. I just want to make sure you know there are no hard feelings if you say you don't want to do this. Now or ever."

"Hun, if I didn't think we'd make it work and be awesome together, I wouldn't be here at all," Alexis said. "The truth is, I've been feeling restless. Itchy, really. I don't know if I need a new relationship, a new job, or something else, but I need a change. This is my sign."

"Weren't you the one telling me I needed a change? Could it be that the wild stallion is ready for domestication?" Mia asked.

Alexis tutted playfully. "Don't go that far. I still haven't met anyone I'd settle down for. Let's just say that this whole 'find yourself' journey of yours has inspired me to do the same. Only without the paranormal crime-fighting."

Mia had been having all sorts of strange dreams since her husband had passed away two years before, and she was convinced there was something to the dreams. Alexis hadn't really put much stock into it at first, but the more she'd learned, the more she agreed with Mia. Something was going on.

"I didn't know you felt that way, but I'm happy for you. Speaking of the paranormal..." Mia explained the latest dream to Alexis, who remarked that it sounded more like a confession than one of her regular creepy dreams.

As if a light bulb had gone off in her mind, Alexis jumped up, hand held out as if she were ready to stop traffic. "Hold that thought. I've got something for you."

Remembering the folded-up town magazine she'd come across recently, she streaked over to the front desk and dug the stuffed pages from her purse. On the cover, printed in bright colors, was a picture of Brad and Emily posing for a photo with David on Emily's hip in front of a newly constructed house. The cover was an ad for Brad's construction company, and from the look of David, the photo couldn't have been taken much earlier than his death.

"She's beautiful," Mia murmured.

"Do you still think he could've done it?"

"I don't know anymore. Did you talk to your cop friend—are you seeing him now?"

"Sort of. About your ghosts, though, he says that if there wasn't a trial, you might talk to the lead investigator on the case, but with no evidence of foul play, there really isn't anything they'll do."

"I was afraid of that. Maybe I'll wait to call him. I'll just sound insane right now, but Emily's journal will be a good segue later," Mia said. She took a breath and shook her head as if mentally changing gears. Knowing her friend as she did, Alexis was instantly suspicious. "Now, how are things going with the new man? What was his name again?"

"Sidney. Things are... interesting, weird, complicated," Alexis said, blowing her breath out through her lips and tossing her curls from her face.

"But not Amanda-ex-girlfriend-complicated, right?"

Alexis knew Mia had never liked her ex, not that she really blamed her, knowing now how it would all turn out. Alexis shook her head, and Mia breathed a sigh of relief.

"By the way, you never said how you met the cop." Mia raised a brow and looked at her pointedly.

"If I told you, I would die of embarrassment."

"Does it have to do with that drunken bar incident I heard about recently?"

"How did you know?" Alexis demanded, sitting up straight in her seat with a huff.

"You have your ways. I have mine."

"It was Sarah, wasn't it?" Alexis groaned and collapsed back into the cushions. Mia smirked but shook her head, frustrating Alexis with her lack of confirmation or denial. "Fine, I'll grill her later. Anyway, complications aside, we're actually going out one weekend soon. You should come and meet him—bring Nick along."

"No, no, no. I think I need to take a step back from him for a while," Mia said.

"Why? What happened? Did you have a fight?"

"Not really." Mia pushed a hand through her hair in frustration and blew a breath loudly from her lips. "Lex, hypothetically speaking, what would you do if your husband died? Would you ever get remarried?"

Alexis laced her fingers together and cupped her knees in front of her. "I think it would depend on how old I was, what happened, whether I wanted to spend the rest of my life alone." She hesitated a moment, her voice becoming just a little softer, a little quieter. "But we're not talking about me, are we?"

"Nick gets this look in his eye sometimes, and I know he wants more."

"And you don't want that," Alexis said. It wasn't a question.

"No, I don't. Is that so wrong? I made it very clear when all of this started. Nothing serious, but he keeps trying to wiggle in."

"Would it really be so bad to let him in, though?"

"Yes!" Mia yelled, and Alexis jerked as if struck. Mia exploded out of her seat and paced in front of her like an irritated tiger, teeth bared and tail twitching. "I've already gone down that road once before, and I don't want to again. I can't do it. It... it hurts too much when they go, and one way or another,

Nick will go." Defeated and out of steam, she sank back down. "You wouldn't understand."

Wait, what? Alexis blinked quickly. Surely she'd misheard. Was her friend, the person she knew better than anyone else in this world and vice versa, really accusing her of not understanding what she was going through?

"I wouldn't understand?" she sputtered. "I was there with you, Mia. Jesus, don't pretend like you were alone because you locked yourself away. People envy you for just a taste of what you had, even knowing it wouldn't last. I envy you, and you spit in our faces by denying yourself any chance at having that again."

Alexis stood, and for a moment she had no words. She stalked across the floor before the urge to commit some type of violence could overtake her. At the door, she turned back to Mia and took a deep breath.

"I know you've been hurting for a long time, and I've been there with you through it all. But Mia, I'm the only one giving and supporting. I'm always there with a smile and a hug to help you pick yourself up or say something motivating. Somewhere along the line here, you stopped giving that back to me. And now you want to turn your nose up at a chance at love again and stay miserable? I'm sure this is just a silly fight we're having, and we'll make up, but right now, I can't talk to you."

Alexis stormed out, letting the door slap shut behind her. How in the world had that just happened? And why did something that really had little to do with her make her so angry? Other than the part where Mia had accused her of not understanding. That was just plain insulting.

But that bit had been short-lived. The larger part of the conversation—Mia wanting to take a step back from Nick— made her angry in a way that was absolutely baffling. She didn't have a dog in that race. What did it matter if new relationships freaked Mia out? Why did she feel so invested in Mia's love life? She blew out a frustrated breath.

"It doesn't matter," she murmured to herself.

She slid into the driver's seat and resolved to take her grumpy self home. Right after a pedicure and a healthy dose of compartmentalization. Her therapist might call it dissociation, but she wasn't here right now, was she?

16

An hour later and Alexis had the softest feet and freshly painted toes. She'd spent her appointment getting her feet pampered while she indulged in an interesting blend of flirting, sexting, and basic kink logistics by text with Sidney. He'd told her to dive into the rabbit hole of it all, and dive she had. It was an interesting experience to hop from topics like bondage and anal sex and all the ways people apparently liked to play with semen to answering questions about safety and her own limits. It gave her a new perspective on just how much went into this type of play.

She found it endlessly fascinating. Which was probably why she and Sidney seemed to get along so well. She was adventurous at heart, and despite her inexperience, she was eager for exploration. Maybe it was the novelty of kink. Maybe it was simply the excitement of a new partner after being in a relationship for so long. Or the safety he was so keen to provide as they explored this together.

Whatever it was, she was enjoying the process.

Despite the good day, she was still only mildly less irritated at her earlier argument with Mia. It didn't help that the moment Alexis had stepped out of the nail salon her phone had vibrated with a text from her.

MIA

I'm so sorry. I have more I need to say, but it's probably better to do in person. Can I stop by tonight? I'll bring ice cream.

"Bitch," Alexis had muttered before shoving her phone into her purse and stomping to the car.

Now back home, she was spread out on her couch wiggling her colorful toes in admiration while she casually sipped an ice water and decided how long she planned to be mad at Mia. Second to that, she needed to figure out the best way to punish her.

Not that she planned to actually hold a grudge or intentionally make Mia feel worse than she already did. Okay, maybe a little. The temptation was there, but only because she was as offended as she was mad. It was more an exercise in venting than an actual plan to be followed.

A series of loud thuds pulled her from her thoughts and drew her eye to the door. It had better not be Mia, she thought as her feet padded across the soft carpet.

"Oh," she said as she swung open the heavy wood and saw Sidney standing on the other side. "Hey."

"Hey yourself," he said with a smile.

"Do you drop by and see everyone you're sending dirty texts to? What are you doing here?"

"Coming to see you. I thought that was obvious."

Alexis sighed and scrubbed her hands over her face. "Not that I don't appreciate the gesture, but I've had the worst day. I know my texts made it seem like I'm fine, but I'm not. And now I'm not really in the mood for company, so unless you're going to fuck the stress out of me, you can kindly go somewhere else."

He cocked his head. "Ah, well."

"No offense," she hurriedly added, already slightly regretting her short tone.

"None taken," he said easily, the corner of his mouth lifting in a smirk. "I was just thinking it's a good thing that's exactly what I'd planned to do." He stepped closer to the open door. "Are you going to ask me in, Lex?"

She blinked, her mouth working, but no sound came out. Without thinking, she stepped back to allow him entry. It was then that she noticed he was carrying a small black bag with him. It wasn't new by any means—the velcro strips that held the handles closed were peeling at the corners and some seams had frayed, small tufts of thread sticking out at wild angles— but it seemed well cared for. No dirt clung to its surface, and the zipper was closed tightly. She wondered what could be inside.

This time he knew the way to the bedroom. She followed him wordlessly. Their footsteps and breath and the swish of their clothes as they walked were the only sounds in her tiny house.

Sidney set the bag down on the bed and turned to her. "Are you feeling adventurous again?"

Alexis licked her lips, her eyes darting to the bag and back to his face. "Yes," she whispered.

She nodded as she spoke it, eyes wide. Butterflies danced in her belly, and her skin prickled with anticipation.

He stepped closer to her. "I enjoyed reading all of your texts. I'm thinking we should try them."

"All of them?" she squeaked.

"All of them."

"Now?"

Sidney nodded, and her mouth went dry. Mind racing, she mentally flipped through the catalog of texts she'd sent earlier like a secretary combing through a vintage Rolodex of cards. There were so many texts, so many activities she'd expressed interest in trying. How could they possibly do all of them? She felt excited and wholly unprepared all at once.

It was one thing to text him all her dirty thoughts... it was quite another to do them.

He cupped her cheeks, his fingers pressing into the skin on either side of her jaw just enough to let her know that soft romance wasn't exactly what was on the table. He drew his hands roughly down her body, his eyes following his hands. She was captivated, staring at the capable way he moved, the strength just below the surface, the way blood pulsed through the veins of his forearms.

He yanked her pants down and before she knew quite what was happening, he panties were ripped from her body. His mouth clamped down on her neck possessively as he pulled her hands behind her back. She moaned at the feel of his teeth and tongue hot against her skin, leaning to the side to allow him even greater access to the sensitive spots along her neck and shoulder. He tied the strings of her underwear tightly around her wrists.

"What are your colors?" he asked before devouring her neck once again.

She moaned again, her mind scrambling to find the words. Sidney bit into her skin harder, and she gasped, instinctively pulling against her restraints. He drew back, his hand coming up to her cheek again. He slapped her hard, and she sucked in a sharp breath as the hot, stinging pain spread across her cheek.

"What are your colors?" he asked again, his voice just as

calm and low as before. He rubbed his thumb across the skin where a pink handprint bloomed.

"Green," she said. A low growl of approval rumbled from his throat, and she felt his other hand press against the folds of her pussy.

"Yellow," she managed, feeling his fingers slide in between the soft lips already slicked with wet.

Another growl of approval, and he pushed three fingers deep into her. She gasped at the rough, sudden invasion. She wasn't ready, and he knew it, but that was part of the allure. Pleasure bordering on pain.

"Red." She was panting as she finally uttered the last words.

"Good girl."

Then he pushed her to her knees and ripped open the front of his pants. His erection was already hard and pulsing, and he shoved his cock deep into her mouth, pushing until it was down her throat, and she was gagging and struggling against the intrusion. He groaned and held her head so that she was forced to take every inch of him. He drew back, allowing her to take a quick breath, then slammed his cock into her mouth. Again and again he rammed against the back of her throat, his fingers clenched around clumps of her hair as he fucked her face, just as she'd fantasized about. The feeling of being used while he filled her mouth and throat, the feral noises that filled the room now. It was enough to have her throbbing and dripping without ever being touched.

"What a dirty little slut you are. Do you like it when I fuck your throat?" he growled. "You take it all so good, baby." He eased up his pace and let the drool drip between them. He sat down on the bed, pulling her so that she had to shuffle on her knees to stay in front of him. "Now clean up your mess."

He pulled Alexis' hair away from her face and held it together at the nape. She leaned forward and began licking and slurping the drool that covered him. Her tongue flicked up and down his hard length, over and around his balls. She relished his gasps and the way he jerked when she licked a sensitive spot.

"Do you want this cock deep inside you, baby?"

Alexis nodded, slipping the tip of him into her mouth. He sucked in a breath, murmuring instructions to tell her exactly how he wanted her to please him. "Let me see you earn it. You've been teasing me all day. It's going to take a lot to get this thick cock where you want it."

He pulled his shirt over his head, letting the fabric drop onto the bed beside him. He leaned back on the bed, pushing his underwear and pants to the floor, and raised one leg so that she could see his whole body exposed from tip to bottom. Grabbing her by the hair again, he pressed her face to the base of him, watching with a satisfied half-smile and eyes glazed over as she lapped at him with her outstretched tongue.

"You're doing so good, baby."

He guided her down even further until her tongue was up against his asshole. He groaned as she tentatively pushed against him, first lapping at him with long, flat strokes of her tongue, then pressing her tongue inside him. She closed her eyes, listening to him groan as she worked his ass.

"Eyes on me. Watch it. Watch me stroke that cock for you," he said, and she could only obey.

All she could think about was submitting to him in that moment. The freedom of it, the absence of deciding what to do next or what she wanted, was more liberating than she'd imagined it would be. When Sidney suddenly stood and yanked her up, she was deliciously powerless to resist. She didn't want to.

He pushed her to the bedroom door and pressed her belly against it, raising her hands up and fitting the panties tied around her wrists over the hook there. His cock pressed in between her thighs, the head of it rubbing along the lips of her pussy, and he pumped in and out. He teased her, whispering in her ear as he drove her wild. Already sopping wet, she coated his cock until it was glistening with wet. He adjusted the angle of his body, and then the head was at the entrance to her ass. He pushed only slightly, withdrew, and repeated it.

Alexis wasn't sure how she felt about it, but she was intrigued. The sensation wasn't bad, and she had experience with anal sex... but he was a fair bit larger than the dainty toys and plugs she'd used in the past.

"Next time," he whispered, as if reading her mind. "Next time I'll tell you to wear a plug and get that pretty little hole nice and stretched for me. Would you like that?" His cock danced around the rim of her asshole, his hand coming around the front of her to trace lazy circles over her clit. "Tell me you want me to fill up that ass, baby."

"I want you to fill my ass," she murmured, arching backwards against him, desperate to take him into her by any means possible.

"That's a good little slut. Let me show you what I'm going to do with your ass," he said.

Sidney snapped the underwear from her wrists, and before she knew what was happening, she was facing him and being shoved to her knees. He slid his cock into her mouth and down her throat in one swift motion, fisting his hands in her hair and bringing her down on his cock so forcefully her teeth scraped at the base of his, her face buried against his pelvis with every thrust. He paused to let her catch her breath, and then he fucked her face until she saw stars. With a noise almost a roar, he withdrew his cock and showered her with hot cum.

His body shook with the force of his orgasm, and for a moment Alexis wondered what else he had up his sleeve. He wasn't the type to be a selfish lover. She didn't have to wait long to find out. He leaned down and grabbed her by the chin.

"Open your mouth," he ordered. She did, and he licked the hot liquid from her face, then let it drip off his tongue and into her mouth. She waited patiently, taking in all the sensations pulsing through her body. "Good girl. Now take it again."

He pushed his soft cock into her mouth, twitching against her as she sucked and stroked the extra-sensitive flesh. She moaned with him in her mouth, imagining what he would do to her next and how it would feel. When he was hard again, he drew her to her feet and led her back to the bed.

"You've been such a good girl for me, haven't you, baby?" It was a question, but he didn't want an answer. Not that she could've given him one. Beyond the colors they'd agree on and a few phrases in reply, she was sure she was incapable of much speech at the moment. Her body was on fire with anticipation and need.

Sidney buried his face in her pussy, his tongue first tracing the lines of it before dipping into her wet heat to taste her. He replaced his tongue with two fingers, pushing into her slowly as his lips found her clit. He closed his mouth over it and sucked gently while he fucked her with his fingers until she was gasping and writhing beneath him.

He lifted his head. "Tell me what you want me to do to you. Beg me for it."

She moaned, her hands fisting in the surrounding blankets. "I want you to fuck me. Please fuck me."

"Yes, ma'am," he said, and he'd barely finished the sentence before he was ripping a condom wrapper open, sliding it down over his cock, and pushing inside her tight pussy. "You like the way I fill you up?"

"Yes, yes, yes," she moaned, her hips lifting to meet his strokes as he slid in and out of her.

"Tell me you want it harder. Beg me to make you come."

"Harder, please. Please make me come. Make me come!"

Alexis' body was slick with sweat where his weight pressed down on her, but she liked it. She liked the weight of him, the feel of his hips undulating as he moved inside her, the way he moved a hand over her belly so he could thumb her clit while he fucked her. Pleasure washed over her in waves until finally she cried out with the explosion of it. She clenched tightly around his cock once hard, then the softer, rhythmic pulses of her pussy coaxed another orgasm from him.

Sidney rolled from her body and collapsed on the bed beside her. His breathing was deep and heavy, his chest was shiny with sweat and rising and falling with every labored breath.

"Still green?"

"Still green," she agreed.

"Good."

17

If there was one thing Alexis didn't want to be doing right now, it was crying. But saying your nasty inside thoughts aloud wasn't the best idea she'd ever had. Telling those thoughts to your friend... well, she had a lot of regrets at the moment, and that could definitely start up the waterworks. A glance in the rearview mirror when she pulled into Mia's driveway confirmed her eyes were glassy and red-rimmed.

She took a breath to compose herself and walked up the porch steps. Her footsteps were slow and measured, as if controlling her pace would help calm her racing heart.

"You've been crying," Mia said, her arms already open wide.

Alexis was done for. Her feet closed the distance between them, and she stepped into Mia's arms, her body shaking with the force of her sobs.

Mia only held on that much tighter.

"I'm sorry I said such awful things to you," Alexis said. "They were true, and I meant them."

"Well, that's nice to know," Mia said with a laugh.

"But I shouldn't have unloaded it all like that," Alexis finished.

"You have nothing to be sorry for. I've been an awful friend," Mia said, and tears pricked at her own eyes. They held onto each other a few moments more before separating and wiping their hands over their faces. Sniffling, Mia wrapped her arm around Alexis' waist and rested her head on her shoulder. "Do you forgive me for being the worst?" she asked.

"Always," Alexis said, leaning her head on top of Mia's.

"I'm glad you got mad at me so we could have this moment," Mia joked.

Alexis laughed. "Anytime. Now, where's the wine and the strippers?"

They walked inside together and took seats in the kitchen. Alexis watched as Mia laid out platters of deli meat, cheese, crackers, and fruit. She brought out a chilled bottle of white wine, setting it on the counter along with two stemless glasses. Alexis plucked a cube of cheese off the tray and popped it into her mouth.

This felt normal, she thought with a wistful sigh. She hadn't realized how much she needed that in her life right now.

"Alexis Donnely, did you get your hair cut?" Mia asked suddenly.

Alexis' hand flew instinctively to her hair. "It's my therapy. Sarah did it for me. You like?"

"I love! She did a great job. It looks fantastic on you."

"Thanks! I'm loving it, too. Who knew that woman could give me a proper cut?" Alexis remarked.

The cut really did look phenomenal on her. Where her tight brown curls had fallen to her shoulder in almost one length, they were now slightly shorter and layered so they almost bounced playfully away from her face, and now with more bangs to frame it. The whole look was fresh and vibrant.

"You should drop in on her. You could use a refresh, too," Alexis said.

"Maybe once I figure out if her husband is an ax murderer or not."

Alexis poured wine into a glass and took a sip. "Better you than me. I'm glad to leave all the ghosts in your head."

She knew she sounded uneasy about the topic. She couldn't explain exactly why, but she hoped Mia wouldn't notice.

"Oh, thanks for that," Mia said.

"Speaking of people who aren't ghosts, are you and Nick going to come out with us this weekend?"

"I'm thinking about it." Alexis raised her brows skeptically, and Mia squeaked, "I am!"

"Have you even told Nick about it yet?"

"Not yet, exactly."

Alexis muttered under her breath, wishing Mia would stop being as stubborn as an ass.

"So is the outing with the guy who's currently scratching your itch?" Mia asked, effectively changing the subject.

Alexis recognized the tactic but ignored it for now. "I haven't decided, but I like him enough to see where this goes. For now."

"But you're still feeling itchy?"

"Yeah, I don't know what it is. I thought maybe it was the guy, but the guy is great. Working with you sounds fun, but I still feel restless, like I'm supposed to be doing something, but I can't figure out what that something is."

"Well, I'm really glad you'll be with me at the shop. It gets kind of creepy in there when it's quiet during the day. When we're slow, you'll have time to explore more and maybe figure out what's causing that itch."

"Maybe," Alexis agreed, and they fell into silence.

"Have you ever thought about writing a book?" Alexis asked suddenly.

"Me? Absolutely not. I was happy enough editing them and happy now to sell them, but I do not want to strap myself to a computer for hours on end trying to drag magic out of my brain and onto paper. Why do you ask?"

"I do," Alexis said, looking somewhat wistfully out the window. She turned her gaze back to Mia. "I've been thinking about it a lot lately, actually."

"What do you want to write?"

"Oh, I don't know," Alexis said, but it sounded as if she very much knew. "Maybe I'd write romance or mysteries, or both. Wouldn't that be fun?"

"It sounds like it might be for you. Have you written anything yet?"

Alexis nodded bashfully. "I have," she admitted.

"Maybe that's why you're feeling restless. You've got a book locked up inside, and it's begging to get out. You've seen that in our debut authors. You can't keep that locked up," Mia said. She picked up the bottle of wine and refilled both of their glasses. "So how far have you got?"

"About half."

"Of the outline or a manuscript?"

"Ha! You know better than to expect me to have an outline, but the first draft is about halfway there," Alexis said. "Would you mind giving it a read when I'm done, maybe giving me some editing notes?"

"Of course. Lex, this is so exciting!" Mia said.

"Hold your horses, Mia," Alexis said breathlessly. She put a hand to her chest, hoping to slow the beat of her racing heart. "I'm still getting used to the idea. I wonder if Nick knows of a good agent. Someone tough but who isn't going to make me cry when they need round nine of edits done."

"I'm sure he does. You should call him later. You know, we'll have to do a big deal event when the book is released to celebrate a local author."

"It's not even finished yet, and isn't Nick a local author, too?"

"Technicalities, my friend!" Mia said with a laugh. "And now we drink to your success! May the book of your heart become a bestseller."

"I'll cheers to that!" Alexis said, clinking her glass against Mia's in both celebration and relief.

18

The sun streamed through the blinds at Sweet Bea's with the same arrogance all morning people possessed. The apple clearly didn't fall far from the tree, Alexis thought, all but glaring up at Ben—with his cheery, almost gleeful disposition—from the rim of her coffee cup. It wasn't like she *wasn't* a morning person exactly... she just wasn't one specifically. She certainly wouldn't identify herself as one in her current mood.

Alexis wasn't even sure why the sun and his smile and this whole goddamn morning bothered her so much. For appearance's sake, things were going splendidly in her life.

The book was coming along, her friendships were not so on the rocks, and her bed hadn't been so empty lately. Truly, there wasn't much to complain about. Good food, good friends, good sex, and all that. So why could she not shake this black cloud?

"What's up, sugar butt?" Ben asked, his cheek propped on a fist. He held his coffee mug in his other hand, and steam poured out of the top of it in gentle waves until it dissipated into the air.

She groaned and dropped her head into her arms on the table. "I don't know," she said, her voice muffled.

"Mmm," Ben said, pursing his lips.

She peeked up at him. "That's it?"

"Honey, I'm a bartender, not a psychic."

The mention of visions and psychics had Alexis groaning and dropping her head back down again. "No woo-woo talk," she mumbled.

"Then you're gonna have to start talking, doll."

Why had she agreed to this again? Alexis wondered. Oh right. Something about the bonds of friendship and reaching out for support when you needed it and all that. She sighed.

"I'm being kind of a brat, aren't I?" Alexis asked. When he didn't respond, she nodded to herself. "Okay, okay, okay. Head out of ass. Ugh. Sorry about that."

"Lex, drink your damn coffee."

Alexis gave him a half-smile and picked up her cup, draining half its contents as quickly as she could. She let the warmth slide down her throat, felt it warm her core, and steadied herself with a few deep breaths.

"Better?"

She nodded.

"Good. Now tell me what's up?"

"I'm not sure. I know, I know—" she held up a hand in defense and continued, "Don't murder me! I think that's actually the problem. Everything is wonderful, but I'm in such a pissy mood about it."

Her phone buzzed on the far side of the table. She glanced down and saw Sidney's name flash across the screen.

"Speak of the devil!"

"You're mad the devil's texting you?"

"Sidney. It's Sidney."

"I thought things were good there. You seemed to hit it off."

Alexis rubbed a finger at her temple and closed her eyes for a moment. When she opened them, she wasn't looking at Ben. Instead, she was looking across the cafe at a couple splitting a muffin.

"You see that couple over there?" Alexis asked.

Ben turned and looked over his shoulder at the pair. He recognized the pair. They'd both known them for years, in fact. They were a couple of high school sweethearts right out of a made-for-television movie. He faced Alexis again, his brows drawn, and nodded slowly.

"They look pretty happy. When we were in school, she used to dream about being a scuba diver and traveling all over the world. They got married right after graduation, and I don't think she's left the city since."

"What does that have to do with anything?"

Alexis merely shook her head and continued. "He looks head over heels for her, right? But I've seen him getting real comfy with home-wrecking Gabby lately."

"Gabby? Gabby Mendez?"

"The very same," she said.

"Bless his heart," Ben said with more judgment than sympathy.

"You're nicer than I am." Ben made a sound in the back of his throat, waiting for her to continue. "Buddy up to Mike, make friends with Lindsey, find the weak spot, and *bam!* Lindsey's going to find herself pushed out before she knows it."

"That's not going to happen."

"Sure, it will. Just you watch."

"How is she going to push out someone he's absolutely devoted to? I've seen the way he looks at her," he said.

Alexis gave him a sideways look. "Doesn't matter. The manipulative ones always know how to maneuver men. She'll start off sweet, but before long that bestie vibe will wear thin, and then she'll be all up in his ear about how awful Lindsey is. He won't even know he's looking at his wife any differently, that she no longer feels like home, until it's over. Maybe not even then. She'll ruin them."

"How do you know?"

Alexis rolled her eyes. "Gabby's twenty-something, goes to the beach in a full beat of makeup, and has lashes as big as caterpillars attached to her eyeballs. All men fawn over the pick-me energy, and he won't even realize he's chosen the two-faced twit over his wife until he's telling Lindsey he just needs some space."

"Your faith in men is astounding."

Alexis shrugged and turned her gaze back to her coffee.

"I still don't really get what that has to do with the point you're trying to make. Are you worried Sidney is like that?" Ben asked.

"Maybe. But it's more the bigger picture. Lindsey gave up everything to be with him. She settled down thinking she'd have her *happily ever after*, and he's over there fucking it up and making it all meaningless. They all do."

"Whoa, okay, no." Ben set his mug down with enough force to have the table ringing and liquid sloshing over the rim. "What we will not do is take this sour mood you're in and assign some asinine childhood trauma to a couple we barely still talk to. So what if Mike's cheating on her? So what if Lindsey decided she'd rather get married and pop out some kids? People grow up. What they want changes. They change. They're allowed to."

Alexis sat back, stunned. A flush of temper bloomed across her cheeks. "I never said people aren't allowed to change."

"Sure sounded like it," Ben snapped.

"Just because I can see the inevitable doesn't mean I'm wrong," she snapped back. She grabbed for the napkins to sop up the coffee sitting around the base of his mug, but her agitated and jerky hands made her knock over her own cup instead.

There was a flurry of groans and motion, and suddenly Ben was pushing her hands away, sopping up the mess with a towel a server handed him. Alexis sat back, her entire system a series of reactions and alarm bells.

Ben kept his eyes on the table and said, "Love doesn't mean losing yourself. Neither does getting married or settling down."

She didn't know what to say, so she simply folded her arms to herself and let the silence fill the space between them. Without question, she'd been thoroughly chastised, but she couldn't bring herself to admit that to him yet. The problem was that she didn't feel wrong. So many of the relationships she'd seen and even been in had all led in the same direction. Two people became some kind of unit, and eventually one of them—and let's be honest, it was usually the woman—gave up who they were or what they wanted to make it all work.

She didn't want to make it work.

She didn't want to face the eventuality that she'd invest in yet another relationship only to be asked to be something or someone she wasn't. It's how it always went. Why couldn't anyone just be happy with the way things are? Why was there always this push for more and more and more? It was exhausting. How could anyone expect her to be more, to give more?

"Am I watching you regulate or spiral out?" Ben asked, interrupting what was absolutely a spiral. "Nevermind, that was a stupid question. Let me try that again. Where are you and Sidney currently? Relationship wise."

Alexis took a deep breath. Pulling her thoughts out of the depths of her brain was like yanking on a boot that had gotten itself suctioned into a pile of mud, but she finally managed it.

"We're just enjoying each other."

"Then maybe stop all this nonsense and go do that."

"You're too smart to be so straight. You know that?"

Ben shrugged. "Not making me attracted to men was definitely one of God's finer moments."

Alexis laughed. "You don't believe in God."

"Hey, I'm just covering all my bases."

"If you were really interested in covering your bases, you'd at least try to be bisexual."

"And live in your special kind of dating hell? Fuck that."

Alexis was still chuckling to herself about that when she opted for a walk down the beach later. There was a pleasant breeze coming off the water, and though she hadn't brought a swimsuit, she'd dressed in a tank top and shorts with sandals that slipped off for easy walking on the damp sand.

Luckily, Ben did not want to hold her words against her, but she noticed she had become involved in two fights with two of her closest friends. Not a great testament to all the time (and money) she'd spent in therapy learning to control her big fat mouth.

It was over now, though. She was thankful for that. Balance had been restored to the universe. Well, at least to her universe. She pulled out her phone, determined to stop overthinking this mess and move on with her day.

SIDNEY

Hey you. Still on for this weekend?

ALEXIS

Of course. I invited Mia and her situationship, too. I hope you don't mind.

To her relief, he responded almost immediately.

SIDNEY

Not at all.

ALEXIS

I figured.

SIDNEY

The more the merrier, and all that. I'm just
excited to see you.

ALEXIS

You had me all to yourself last weekend,
cowboy. Careful or you'll start accidentally
dating me.

SIDNEY

Ok

"Okay?" Alexis read aloud. What was that supposed to mean? She knew she wasn't the most eloquent texting companion, but at least she was consistent. Sometimes he was so short and to the point that she wondered what exactly his point was anyway. Did he know "ok" was almost the most passive-aggressive thing you could text? It was second only to "Fine."

She shook her head. It didn't matter what he meant, she told herself, or how infuriating she found his text communication style at this moment. The conversation was over.

No sooner had the thought crossed her mind than her phone rang, the screen lighting up with Sidney's name.

"Really?" she asked aloud, but she answered because of course she did.

"Can you talk?" he asked.

She looked around the beach. It was quiet today, and she was relieved about that. "Sure. What's up?"

"What are we?"

"That's how you want to start that conversation?"

"Yes."

Ah, so she was talking to the decisive man today, not the charmer. His tone only made her want to punch him in the face a little, but she sucked in a breath between clenched teeth.

"Okay, then. Well, we are seeing each other. Enjoying each other."

"Dating?" he asked.

"I guess you could say that, yeah." Warning bells were going off in her head. She looked out over the water, and the breeze made her baby hairs dance across her face. She'd pulled her hair into two low bubble braids, one on either side of her head, just before her walk, expecting casual peace, a little serenity. Not this. "Why do you ask now?"

"I don't know."

She resisted the urge to groan. Why did men always do this? Anytime one of them was asked about themselves or their feelings that they didn't know, they just stopped there. No introspection. No motivation to do the work that would be required to actually figure out that answer. Just, "I don't know."

She was remembering why she preferred dating women.

Okay, maybe that wasn't fair. Completely. Maybe she was a little on edge, and she should cut him some slack. Alexis knew things had been stressful at work—stress was basically his entire job—and she was not happy about her calm being interrupted. She stared over the water and timed her breathing to the lapping waves. She wanted them to take a step back and move out of hostile territory.

Somebody had to do it.

"Do you want to be something else?" she asked. *Like single*, she snapped in her head.

"No, dating is good."

The warning bell rang again. She didn't consider them to be dating. Not really. Seeing each other, enjoying each other... that's how she described whatever they were to other people. It's how she thought about it herself. She wasn't really ready to be dating yet. She hadn't even really settled into being single.

But she didn't want to make a fuss and ruin a good thing

either. She liked their connection. She liked what they were exploring together, how he was allowing her to open parts of herself she hadn't let herself see yet. If he needed to consider them a "together" right now, she thought she could do that until it felt right. Technically, that was dating. Perhaps they just saw it as different levels right now. That could be fine.

"Are you trying to ask if we're official?" she asked.

There was a pause on the other end of the line. She could hear him breathing, but she could've sworn she also heard him thinking, weighing, considering.

"I think so," he said finally.

"And that'll make you feel better right now so I can keep walking down this beach in peace?" she said, hoping her sarcasm would lighten the mood.

He laughed, and it sounded like amusement wrapped in relief and gratitude. "Yeah."

"We're together. I'm not sleeping with anyone else. You're not sleeping with anyone unless I'm invited to the party, I hope. And we're about to spend another weekend together. Is that good for you?"

There was another pause, though shorter this time, and Alexis wondered if he wanted more. But he said, "Yes, that's good for me."

"Good," she said, relief flooding over her. She wasn't sure if she was relieved they'd avoided conflict or at the solution they'd come to, but peace was peace.

"And sweetheart..." he said, the playful charmer back. "If I want to sleep with anyone else, you're definitely coming to that party."

19

Everything burned—her eyes, her back, the muscles in her fingers for god's sake—but it was not the pain that finally interrupted her hours-long writing session. It was the sharp, insistent knocking on her door that started and didn't stop until she practically threw it open.

"What?" she all but screamed.

Standing on the other side was Harper wearing almost nothing but a smirk on her face. Her crop top was damp beneath her breasts, and the cut-off shorts rode high on her hips.

"Sorry." Alexis cleared her throat, squinting against the afternoon sun. "Uh, what are you doing?"

"Saving you from yourself," she said, grabbing Alexis' t-shirt in a fist and yanking her through the doorway.

Alexis stumbled and sputtered. "But—wait—I need to save it at least!"

But Harper was relentless.

"Autosave exists!"

Alexis found herself pulled across her lawn and the one

next to it, then sat down in a white plastic chair on the porch next door. Harper shoved a neon green plastic cup into her hand and plopped herself into the chair beside her. The cup was the worst shade of green imaginable, Alexis thought, but it was a cold and welcome respite. She smiled to herself and took a sip. The beads of condensation dripped onto the thin cotton of her house pants, and the ice chinked and rattled in the cool liquid.

"Better?" Harper asked, a smirk still plastered across her face.

"Yeah, yeah, yeah." Alexis laughed. "How did you know I needed a break?"

Harper relaxed into the chair and propped a bare foot on the seat next to her. Her arm draped across her folded knee as she swirled her tea. "It might've been the fact that you ignored my cat howling at your back door for over an hour. Or the postman acting like a lunatic trying to get your signature."

Alexis opened her mouth, but Harper raised a hand to silence her.

"Don't worry. I signed for it. It's on your kitchen counter."

When Alexis' brows drew together, Harper laughed. "You left your back door unlocked. Didn't even notice when I let myself in to give you the package."

"Then why all the knocking?"

"Oh, that was just to mess with you. I wanted to see how long it would take you to open the door."

Alexis chuckled with an exasperated sigh, turning her face up to the sun and closing her eyes. She let her head fall back and rest on the wooden siding behind them. She didn't want to admit how good it felt to sit outside in the sun. Maybe she'd been a solar panel in another life. It made little sense if you thought about it closely. As far as she knew, solar panels were a newer technology and hadn't been around long enough for that. But it felt right if time didn't exist, and her mind was mush enough from hours of writing to be satisfied with that.

"Six minutes and twenty-seven seconds."

"Is that a fact?" she said with her eyes still closed.

"Mmhmm."

"Thank you, by the way. For the signature, yes, but also for dragging me out of there like a wild woman."

"That's what friends are for."

The first thing Sidney saw when he arrived was two gorgeous women sitting together just like that, a picture of slow southern afternoons taken right out of a magazine. The porch might be smaller, the house less grand, and the lawn less manicured, but it was quite a picture all the same.

"So you're the man I keep seeing coming and going lately," the woman said to him with a grin.

"Yeah, that'd be me," he replied. He walked over the grass, feeling it crunch dry beneath his shoes, and stopped short of the porch in the shade of a nearby tree. They needed some rain soon, he thought to himself.

"What are you doing here?" Alexis asked.

Sidney shrugged. "Just dropping by."

He tucked his hands into the pockets of his shorts and rocked back on his heels, taking in the sight of her. Even in a loose-fitting shirt and what looked like pajama pants, with her hair tousled and no makeup to speak of, she was breathtaking. Tired, too, though. He noted the bags under her eyes and wondered how she'd filled her day.

"Is that so?" Alexis asked. She set her cup on the table next to her and stood, brushing at the back of her pants.

"It is," he said.

"Welp, this has been super fun, but I'm going to go inside now and leave you two crazy kids to finish this awkward conversation without me."

Alexis laughed as Harper gathered their cups and made her way inside. She walked down the few porch stairs and moved past Sidney. She said nothing, didn't even give him so much as a look, but still she looked pleased when he turned and began walking in step with her.

"Are you hungry?" she asked.

"How did you know?"

"You're a man," she said simply. "You're always hungry."

"I could take offense at that."

"But you won't because you are, in fact, hungry." She shrugged and smiled, continuing into her house and expecting him to follow. The cool air slapped him in the face like walking into a literal wall of air and was a welcome respite from the humidity outside.

He gave her a lopsided smile and shook his head. "Starved," he laughed. "I was hoping I could stop by and grab some dinner with you."

"Let me go change and freshen up first. Make yourself at home." When he moved to follow her into the bedroom, she added with a pointed look, "On the couch."

She laughed when he slumped his shoulders like a cartoon dog being told he couldn't have a treat. It echoed through the house as she walked around the corner, and Sidney shuffled back into the living room. He dropped onto the couch and listened to the sounds of water running, of plastic and glass clanking on countertops, drawers opening and closing.

Women were amazing creatures who could take two minutes or two hours to get ready, so he amused himself by trying to decipher what was happening by sound alone. He supposed it could be considered job training, depending on your perspective. His job as a detective certainly hinged on noticing details out of context and then putting them together, deciding what mattered and what didn't.

Without warning, a clatter of sounds pulled Sidney out of his thoughts and had him scrambling down the hall. "What was that? Alexis? Are you okay?"

He found Alexis hunched over the sink, shaken but unharmed. Various bottles and jars littered the floor around her feet, but she seemed unfazed by the mess. When she didn't respond to his call again, he slapped the faucet on, wet a cloth, and shoved it into her hands, moving them up onto her neck so that she held it there. He maneuvered her to the toilet and pushed her onto the closed seat.

He knelt in front of her and watched as the pulse hammering at her throat slowed and her breathing steadied. "What happened?"

She shook her head slowly, and her tongue darted out to lick her lips. "Nothing. Just a spell."

"Nuh uh, nothing about this was fine."

"I'm fine, really. Sidney. I'm fine," she assured him, though her voice sounded far less firm than he thought she'd intended.

His eyes narrowed.

"Does that happen often?"

The question had an immediate effect, and she stood abruptly, pushing past him on her way right out the bathroom door.

"No, yes, sometimes. Not so much, really." She pushed a hand into her hair, a habit of hers he'd noticed. She did it more when she was frustrated.

His eyes stayed zeroed in on her.

"You're not going to let this go, are you?" she asked.

His head moved slowly from side to side. He drew himself up to his full height and moved to the doorway of the adjoining bathroom. Propping his shoulder against the frame, he waited.

She held out a hand and said, "I'm not crazy. Whatever you're thinking, I'm not. I've never been diagnosed with anything other than anxiety, and I've never been hospitalized."

Intrigued by her defensiveness as much as by plain curiosity, Sidney inclined his head slightly, prompting her to continue. He was like a hunting dog once it caught an interesting scent. It was what made him a good detective.

"Sometimes I have these—" she paused as if to find the right words. "Visions. Like waking dreams. Disorienting but harmless."

"Mmm. This isn't some weird cancer thing where I'm going to fall in love with you and then you'll tell me on our wedding day that you can't marry me because you're going to die."

"Whoa there," she laughed despite herself, pushing a hand through her hair. "It really is harmless. Usually."

Sidney looked pointedly toward the mess of a bathroom and then back to her. "I see."

Alexis stood in a huff and paced the room. "Don't you dare judge me!"

"I didn't say anything."

"You didn't have to."

Sidney held up a hand. It wasn't worth escalating her simply to satisfy his curiosity. "Come here."

She stopped pacing and stared at him, but her body remained rooted to the spot across the room. He gestured with an outstretched hand, a quick movement of his fingers that begged no argument. She hesitated a moment longer, then her shoulders sagged, and she dropped onto the bed beside him.

"Do they bother you? The dreams," he clarified, reaching out and pushing her head onto his shoulder.

He could sense that Alexis wanted to feel comforted, and to her credit, she tried to relax against him. She shook her head. "Yes and no. They're confusing but mostly inconvenient." She gestured toward the bathroom. "And messy."

Sidney nodded with a small smile. "True."

"The worst is when I'm going somewhere new, trying to remember directions, and a flash of random street signs interrupts my day."

"Street signs?" he asked.

"Yeah," she laughed. "You have no idea how annoying it is to be blessed with a sense of direction so bad that the idea of another street name is enough to get you all turned around."

"Is that what you saw just now?"

He was kicking himself as soon as the words left his mouth. She'd just relaxed again, and in truth, his curiosity was already fading as quickly as the rumbling in his stomach grew. He really was starving.

"Just now? Um, yes. Live Oak Lane and Baker Street, actually."

"Live Oak and Baker..." his voice trailed off. He'd just been at that cross street working a case, and a nasty one at that. They were at a standstill at the moment, a frustrating place to be where evidence was scarce and leads were few.

Alexis seemed not to notice the way he was retreating into his thoughts, but that was certainly preferable to the alternative. He'd found that relationships didn't last long when his partner peppered him with questions they really didn't want the answers to. Actual crime fighting was nothing like the shows portrayed. Progress was slow, and detectives were always working a dozen cases or more. Their solve rate was abysmal compared to their television counterparts, even with all the advances in investigation techniques and forensics.

But while her lack of interest in his work was a relief, he still wasn't sure what to make of her or their situation. She was certainly an interesting creature, that was for sure. Interesting enough that he was happy to spend time with her and let the chips fall where they may. Dating, they'd agreed. They were dating. Maybe he'd want more one day, but for now, that was enough for him.

"—also get snippets of things like clothing or a feeling. Being cold or wet, scratchy or hot," she was saying. "Like this time I saw the street signs and then felt all constricted by my clothes, as if my pants or something were just a little too tight. Then I come to again, and that's that."

Something about the way she described the clothing nagged at him, as if tugging on a memory locked away somewhere in his mind. Clearly, this was a disorder of some kind, which under normal circumstances would be fine. People walked around living full, happy, functioning lives with all manner of diseases and diagnoses, and no one the wiser. He only needed to know if this was the lucid dreaming type of situation or that of the psychosis variety. He doubted the latter, but he needed to be sure.

The logic made sense. Weird dreams plus gorgeous woman meant trauma and therapy, maybe some medication. No big deal. Still, something nagged at him. The street signs and the clothing. Wasn't it strange to have waking dreams about that kind of thing instead of—oh, he didn't know—going to work with no pants? He couldn't put his finger on it, but his weird meter was spiking.

His stomach growled, and he looked sheepishly from it to her. "How about we order in?"

Alexis laughed and stood. "I think that's a perfect idea. I'll take care of this mess in the meantime."

Snagging her about the waist, Sidney tossed her back onto the bed and covered her body with his. "I have a better idea."

20

A dull thud, the scratching of dirt scraping against metal, the distant rumbling of cars and conversation. She lay flat on her back somewhere in the dark. Her body was motionless, limbs heavy, eyes wandering. Warmth emanated up from the ground beneath her while cool air stroked her skin from above. It was night, and still her vision darkened as if every moment was a still from a silent film fading into black at the edges.

A metal sign adorned with an image of railroad tracks creaked as it swung back and forth in the hot breeze, ringing out each time it slapped against the brick wall it was mounted to. The sound startled her, made her skin prickle with awareness, and yet she couldn't summon the will to move. A figure cloaked in the night itself loomed above her. It lifted her body, and for a moment, she was weightless, flying until the ground slammed against her back.

She felt no pain, only a jarring sensation of movement suddenly stopping and the dirt beneath her. It was cooler now, the chill seeping up from below and consuming her inch by inch.

Dirt scraped metal once again. Thud, scrape, thud, scrape. A shower of itchy crumbs rained over her body. She tried to blink them *away, clear her vision, shake them from her nose, but her body refused to cooperate. So heavy were her limbs, so heavy and so cold.*

More dirt.

She tried to scream, move, claw her way to fresh air. If only she could beg the shadowy figure to help her, but the weight of the ground pressed in around her, suffocating her.

She couldn't breathe.

She couldn't...

Alexis sat up in bed with a gasp, her hands clawing at her throat, wiping at her eyes. She gulped down air as if she hadn't taken a breath in hours, her chest heaving with the effort of it. Sweat slicked her body, casting a shine on her skin in the morning light that streamed through her bedroom window. She pushed a hand through her hair, frantic to get it out of her face, to get everything away from her face, and gulped. Her hand moved to cover her heart, the pounding of it all but beating through her chest.

She glanced down at the figure stretched out in the bed beside her, her eyes following the line of his legs to a face as wide awake as hers. Her cheeks flushed as she realized the state she was in. After last night, there was no doubt in her mind that he probably thought she was certifiable.

"Bad dream?" he asked, his voice husky with sleep.

Alexis took a deep breath and shook her head. His raised brow had her wanting to both roll her eyes and slug him in the jaw, but when she thought about it, she wasn't actually being untrue. It hadn't been a bad dream. Strange and unsettling, sure, but that was the extent of it.

She swung her legs over the edge of the bed and muttered something she hoped was coherent about taking a shower as she padded into the bathroom. She just needed a moment to settle, and she couldn't do that with him staring at her.

Sidney wasn't sure exactly how he felt. His first bleary

thought of the day was concern, obviously. The woman he was sleeping with—and enjoyed the company of, thank you very much—was clearly going through something and was determined to keep him at arm's length. Whether it was because she was just the type with sky-high walls, he wasn't sure. He certainly would not risk his own peace and sanity to live out some Captain Save-a-Ho fantasy, but he wasn't a complete ass. So long as she wasn't losing her marbles, he was concerned and curious enough to want to know what was going on. Feeling helpless wasn't his favorite feeling in the world.

Not to mention the way she pulled at him. There was the physical attraction, of course, a fact he was well aware of. It only took a glance down at the covers pooled around his waist to confirm that. He wanted to enjoy this, whatever it was between them, as much as he wanted to enjoy her. Doing that safely and with their sanity intact was a top priority.

Movement outside the window caught his eye. The early morning light was still soft against the retreating night, but he could still see fairly well. He smiled to himself as he saw a figure no longer a little boy but not quite a teenager hauling a trailer with his bike.

The boy slowed long enough to stand on the pedals and throw a newspaper at the driveway before his legs were pushing down again, and he was on to the next house. Sidney found it strange that the boy hauled a trailer behind him, that it contained such a large and presumably heavy duffel bag, but he supposed that's what happened when you were probably the last small town to have kids delivering papers at dawn. Likely there weren't many volunteering for the job, and routes were long.

Sidney contemplated getting dressed and retrieving the paper while he waited, but it turned out Alexis was already out of the shower. Barely any steam escaped when she reopened the bathroom door, and she emerged with dry hair wearing the same loose t-shirt she'd gone to bed in. He wondered if she'd actually showered or just sat in the bathroom collecting herself instead.

"Better?" he asked.

"Yeah, sorry," she said in a tone that practically begged for the subject to be changed.

"It's no problem," he said, propping an arm on the pillow behind his head. "Do your visions come as dreams sometimes, too?"

"They're not visions." She held up her hands and gestured with air quotes when she said the word.

The mattress dipped when she slid back into bed, and Sidney instinctively opened his arm in invitation. She hesitated a moment before coming to him.

"Good, I was worried you weren't the morning cuddles type," he said.

"Why wouldn't I like morning cuddles? Doesn't everyone like morning cuddles?"

Sidney shrugged. "I don't know. I haven't slept with them all to find out."

Alexis smiled and looked up at him. He couldn't help but grin right back. It was nice to see her smile. Maybe this would be closer to their normal. That could be a nice thought.

"Well, I do."

"Perfect. Now I can hold you while you tell me about these visions," he teased.

"They're not visions," she said with a breathy laugh.

"You called them visions," he reminded her.

She groaned. "I know."

"So, they're something. Why don't you tell me about this one? Unless you're scared."

"Are we in kindergarten?"

"Christ, woman, just tell me what woke you up like that," he said, enjoying the topic now with this playful banter much more than he had its more serious twin last night.

"Okay, okay, okay. Just hold your horses," she said.

He held up pinched fingers. "Holding."

Alexis rolled her eyes at him, always a sign of a successful dad joke if he said so himself. Then she finally recounted the vision, dream, whatever she wanted to call it. She spoke of the sounds of digging, creaking signs that slapped against brick, the heaviness of her body, and more. It was certainly an interesting mystery, and mysteries had always fascinated him.

"You don't look as freaked out as yesterday."

His shoulders rose and fell beneath her head. "I told you I'm good with weird. What do you think they mean?"

Alexis shifted her position so that she was facing him, her body pressed along his in a long line under the covers. All the places where their bare skin touched suddenly felt ten degrees hotter.

"You mean in general, or this one?"

"In general."

"I'm not sure," she said, her face tipped up to his as her hand wandered down over his stomach to what was already hard and waiting below.

His pulse hammered at his throat, his heart racing in anticipation. Jesus, you'd think he hadn't been with a woman in months by the way his body was reacting. It was, frankly, kind of embarrassing. He would consider himself more of the stoic type, yet his body was responding to her as anything but.

"I try not to think about them too much, honestly. They're silly and annoying, and that's all there is to them," she said, her volume dropping more and more into a whisper with every word.

Her breath was hot on his jawline as she traced it with her

lips, settling them on the skin below his ear while her hands drove him mad beneath the covers.

He groaned when she trailed her mouth down his chest, over his belly, and wrapped those perfect lips around his cock. She pushed the covers away from their bodies as she took him deep into her throat. He watched as it disappeared and reappeared, her hands working in time with her mouth to stroke him from base to tip. He knew she was distracting him from asking anymore prying questions, but goddamn, right now he didn't care.

"Fuck. You're so good at that."

Alexis murmured in acknowledgment, moving away from his cock to take his balls into her mouth. He gasped at the sensitive play, his head falling back and his eyes closing as her mouth and tongue and lips and hands worked over him. Then her mouth was around his cock again, and he was deep in her throat. His hands fisted in her hair, and he pushed his hips against her face, his movements matching the rhythm of hers. Her eyes watered, and he could feel her throat contracting around him, but still she continued.

"Yes, baby. Take it, take it, take it," he growled as they moved together, his cock slamming into the back of her throat again and again. Their gazes locked as his body drew closer and closer to climax. "You gonna make me come?"

She nodded, and the pace of her mouth and hands grew even more frantic. His entire body bucked against her, all of his muscles tensing. His breath was coming fast and harsh, his cock pulsing with every choking sound and gurgle she made. With a feral roar, he pushed himself as far down her throat as possible, relishing the feeling of her teeth straining against the base of him, and he exploded inside her.

Sidney collapsed as the powerful throbs subsided, twitching and groaning as she worked to swallow his cum. She slid her lips off him with an excruciating slowness that had him gasping. He supported her body as she settled back against him, cupping her cheek and tipping her face up to his. He captured her lips, relishing the way she moaned into his mouth, and kissed her deeply. His tongue danced with hers until she was writhing against him.

He held her in a side-facing position, scooting his body down the bed and pushing her leg onto his shoulder. His teeth scraped down her side and belly until he was hovering just above the warm, sensitive flesh between her legs. His tongue traced the curves of her, dipping into the folds of her lips until her hips were straining against him and he could hear her panting.

"Beg for it," he said, his lips barely touching her clit.

She groaned, and he couldn't help but smile at the torture. She was stubborn enough to resist him out of spite, he was sure, but she was also glistening with wet, her body hot with need. As much as they'd tried the night before, an orgasm had eluded her, a subject of much frustration that he was sure she was dying to remedy now.

And he was determined to give it to her.

"Beg me to make you come," he ordered, his tongue pushing into her as deep as he could go, then withdrawing.

Her hands pushed into his hair, her fingernails digging into his scalp as she strained to pull him in again. "Please," she panted. "Make me come. Please."

It was exactly what he wanted to hear.

He filled her with his tongue, lapping her up like a man in the desert dying of thirst. Then his fingers replaced his tongue, and he moved his mouth up to cover her clit. He pressed it flat against the swollen nub and rubbed it up and down, keeping pressure on it as his fingers hooked inside her and found the soft cushion of her g-spot. His lips formed a tight circle around her clit, and he sucked. Gently at first, then harder and faster while his fingers pressed up inside her, his hand sliding them in and out.

Her legs shook as liquid poured out of her, spraying his face and soaking the bed beneath them, but he didn't stop yet. There was more pleasure to be wrung from her body, he knew it. Seconds later, she cried out. Her hips bucked against him, and the walls of her pussy clenched hard around his fingers again and again. She held onto him for what seemed an eternity until the spasms finally ebbed, and her body melted into a puddle.

He rested his head on her inner thigh, sated and pleased at the delicious mess they'd made of each other. It was going to be a wonderful day. He was sure of it.

21

This woman was going to be the death of him. It was all he could think as he walked out of the cafe. He was good with weird, he reminded himself, but he hadn't realized just how much that statement would be tested. There was Alexis with her visions—and he was doubting whether he believed that's all they were—and now her friend Mia was off ghost hunting. At least he could be a voice of reason in all of this. He hoped.

Alexis followed him outside, stepping to the side of the sidewalk with him when his phone rang.

"Neal," he answered.

The voice on the other end of the line was curt and straight to the point. There had been a murder. Behind The Raleway. He needed to come right away.

"I'll be right there. Another kid?"

He inhaled sharply and mentally prepared himself. Alexis was watching him, a little wrinkle forming between her brows. He hung up the phone, sliding it into his pocket and patting his jeans as if that would help him know what to do with his hands.

"Duty calls," she said.

He nodded, his mind already elsewhere.

"I'll see you later?" she asked.

He nodded again. The air between them suddenly felt tight, the atmosphere stiff. He leaned down to kiss her cheek, his movements awkward and stilted.

She shook her head with a small smile, something between amusement and pity, maybe pity for his entire species. "Okay then. Don't die."

That teased a chuckle from Sidney, and he answered, "I'll try."

They parted ways, and he spent the drive to the bar locking his emotions down. It wasn't as hard as he knew it should be. He often joked that he didn't have feelings, though he knew that wasn't exactly true. He just knew that he needed to keep his under control. Control eliminates chaos, and that was how he preferred his life: chaos-free. He had enough chaos to deal with at work. Kids were always the hardest cases, and he didn't like the pattern that was emerging as more tiny bodies piled up.

He arrived at The Raleway and saw that officers had already taped off the back of the building. A camera crew was standing at the front of the bar, just behind an officer likely stationed there to keep them from getting too close. Thankfully, he couldn't see much from the street.

Detective Connor hailed him, "Hey Sid. It's not a good one."

Ignoring the nickname, he said pointedly, "They never are, Lewis."

It was the first time he'd used Connor's given name, and the younger man stared at him with an odd look in his eyes for a moment longer than was necessary before shaking his head. He leaned down and lifted the white cloth covering the body.

"Shallow grave. Barely a grave at all, actually," Connor said. "Signs of strangulation, possible assault."

Sidney looked down at the small body, pale and lifeless with speckles of dirt all over his skin. There were bruises on his neck, and the hem of his t-shirt was stretched. "Looks about seven or eight years old. Have we identified him yet?"

"Yeah, Walker Evans. It's written on the tag of his jacket."

"How long has he been missing?"

"That's a thing. He hasn't been. Not officially, that is."

Sidney stopped looking at the body and turned his attention back to Connor. "They haven't reported him missing? He hasn't been dead long."

"Medical Examiner said less than twelve hours."

"I'll talk to the parents."

"Officers are with them now. To inform them and all." Connor looked at the boy, lowering the white sheet back over the body. "Poor thing."

"I'll head over shortly." His voice took on a far-away tone, a strange sound drawing his attention up and away from the man. It was The Raleway sign slapping against the brick siding as the warm summer breeze blew through the gap between buildings. He couldn't help but think of Alexis' dream, and that same feeling tugged at his brain. She'd talked about the sound of digging, the feel of dirt, a cold heaviness, and the sound of metal ringing out ominously as it struck stone. He was good with weird, but this? Psychic visions of murder? This might be too weird.

Shaking his head, he turned his attention back to Connor and asked, "Have we found anything else?"

Connor nodded and stood from his crouched position. "Let me show you."

"What are you doing here?"

Pulling into her driveway to see her mother, of all people,

was the last thing Alexis had expected, and she wasn't sure how to react. They hadn't spoken since that phone conversation months ago. Her mother had sent a few text messages, of course, but she hadn't been ready to really engage with her yet.

Genevieve wore what Alexis would call her Sunday church clothes, even though she was sure she hadn't attended church in some time. The dress was thin and clung to her body, though no one would call it immodest. The chiffon hem danced in a breeze so hot it did nothing to whisk away the effects of the blistering sun. A hat with lace and feather decorations shielded her mother's eyes from the sun's brightness.

"I was in the area and thought I'd stop by," Genevieve said carefully.

"No, you weren't," Alexis said, her blunt, sardonic tone betraying her mood.

Her mother pursed her lips. "Well, I was, and I wanted to check on you. Make sure you're okay. You haven't responded to my messages. You look tired."

"Thanks, Momma."

"Hmm," her mother grunted, adjusting her grip on her purse as if she needed something to do with her lace-gloved hands.

"As you can see, Momma, I'm fine, but I *am* sweatin' like a sinner in church. So, would you please tell me why you're really at my house?"

"I was sorry for the way our last talk went, for the way you've felt." Genevieve cleared her throat delicately. "For the way I've made you feel."

Alexis pulled open her shirt and fanned her torso with the fabric. Sweat pooled under her breasts and dripped down her belly. She thought about asking her mother in. It would be the polite thing to do. She supposed there was a little bit of a sadist in her that enjoyed knowing how uncomfortable her mother was and how she would be far too polite to say anything about it.

"And you came to this conclusion all by yourself?"

The ground scraped beneath her heels as Genevieve shuffled uncomfortably. "Not quite. My therapist may have helped a little."

"Therapy? Wow, should I call the Pope and tell him the news?"

"We're not Catholic," her mother snapped. "And no, it's nothing to celebrate. Not yet. But I'm working on things, and I wanted to tell you I'm sorry."

"That's amazing, Momma," she replied dryly, taking this moment to walk past her mother and toward the house.

She was done with this conversation.

She didn't want her mother's apology, not after all these years, not after she'd been robbed of what a mother-daughter relationship should've been. There was too much hurt. Better to continue to exist in this limbo of obligatory familial love. She threw open the screen door.

"I'm singing again," her mother called out. She faced the street.

Alexis stopped and looked over her shoulder. She couldn't see her mother's expression well enough to know what it meant, but it wouldn't have mattered. Those words were the last she'd expected to hear, and there was so much more said in them.

All the years of fighting, all the times she had shamed her mother for giving up her dreams of performing, told her mother that she never wanted to be like her. All the tears and disappointment, the shame and the hurt. It all bubbled to the surface with those three words.

Alexis turned, letting the screen door close gently against her side, and she looked at her mother. Really looked at her.

Before her was a woman who she would've considered a man's woman, the kind who chose everything from the style of her hair to her career in order to conform to the standards set by her husband. Much as it shamed Alexis, she'd looked down on that kind of woman. Maybe unfairly. Not everyone had the resilience or the strength to swim against the stream. Not everyone was even aware they were swimming according to a current that wasn't their own. Hell, some probably genuinely liked it. Who was she to judge?

She hadn't really thought about what kind of woman her mother really was, or the pressures that had pushed her to make this choice or that one. She hadn't thought about it, and she hadn't asked either.

"It's not much. This Saturday at Mary's. It's just for one night, but..." her voice trailed off, and for a moment her whole body drooped, as if all the years were weighing on her in that moment.

Then her mother cleared her throat, straightened her shoulders, and brushed at some invisible debris on her shirt. "Well, I thought maybe you'd like to come."

Alexis wanted to close the gap between them, to reach out and grab her mother's hand, but she wasn't ready. Not yet. There was too much left unsaid. There were too many questions unasked. But if this was the olive branch, maybe she owed it to them both to take it.

"I'll be there, Momma."

22

"You look like hell."

It was the first thing he heard when he stepped out of his car and into the sweltering August heat, and he wasn't sure why the words crawled under his skin like burrowing insects.

"Hello to you, too," he muttered.

"Um, nope. You can turn right back around with that nonsense," Alexis said as she stood up from the chair. She walked the few steps across the concrete pad to her front door, opened it halfway, and stood in the gap between the door and its frame as if to physically keep him from coming inside.

For a moment, his steps slowed, and he considered turning right around and going back to his car where he could sit in the air conditioning and not deal with whatever this was. Then he remembered the day he'd had and the mountain of work waiting for him. He thought about the evidence that continued to pile up with no solid leads, and the new cases being dumped in his lap every week. His head throbbed at the temples.

Maybe she was right. Maybe he looked like hell.

He felt like it.

So instead of turning on his heel and huffing off, he took a breath and rubbed his hands over his face, trying to scrub away the day. He looked up at Alexis, still waiting in the doorway. She didn't seem bothered or impatient, simply watchful.

"You're right. I'm sorry."

She put a hand to her ear dramatically. "I didn't hear that. I'm what?"

A smile tugged at the corner of his lips, and he repeated the words he knew she wanted to hear most. "You're right."

"And?"

"And I'm sorry," he finished with a laugh. "Can we start over? Preferably inside? I'm sweating in places I'd rather not discuss right now."

"If you must," she teased in a breathy voice, pushing open the door fully and stepping back into the house where it was blissfully cooler. "Rough day?"

"You could say that," he said. Then he told her of the boy they'd found—nothing that hadn't already been reported on the local news, of course—and of his frustrations with the slow-moving investigation.

As he spoke, Alexis moved into the kitchen, shuffled around between the cabinets and the sink, and came back with two cups of ice water. She handed one to him and then plopped herself onto the couch, drawing a leg up under her body. She wore a loose t-shirt that billowed over what looked like linen shorts, her hair pulled back into a thick puff at the crown of her head.

"How was your day?" he asked, not wanting to ruin hers with the horrors of his.

She shrugged, adjusting her body slightly when the weight

of him sank down the couch cushion next to her. "Not terrible. Not great, though. My mother stopped by, and that was a whole thing. I'm worried about my best friend, and I keep having bad dreams, so I'm not sleeping well on top of all that."

"Your friend, Mia? You two seem like two peas in a pod with those visions."

"Maybe, but at least mine aren't real."

He wasn't sure about that. "You believe hers are?"

"Mia does, so yeah, I guess I do."

"What if yours are, too?" he asked, shifting in his seat. He'd been giving this a lot of thought lately, more and more than his investigation floundered. Connor poking him to go talk to "his psychic" wasn't helping.

"They're not," she said in a flat voice. She took a sip of water and turned her gaze away from him.

"Hear me out. What if they're more than bad dreams? What if you're seeing what's really happening, or happened?"

"No. Nope, no, no. Absolutely not." Alexis stood up so quickly she knocked over a cup of water on the side table, but she didn't seem to notice.

It was better for his survival that he didn't point it out. He probably should've also dropped the subject, but he couldn't bring himself to let it go. Because what if her visions were more than just bad dreams? What if Connor was right, and she was some kind of psychic? He didn't live under a rock. He knew the stories of cops working with psychics. Maybe he was skeptical in the past, but after today and all the eerie coincidences between her last vision and the latest crime scene...

Well, he figured there had to be some truth in the stereotype. At least some of them had to be real, right? Otherwise, there wouldn't be so much press about it.

With no real leads so far, three bodies—of children, no less

—piled up, and one still missing, he would put his money on anything.

"Really, Alexis. You've never thought about it once? Imagine what you could do! Think of the help you could be to people like me. Think of the families…"

His voice trailed off, and at some point he stopped seeing the effect his words were having on her and could only barrel through the fog of desperation. This was the key. He was sure of it. She could be the edge he needed to crack this thing wide open, to figure out what was happening to these kids and who was behind it so he could stop it from happening again.

He didn't realize he'd upset her, or even that she'd left the room, until the screen door slammed. The front door stood open, but he hadn't seen her open it. Or walk out.

He could see her silhouette through the front window. She was sitting in the chair, motionless, staring out at the setting sun.

"Fuck," he muttered.

Now he'd gone and done it. He'd pissed off the person who was both the woman he was seeing and also the psychic he desperately wanted on his case. He needed her. In more ways than one.

He shuffled outside, shoving his hands into the front pockets of his jeans. "I'm sorry. Again," he said.

"You don't understand." Her voice was quiet, and she wouldn't look at him.

Sidney said nothing, simply waiting for her to continue. To his mind, he'd already said enough. He stood next to her seated form, and it reassured him when she leaned her head against his thigh.

"They can't be more than bad dreams, visions, whatever. They can't be real. They just can't," she said.

"Why?" he asked.

"Because if they're more than that, I have to do something about them. If they're more than that, then I have to open myself to them, and I don't want them. I want them to go away."

"Even if they could help someone?"

Alexis nodded, her head rubbing against the denim on his thigh. "Even then."

"I don't understand."

"You wouldn't. Someone like you? A fucking cup. How could you understand? You got into this to help people, right?"

Sidney nodded, his brows drawing together at the way her voice was thick with emotion.

"The best way I can help people is by turning it off. Sure, sometimes I see things in my sleep, like a bad dream. But most times I'm just going about my day. What if I'm holding a knife or cooking? What if I'm driving?" She paused and drew in a deep breath, her eyes closing and staying that way. "I have to keep them in. I don't know why it's getting so hard, but I have to make them stop."

He didn't agree, nor did he like it, but it didn't seem like he had much choice. It wasn't as if he didn't understand where she was coming from, and he certainly would not change her mind overnight. Better to let it lie for now, he thought as he took her hands and drew her up, pulling her into the comfort of his arms.

Maybe this was what she needed—to feel safe enough to let down her guard. If he could do that, he could kill two birds with one stone. She'd process her visions and find some sort of relief. He was sure she would appreciate her gift when she could do so safely. He would get a leg up on this investigation, maybe future ones, too. It was a win-win situation.

It wasn't as if he was only with her because of the visions. It was simply a perk. Deepening their relationship right now only helped them both, he reasoned, and now was as good a time as any. Lives were at stake, whether or not Alexis wanted to believe it. He was sure they'd have gotten here.

Eventually.

Of course.

23

———

"Did you hear what happened here?"

"Of course. Some boy was murdered. It's all over the news."

"I'm surprised they're already open."

"Money doesn't make itself."

"It's crass, is what it is. I don't even know why we're here when—"

The hostess arrived and abruptly cut off the older couple's whispers. She took a deep breath as if she'd overheard far too much of a conversation likely on repeat all day. Then she asked if they would prefer to sit at a table or at the bar.

They chose the only option she hadn't mentioned.

Alexis and Mia shared a look that said, "Of course."

Poor thing, Alexis thought. She didn't envy the conversation happening now as the couple argued for a booth that wasn't available and wouldn't be for quite some time.

Mia raised her hand and wordlessly caught the hostess' attention, motioning to the bar and giving a thumbs up. A brief look of relief washed over the young girl's face, and she nodded. At the very least, they could take themselves off her mental to-do list.

Alexis followed her to the bar, pausing on the way to wave to Harper, who was sitting at the far end. Mia turned to see who she was gesturing to and smiled.

"Looks like Harper is on a date with that new guy she was talking about," Mia said.

"What new guy?" Alexis settled herself onto a barstool and grabbed the drink specials menu.

"The one she was just talking about, obviously."

"Very helpful," Alexis remarked dryly. The bartender came by and took their orders and then pushed a white napkin in front of each of them. Out of the corner of her eye, she glimpsed the side profile of Harper's date and gasped. "Is that Ben?"

"The very same." Mia smirked.

"You could've said it was Ben," Alexis grumbled.

"But it was more fun this way. I don't think it's going to last."

"Why do you say that?"

Mia smiled and propped her cheek on her palm, a conspiratorial look on her face. "Look at Harper's face. She's not into it at all, but she's too polite to be mean about it."

"Then why are you smiling about it? Don't we want our friends to be happy?" Alexis asked.

"Harper will be. Once she puts an end to it. She'll be all milk and honey sweet about it, too."

"And Ben?"

"Oh, he's a guy. He'll be fine," Mia said with a flip of her wrist.

"Speaking of guys, how are you doing about yours?" Alexis twirled the thin square of paper masquerading as a napkin in circles on the slippery bar top.

Mia groaned. "I don't know. He's still out of town, though, so it doesn't matter. Yet."

"Men are trash."

"Amen to that."

The bartender set their drinks on the napkins and moved to the other end of the bar. They contemplated ordering meals or appetizers and decided on a basket of fried pickles, agreeing that the dipping sauce they made in-house was superior to any other in the area.

The conversation wound around from updates about the bookstore to Mia's little ghost dreams, and Alexis considered telling her about her own dreams. In all these years of friendship, she'd said nothing. She suspected Mia had seen some strange behavior but had let it be. Or maybe her friend simply thought she was dissociating. She wasn't sure what her visions looked like on the outside.

Eventually, they talked about men again—because, of course—and the dumpster fires they called their dating lives.

"At least you have more than one gender to choose from," Mia said.

"Not that it's helping me much right now."

"What do you mean? You and Sidney are a thing now. Isn't that a good thing?" Mia asked slowly, taking a sip of her margarita.

Alexis had ordered the same and followed suit, though she sipped more to buy herself time to respond than out of a genuine desire for a drink at that moment.

"It's hard to explain. Everything seems fine. It's great, even. Something's just off, but I can't figure out what. Maybe it's nothing..." Alexis said, her voice trailing off.

"That doesn't sound like nothing."

"I don't know. Maybe it's just that he's a cop. Or that he's really stressed about this murder case."

Mia shivered. "Kid stuff gives me the heebie-jeebies. I think it's got everyone on edge."

Alexis nodded and said, "Big time."

"Maybe your picker is off," Mia suggested.

"About murder?"

"No, about men."

"Same thing," Alexis snorted. That earned her a backhanded smack on her arm from Mia, but she rolled her eyes and played along. "Okay, okay. What is a picker?"

"The thing that picks out terrible partners for you and then convinces you to sleep with them."

"Oh, that. What happens if someone doesn't have one at all?"

"That means you're a widow," Mia said. She grinned to herself in a way Alexis knew meant she thought she'd just been so clever. It was utterly adorable.

"How does that work?" she asked.

Mia shifted on the stool so that her body was facing Alexis. She gestured to the bartender for another round of drinks, then turned her attention back. Alexis could smell the tart citrus on Mia's breath when she spoke.

"We're so love-starved that the universe just takes it away. Then it waits until we're so lonely that we'll take anyone so long as they look pretty and say the right words."

"I don't think that's how it is, Mia." Alexis patted her thigh, letting her hand linger a little longer as if she could imbue her friend with all the healing she wished for her. She couldn't imagine becoming a young widow like Mia, building a life with someone you thought you'd spend your twilight years with, and having it all ripped away from you just a few years after it all began.

"No, it's not," Mia agreed, albeit somewhat reluctantly.

"You're in a mood."

Mia huffed but moved her head in the affirmative. She took a gulp of her drink and then sat up straight on the stool, squaring her shoulders and shaking her head and hands together as if she were shaking off droplets of water. She made a sound in the back of her throat and said forcefully, "Not today."

Alexis laughed. "You good now?"

Mia nodded and pushed a hand through her hair. "I'm perfect. Never been better."

"Okay," Alexis said, stretching out the vowels of the word.

"Have you heard any more about the murder?" Mia asked.

"No." She really hadn't, though she wasn't sure she'd want to talk about it even if she did.

Mia made a noise in her throat. "It's funny how it's all happening at once. Ghosts, murder, your boyfriend being a cop."

Alexis wasn't sure if "funny" was the right word to describe it, but she knew her friend had far too much on her plate to debate word choice, so she kept her thoughts to herself. She was determined to have a good night, whatever the cost.

24

Sidney watched the kid through the glass of the interview room for the third time and felt the same icy knot in his stomach he got when a case went sideways. The kid was young, thin, all elbows and knees. His hair looked like someone had stolen a style from an old punk record and never updated it. He kept his head down, hands stuffed into pockets of a hoodie that had seen better days. A woman hovered just beyond the doorway, arms folded tight across her chest, though she looked more like a parent who was angry she'd been bothered rather than one who was there to protect her son.

The longer he looked, the tighter the knot got. He'd do his job and interview this boy, but he didn't really think this was his guy. This was a child. Troubled, yes. But a child.

The kid delivered papers in Alexis' neighborhood, Sidney remembered. He'd also been seen near where the bodies were found, and he had a history—animal killing mostly, and a string of small, cruel incidents at school where he had gotten little more than a slap on the wrist and a few days of suspension. That pattern could mean nothing... but it could mean everything.

Sidney would take that chance, and really, he had to. He had nothing else.

Sidney had read the reports, combed through school records, then talked to a counselor who said the kid was an "at-risk youth" and a teacher who referred to him as "lost." Lost was the kind word for kids you expected society to shrug off. Sidney didn't believe in punishing kids in an adult system, but he also owed it to the victims and their families to find out what happened to them. Even if it was at the hands of another child.

Still, he wasn't holding out hope. Witnesses were notoriously unreliable, but they were also what drummed up leads when forensics produced nothing. Well, not nothing. They'd gathered plenty of evidence, in fact, but none of it led to a potential suspect. Not yet.

He walked into the room with stiff, precise movements. The metal legs of the chair scraped across the tile floor as he took a seat at the table. With an adult, he would've sat across that very table, a position of power. But this was a kid, not an adult, so he pulled his chair around and sat to the side. In the small, fluorescent-buzzing room, he watched the way the light cut across his cheekbones, watched the eyes that darted across the floor like minnows at the edge of a net.

"You can come sit, mom," he said to the mother who still stood by the door with her arms crossed tightly.

She shook her head, and he couldn't help but judge her. What kind of mother didn't want to be near her son at a time like this? To offer him some kind of support or even comfort?

Sidney asked the boy if he wanted some water. He said nothing but shook his head. He told him all the standard stuff, trying to use simple language whenever he could.

"Have you ever hurt an animal, Colby?" Sidney asked. His

voice was careful, less the clipped command he used on career criminals and more the needle you used to find where someone bled. The kid shifted uncomfortably.

"No," the boy muttered.

"You deliver papers around town. Is that right? Little league fields, cul-de-sacs. You ever go to the park after your route? Maybe hang out there after school?" Sidney kept it simple. People liked to get tangled when they heard too much at once. He liked to let them trip over the truth themselves.

The kid swallowed, eyes flicking to his mother, then down to his hands. "I guess," he muttered.

He asked a few questions about specific days and times, working to establish where the boy was during the moment each murder had happened. He asked other questions, some more to the point than others, but he couldn't get anything concrete enough to tie the boy to the murders.

Sidney could have pushed, used the old tricks—threaten, cajole, promise leniency—but with nothing tying Colby Marshall to the victims specifically, there really wasn't a point, and he didn't want to traumatize the boy. Innocent until proven guilty. It still meant something to some cops, he thought.

"Okay," Sidney said finally, and meant it. He looked between the kid and his mother. "You can go, but we might need to speak again."

The mother opened the door without a word, not even waiting for Sidney to do it for her. And he would've. The kid followed her in a posture of defeat and dissociation that made you pity and worry in equal measure.

Sidney followed them part of the way, stopping when he reached Connor. "Detective," he said with a nod to his friend.

Connor leaned against the far wall, arms crossed, a smirk already forming before the words arrived. "Sid," he said in reply. "Not much like with the paperboy, I see."

Sidney ignored the nickname as he usually did and kept his attention on the departing pair until they disappeared out of sight. He turned to face Connor. "Do you know anything about him?"

"Enough. He's got the history. Heard about the lurk. But I know the drill. No proof, huh, Sid?"

Sidney felt the old muscles around his mouth tighten. It wasn't just a scrap of frustration; it was a rawness. The way Connor said Sid, the tone of his voice, worked like a cattle prod on his nerves. He didn't even know why he hated being called Sid so much, though he supposed it didn't matter, anyway. It was enough that he hated it.

"No proof. No leads. Nothing we didn't already know," Sidney replied. "I feel like I'm missing something that's right in front of my face. I hate that feeling."

Connor tilted his head, the bright look of remembering lighting up his face. "What about your friend? The one with the psychic thing. Could that be real?" He hesitated. It wasn't as if cops really enjoyed admitting they believed in that kind of thing. They'd rather trust the facts and sometimes their gut.

"I don't know. Maybe," Sidney said. "Some things she sees seem so real when I look at this case, things she couldn't have known or seen yet. Or it could be coincidence." He wasn't ready to admit how ready he was to believe in her visions, how desperate he was to use them.

He'd told Connor about the visions then. Now he almost told about the way Alexis' face appeared to him when she tried not to talk about what the dreams did to her, the way those images had lodged themselves in his mind and refused to move. He almost told him how he'd used those visions the way other men might use a drinking buddy, as a tool, a way to pry open a closed case by dangling something dangerously human in front of a woman and watching what she gave up to keep the world from spinning. He almost told him of the shame he felt at it all.

"I mean, you're dating her, right? So she trusts you? Who knows? Maybe she can force a vision or something."

"I don't know."

"Push her a little. Not a lot. Just get her to help with the case, Sid."

He snapped before he meant to. "Don't call me Sid!" he snapped.

It came out shorter and louder than he wanted, a yell with a clipped edge that surprised them both and had half the guys seated at nearby desks looking up at them.

Connor's eyebrows shot up. "Hey, I—"

Sidney bit his tongue. He hated the way he sounded, hated the way he'd yelled, his voice tight. He hated the heat climbing up the back of his neck, the way it felt as if his anger revealed who he really was. Not just annoyance. Not just the name.

He let out a breath that was a near-apology. "Look. I'm sorry. Stress. No leads. Bad night." He kept it to a vague explanation, something that would allow him to keep the pieces of himself in place.

Connor shrugged, but the look of hurt turned to one of concern. "Are you okay? Really?"

"I'm fine. We'll get the guy who's doing this. For now, we watch."

Connor's face went thoughtful. "You're not going to use her then?"

"I told you I don't know."

Sidney felt something tighten in his chest—the old, pragmatic part of him that cataloged assets and angles. Alexis was an asset in the sense that her visions could point to how the killer thought who the killer was. She was also a person with feelings and needs and pain and a visceral need to be left alone.

That ashamed feeling reared its ugly head, but he pushed it back down with the weight of his determination. He could balance it all if he just stayed focused. He just had to keep that line straight in his head or he would lose it all.

The case and her, and he wasn't sure he wanted to lose either.

Connor looked skeptical. "Just be careful then. Don't break yourself over this."

Sidney swallowed. "I won't." He knew how hollow that sounded. Hell, he didn't know if he believed it himself. "For now, I need something else. Did you turn up anything on the Williams family I asked about?"

The Williams file was a more recent splinter under his skin, a favor for her friend Mia who was apparently balls deep in a cold case about a ghost kid and some mysterious deaths—what was it lately with this town and dead kids?

Connor's face went neutral, then apologetic. "Yeah, I dug up the old case file. It's on your desk."

Sidney let out a breath of frustration. "Thank you."

Connor nodded. "No problem." He glanced back toward the exit where the kid had disappeared. "Do you really think he's our killer?"

Sidney didn't want to say what he thought, but being desperate for leads didn't make a bad one suddenly turn good. No matter how much he wanted it to be. He didn't want to admit that no matter how stubborn and persistent he was, sometimes things just didn't pan out.

"No, I don't," he said reluctantly. "He's just a kid. Our guy isn't a kid, at least not one like that. He's methodical. He plans. He hasn't left behind any evidence that would tell us who he is."

They stood in the station's quiet for a long minute, the hum of fluorescent lights filling the space between them. Sidney wanted to be harder, colder, and more precise. He wanted his anger to be the kind that galvanized rather than pushed people away. He wanted to be the man who could walk into a room and take what the job demanded without leaving pieces of himself on the floor.

Instead, he pocketed the small, dangerous truth that Alexis' visions gave him and folded it into the day's work. It felt like an incalculable risk, but he'd never been much for safe bets. If Alexis could give him even the smallest direction to go in, it might be worth the cost in the end.

"Well, onward and upwards," Connor said finally, breaking the silence. "Keep an eye on your paperboy, just in case."

Sidney nodded. "Of course."

He walked back to his desk, his mind already scanning for the next thread, the missing piece he was sure he was overlooking. The case didn't stop because he needed to take a breath. It didn't care about his flaws or his faults, or his lack. What it required was his focus, and for now, that would have to be enough.

25

The rake bit into the loose pile of leaves with a satisfying scrape, the sound oddly domestic against the distant hum of the cars driving by. As fall pushed out a reluctant summer, the green leaves turned amber and gold, then dropped to blanket her yard. Alexis was deluding herself into thinking that if she started raking now, she could stay on top of the chore for once in her adult life.

She worked the yard in a rhythm she'd inherited from years as a child, mowing, weeding, raking, and more. It wasn't so much a love of gardening or even being an outdoors sort of girl. More out of habit after living with a strict military father. When you grew up like that, some things you avoided as an adult. Others you learned to appreciate the rhythm of.

She was grateful her little house had only a small patch of grass, and though late September still held a stubborn warmth that made the temperature swing from morning to afternoon feel like an argument between seasons, there was the first hint of a bite when the breeze moved through the trees. She tugged off one glove and brushed a curl from her forehead, the scent of cut grass and old citrus hanging faint in the air. Harper must be baking lemon pie again, she thought.

Mia's little car pulled up to her mailbox before Alexis realized she was even coming, tires crunching over the loose leaves. The car door popped open, and Mia, her hair pulled into a messy knot and sunglasses perched on her head like a crown, hopped out with a brown paper bag clutched in both hands.

"Surprise!" Mia called, her voice carrying a bright bell tone.

Alexis laughed, dropping the rake against the column at the corner of her patio and wiping her palms on her jeans. "What are you doing here?"

Mia trotted across the grass and handed her the bag. Inside was a net bag of flower bulbs, dark and firm as closed lips. Snowdrops, the tag read. Alexis held them as if they might be fragile heirlooms.

"Mia," she said, softening, "this is a beautiful surprise."

Mia smiled, pleased with herself. "The tag says snowdrops symbolize innocence and hope. I thought you might like to plant some by your mailbox since you don't have beds."

Alexis felt something warm and quick in her chest at the words. She glanced at the mailbox. It was an old wooden post painted teal, leaning slightly as if listening to the road. All she had were a few holly bushes flanking the house and the stubborn rosemary a previous owner had planted that refused to die.

She grinned. "You're such a sap."

Mia waved off the playful insult. "Yeah, yeah, yeah. I can't stay. Got a million things on my to-do list. Plant them and send me a picture. I want full bloom proof."

"Promise," Alexis said, already picturing the bulbs popping up like tiny white flags. The idea of hope tucked into the soil felt almost dangerously literal, but that was what she liked about it.

She wanted to put them in the ground right away but belatedly realized her grass grew around every inch of her mailbox post, so she set the bag down, walked around back, and brought out a shovel to prep the ground. It took far longer and required far more sweat than she'd expected, but finally she'd cleared a somewhat even little circle around the base of the post. She marveled at how hard it was to dig up grass. Who would've thought?

From her periphery, she saw Harper emerge from the next-door house with a pitcher of sweet tea, hair pulled back in a cotton scarf, red lipstick catching the light as she smiled.

"You're sweating like a sinner in church," Harper said.

"I *am* the sinner in church," Alexis replied with a laugh, but she knew an invitation when she saw one and dropped the shovel right where she stood and met Harper on her porch.

"Do you want to go inside the A/C?" Harper asked. "It's about ninety out here even in the shade."

Alexis shook her hand and plopped down in a chair. "No, this is just fine."

The porch smelled faintly of lemon oil where the sunlight hit a table between the chairs, and Alexis wondered if she'd been cleaning recently or if that was just its natural state. Harper poured the tea into tall glasses, the ice clinking like little bells, and handed one to Alexis.

"It's Georgia," Harper said, lifting her glass. "We'll shiver in the morning and sweat by noon. Always have, always will."

Alexis inhaled the tart citrus of the tea and closed her eyes. It should have felt ordinary: the neighbors, the idle chat, the small domestic rituals. Instead, under the surface of her calm, a familiar pressure budded at the edges of her mind. There it was, behind her eyelids—a hand, pale and too thin, with fingers reaching, pushed at the rim of her awareness like a child pressing against a screen. She blinked hard, forcing it back like a tide she didn't want to rise. Not today. It would not ruin her day today.

"Is everything okay?" Harper asked, brow knitting.

"Yeah," Alexis said quickly, too quickly. "Just—déjà vu, I think. Weird dreamy stuff."

Mia glanced at her, concern pinching her face for a second. "You sure? You looked like you saw a ghost."

Alexis shaped a smile and accepted the label as a joke she would own. "Ghosts, déjà vu, Tuesday. Same difference." She shifted in her chair to make it obvious she was present, focused, like someone pushing a sticker back on a window.

"It's probably the heat," Harper said, taking a sip of her drink and turning her attention back out across the yard and the street beyond.

She had been better lately, better at pushing the visions away when they threatened the surface. Sidney had become a steady part of her life, something that still surprised her, but it gave her a reason to keep her feet planted when the earth seemed to tilt. She was still careful, enjoying their adventurous sex life at a fast pace while not rushing through the small stages of intimacy, but she felt grounded. She was happy.

Her phone buzzed, and she did a little wiggle in her chair to get it out of her back pocket. Sidney's name lit up the screen. She propped her feet up on the wooden porch rails in front of her and answered.

"Hey, stranger," Sidney replied, his voice warm and close through the tinny speaker. She could hear a car door in the background, the everyday sounds of a life that was not her own but into which she enjoyed being invited.

"You're on speaker so you can say hi to Harper," Alexis said with a smile.

"Hi," Harper chirped, waving a hand at the phone, even though she knew he couldn't see her.

"Hey, Harper," he said. "How's the front porch gossip?"

Harper clicked her tongue playfully. "We haven't gotten to it yet. We demanded sweet tea first."

"I'm taking you off speaker now. Say, 'Bye, Harper,'" Alexis shouted.

Both Harper and Sidney shouted, "Bye, Harper!"

Alexis laughed and tapped a button on the phone, moving it to her ear. "Okay, just me now."

"Hello again, just me."

"What's up?" she asked. "I don't mean to rush you, but I do have tea and tea, if you know what I mean, waiting on me and some flower bulbs to plant before you get here later."

"Sure. About that—listen, when I come over tonight, would it be okay if I bring a few things to leave at your place? A toothbrush, a change of clothes, that kind of thing?"

Her heart did a tiny, traitorous flip. The idea of his things at her apartment felt like a step. It felt like relationship progress, the kind you measured over time to gauge how serious things were getting. On the one hand, that was good. She wasn't a commitment-phobe or anything. Not exactly. At the same time, it felt like an enormous cliff edge she wasn't sure she wanted to look over. Yet.

Alexis felt Harper's eyes on her and watched the way the red of her lipstick flashed as she mouthed, "What's wrong?"

She almost laughed at how ridiculous it all was. "He wants to leave stuff. At my place," Alexis mouthed back, eyes wide and expectant.

"Mute him," Harper mouthed, then pantomimed pushing the mute button on her phone. When Alexis turned, she raised her voice a fraction. "Is that what you want?"

Alexis hesitated. Her mouth suddenly tasted of copper. She knew, logically, that it was a small step. A toothbrush lived in a bathroom drawer or on the counter pretty easily. Jackets could hang on coat hooks; a change of clothes didn't take up much space. But things had a way of multiplying, she thought, and not just in terms of space. What started as a toothbrush could become an engagement ring before you knew it.

Harper watched as a flurry of emotions washed over her face. "Alexis, honey, it's fine. This is good. You two have been good. You want him to be around. Let him be."

Alexis chewed the inside of her cheek. "I don't know. It just feels like a big step."

"Because you're making a mountain out of a molehill," Harper said bluntly, and there it was: the honesty that was both a scalpel and an antidote. "Take that man off mute and tell him it's fine."

Alexis blinked and was once again grateful for her friends. Harper's pragmatism, a rare moment away from her usual sense of whimsy, was a rope she could cling to. "You're right," she admitted. "I am making a mountain out of a molehill."

She unmuted Sidney. "Hey, sorry. Yeah, that's fine. Bring whatever you need. We'll see what you've got and find a drawer or something when you get here."

There was a small, pleased sound on his end. "Thanks. I'll be over around seven?"

"Seven's perfect," she said. "I'll see you later." She hung up with a little more lightness than she expected and sat back into the chair.

"How you feelin'?" Harper asked, a teasing undertone in her voice.

Alexis laughed as she let out a breath. "Fine. I'm fine. I'm..."

"Fine," Harper finished with a laugh of her own.

"Exactly," she responded.

For a second, a familiar pressure pushed at the edges of her mind again—the same hand, a thin upturned palm like a memory reaching forward. It was clearer this time: fingers, knuckles, the pale of the underside of a hand. Her breath hitched.

"Lex?" Harper's voice was immediate. "You okay? That's not fine."

"Yeah," she said too quickly. Harper's voice sounded so faraway, like a distant echo. She forced herself to breathe, slow and deliberate, and grounded herself in the smell of earth and the feel of smooth wood under her fingers. She traced the lines of the wood, imagining the tree that had made them.

Harper was watchful. "If you need to lie down, do it. Don't be a hero."

She was about to respond when suddenly the feeling stopped, and the world roared back to life. Her phone buzzed on the table beside her, and she glanced over at the screen. She expected to see Sidney's name.

Her stomach clenched before she answered. She had a bad feeling. "Nick? Everything okay?"

Harper mouthed to Alexis, "Mia's man, Nick?" And Alexis nodded.

"Alexis." Nick's voice was tight, the words tumbling out one over another. "Mia's at the hospital."

"What? Why?" Alexis said, the word a small bullet.

"I don't know. It's hard to explain. Just—" He swallowed audibly. "I thought you should know."

The world beneath Alexis tilted like a table kicked from under it. The air was too heavy, the sky too bright, and the sound of distant traffic was like a horn blowing right in her ear. Mia's laughter, the unwavering friend who'd just delivered flowers, was at the center of something sharp and urgent.

"I'm on my way," she said, voice steady only because her body demanded movement. She looked up at Harper, who didn't know what was happening, but she could tell by the look on Alexis' face that it was emergent.

"Thank you," Nick said softly, as if he could hold the scene together with the sound of his voice. "I'll text you if anything changes in the meantime. But please get here."

"I'm coming," she said. She turned to Harper, to the bulbs she'd just tucked into the earth like promises. "I need to go."

"Go," Harper said without hesitation, rushing forward to loop an arm through hers. "Are you okay to drive? Do you need someone?"

"I've got it," Alexis said with a shake of her head.

"Are you sure?" Harper asked.

Alexis nodded and the two parted ways with the promise of updates and that Alexis would let Harper know if she needed anything at all. She left the mailbox planting project half-done, the earth dusty on her fingers, snowdrops sitting in their paper bag on her lawn. Hopefully, that wasn't some morbid metaphor for something.

She started the car and pulled out her phone to text Sidney before leaving.

ALEXIS

May need to reschedule plans tonight. Mia is in the hospital. On my way there now.

SIDNEY

Of course! I can meet you there.

Alexis groaned. It wasn't as if she didn't want him to be there for her, but... okay, it was exactly like that. She didn't want him to be there for her. Not like this, not right now.

ALEXIS

Maybe you should come a little later.

SIDNEY

What happened to her? Is it related to the case she's been poking around in?

ALEXIS

I'm not sure. Nick didn't say.

SIDNEY

I need to go. I need to check on her, ask
questions. I put my neck out there digging up
that cold case. If it's related, I need to know.

ALEXIS

It could be anything. An accident, a car wreck.
I don't know. I have to go.

Okay, okay. I see what you mean. You can
come. Just later, once I find out what's
going on.

SIDNEY

Fine.

That was what he was going to send to her. She all but threw her phone into the passenger seat. Backing her car out into the street, she cursed him. Colorfully and thoroughly.

She had more important things on her mind. The last thing she needed was a man and his tantrum to deal with, too.

Fine?

Fine.

The fluorescent light above them hummed quietly, and the chair inside Mia's room sat in that exact unpleasant way hospitals designed them. It was too straight and too unforgiving despite its comfortable appearance.

Alexis had been there long enough to have memorized the slow swing of the privacy curtain and the way the machine's soft beeps were a metronome for a life paused. Mia lay small and pale under a blanket, hair tangled and knotted across the pillow, oxygen tubing resting against her lip. Bruises and blood covered her, but her chest rose and fell in a steady rhythm. Still, Alexis counted each breath as if each one were a victory.

Nick hovered at the foot of the bed, his jaw tight, hands deep in his pockets. He kept glancing at the door the way someone waiting for a verdict watches for the judge. There was a police officer in the corridor sitting in a chair positioned against the wall right outside the door. When Alexis had first arrived, she'd asked him what happened, and he'd simply folded his arms and given her an official spiel that promised no answers.

"Can you tell me anything?" she'd asked then.

"I can't tell you anything, no," he had said, his voice flat.

Instead of a bitchy retort, Alexis had snapped her mouth shut, and then felt like an idiot for saying anything at all. She didn't yet know most of what happened to Mia—and she still didn't know now—except that someone had attacked her. The cop waiting to question Mia when she woke up wasn't any help. Nick wasn't much better. Alexis was sure he knew more, but he was too anxious to talk about it, and she didn't want to push him. There would be plenty of time for details. Right now, they needed to be there for Mia.

She'd been sitting in the chair, hands banded around a paper cup of stale-tasting water that did nothing except cool her fingers. She imagined all the worst things on a loop. The not-knowing was a physical thing, a pressure that made her scalp hum and her mouth taste metallic.

She wanted to call Sidney, wanted his determined, procedural mind to take the edges off the panic, but their last texts felt like a wedge between them. Alexis imagined Sidney barging in, the authority he carried wrapped around him like a dark coat. She thought about how he'd switch off the charm and demand to know, to do. But part of her felt overwhelmed by the idea. All she could think about was Mia. There was no room for anything or anyone else.

And she didn't want to talk to him right now.

Her phone buzzed in her lap. Sidney. She stared at his name—Sidney Neal—until the glow of the screen blurred. She shoved the phone face down against the chair, as if that would muffle the noise, keep him from reaching her.

She kept telling herself she wasn't ready to talk. Angry, yes. She was angry that things felt too fast, that he was pushing her, and them, to be more and more and more. She was angry that he'd presumed access to every part of her life would come with a toothbrush and a spare sweater.

And yes, she was also scared. Of the visions, scared of how quickly her life could tip from ordinary to something she had to guard against. She was scared of what it all meant. Her wings were meant to soar, but it felt as though they were being clipped.

Mostly, beneath the anger and the fear, there was a steady drumbeat of need. She needed to focus on Mia, to be present for the friend who had been a constant, luminous thing in her life. She minded that need like a delicate vase, while Sidney felt like someone trying to rearrange the room without asking if she wanted the furniture moved.

Sure, in the bedroom she'd been all for handing over control. It felt invigorating and exciting to give herself over to the whims and wishes of someone else. The sense of release and euphoria was unmatched. But relinquishing control in the bedroom did not mean she was comfortable doing so in other areas of her life. That she had not consented to, and that was what it felt like he was pushing for.

Whether real or imagined, she had to listen to her body, to her gut. She thought about telling him to stay out for a while, to let her breathe. She pictured his face. The flash of his crooked tooth drawn into that half-grin of his would disappear, and his jaw would clench. That image made her stomach clench. She hated conflict, and she'd had too much of it lately.

Nick watched her. "Are you going to answer that?" he asked, voice low. He didn't look accusatory. It was a practical question in the face of the emotional.

"No," she said. Her voice came out small.

She clasped Mia's hand, cool and sure in hers, and felt all the reasons she'd come here like a warm weight. Nick didn't ask who was on the phone or why she was ignoring it. He simply nodded once, as though he understood some things needed to be kept for later.

"Do you want something else to drink?" he asked.

Alexis nodded, setting the cup of water she had no intention of drinking off to the side. He rose and shuffled out of the room toward the vending area, and Alexis watched the door close behind him.

She tried to keep her gaze from resting solely on Mia's too-still form. She looked outside the room, noting how the corridor outside was full of small things like posters for flu shots, a clock with a second hand that ticked loudly, and a nurse pushing a cart of linens.

She studied Mia's face again. In sleep, Mia's features smoothed in a way that made her look ten years younger, edges softened. She wondered if that happened to everyone, if comatose patients had somehow unlocked the secret to eternal youth. Alexis pressed her thumb to Mia's knuckles and felt that fragile pulse, but she didn't want to think of her as fragile.

From the scant details Nick shared, Mia had been attacked in her own home by the very woman at the center of the murder mystery she'd been poking around in, and she'd fought. She'd fought hard. Alexis wanted to think about Mia like that, as a woman dedicated to solving a ghost mystery, if for no other reason than to bring peace to the restless soul of a child and his mother. And a woman who'd fought for that peace.

Alexis remembered their long-winded talks, how she'd pushed Mia to live again after the death of her husband, the late nights they'd spent together opening Mia's new bookstore. If anyone deserved to live a life of peace and happiness, it was Mia.

Her mind drifted back to Sidney. Each thought felt like a

little poke, a tap on the shoulder she was trying to shrug away. She could see the future that might come if she called him to come right now: Sidney steady, concerned, maybe a little paternal as he tried to navigate her boundaries with the certainty of a man used to maps and rules. Her chest tightened at that thought, because she didn't want his certainty to feel like an obligation. She didn't want support and...

Her phone buzzed again...

Couldn't the man take a fucking hint?!

She knew what he was doing. Either wanting to talk to her or give her a heads-up that he was coming, no matter her thoughts on the matter. He was impatient to be helpful where she needed space. The phone vibrated, then stilled. Her thumb hovered over the screen and then hovered away. She thought of the toothbrush, of the small step it represented, and all the little moments that led up to that.

She needed to take some time for herself, to sort it out without stringing him along. He deserved to know that, she told herself. He deserved an explanation clumsier and more human than silence.

Before he could call again, she thumbed the phone awake and dialed his number.

"Alexis," Sidney's voice sounded immediate, as if he'd been ready at the edge of the line.

"I—" She swallowed, the hospital scent and the sharpness of her worry closing in. "Sidney... I need to stop. For a little while. I can't—" The words were a tumble. "I can't have this, us, on my mind right now. Not with everything else. I need to be here for Mia without wondering if I'm letting you down." She paused, looking at Mia's face as if it would give her the right words. "I need to put things on hold. Maybe not forever, but for now."

"Where is this coming from?"

"I'm just overwhelmed. You're great, really. This is a me thing." Alexis cringed. No matter how she dressed up the words, she was giving him the old "it's not you, it's me" cliché.

There was a pause, and then he asked bluntly, "Is this about the toothbrush?"

She took a deep breath and answered in kind, "No. Yes. Not completely."

There was a long, strange silence on the line. In it she could hear a muted shuffle, a sound like someone rearranging paper. When Sidney spoke, his voice had an element of control, of distance she hadn't expected. "You want a pause," he said. "A break until Mia's better and you sort through your stuff."

"Yes." She heard the thinness in her own voice and found it almost intolerable. "I'm angry and frightened, and I just have a lot on my mind. It's all back and forth—what I want, what I don't want—I just don't know right now, and I don't want to drag you into that. I want to be alone in it for now. I just need some time, that's all."

Sidney's reaction was not loud, but it was clinical, measured. "Alright. I'll give you the space you need. What's meant to work out, will. I'll be around."

Something choked in her throat. Relief sharpened fast into a small, bitter shard. "Thank you," she said, and meant it, though it tasted complicated.

"I need to be there when she wakes up. I need to ask her some questions."

"Of course." Her answer came quickly, automatic and fierce. "I'll be gone by then."

"Alright," he said, quieter than before. The word was simple, solid, but the tone had gone cool, a reservedness she had no shape for. "Do what you need to do, Alexis."

She felt the distance then, like a physical displacement, a chair pulled back at a table they had once shared. Her chest tightened. For a moment she imagined him in his car on the way to the hospital, headlights cutting through the night, jaw set. For a moment she both wanted him there and wanted him as far from her as possible, and she felt ashamed of that.

They hung up, the phone's screen a black rectangle in her palm. She let out a breath and collapsed back into her chair. Nick returned with two cans of soda dotted with beads of condensation and set one down on the table beside her.

"Here," he said simply. "Are you okay?"

She thanked him for the drink. "Yeah. Sidney," she paused and corrected herself, "Detective Neal will be here later." Saying his professional name made it less personal, less vulnerable, and she needed that measure of distance in the fluorescent quiet.

Nick's face scrunched with confusion, but he stayed silent. "That's good," he said.

She looked at Mia again and nodded. "I'll stay until she wakes. Tell her I'll help with the shop while she recovers. She's going to be worried about it. I don't want her to worry."

"Thank you," Nick said, and she could hear the gratitude stretching like an unspoken prayer. He meant it. Through the mess of emergency protocols, worry, and everything else, someone needed to keep ordinary life standing.

Alexis sat back and folded both hands over Mia's limp fingers. She felt a weird steadiness settle into her bones, a kind of certainty that she was doing the right thing for herself that she rarely felt.

She'd asked for space with Sidney, not because she wanted him around less, but because she needed to make room to love herself more, too. There would be time for toothbrushes and relationship things and the slow growth of a shared life. For now, she would keep the vigil, count the breaths, and hold the small, living things in her hands until they woke.

27

THREE MONTHS LATER…

Alexis moved through her days much like the months moved through the seasons, a slow shifting from one thing to the next. Where September had been a slow, humid drag that made paper stick to your palms, December drew the air taut and clear, as if someone had wiped the sky clean with a cloth.

She'd slipped into a rhythm that felt steadier, spending most mornings at the bookshop and her evenings lost in writing that stubbornly refused to bend to her will. In between, she spent her afternoons with Alan, sitting on the benches between their stores when the weather allowed and enjoying lunch. They talked some days and traded recipes others, and sometimes they just sat in companionable silence.

Alan had a way of making the mundane feel cushioned—his laugh was soft as a hand on your shoulder, and he asked questions that made you feel like he was actually interested in your answers. Because he was.

It was just another Tuesday, but there was at last a bite of real winter in the air, and holiday shoppers buzzed up and down their little street. She and Alan sat on the wooden bench between the bookstore windows and those of his antique shop. There was a plate of half-eaten sandwiches between them and two steaming cups of soup to chase away the chill. Alexis dug into her bowl and felt the comfort of a small town that still enjoyed knowing its neighbors.

"It's finally feeling like snow," Alan said, eyes on the narrow street where leaves skittered along the curb. "Weather people are saying we might actually get some this year."

Alexis rolled her eyes. "It's global warming. We've started getting some every year. A little, at least."

"I remember a time when snow in the south was a freak event of nature. The blizzard of '94 was one to remember."

"Until Snowpocalypse, maybe. Now that's the one they all talk about."

"For good reason," Alan said, gesturing with his sandwich toward the people walking around as if the movement meant something.

Alexis smiled at the old man. He was a little strange, a little kooky, but she liked him more than she'd thought she would.

Alan nodded at everyone and no one in particular. "Wouldn't surprise me. This year's weird."

She wondered what he was talking about. Did she miss part of the conversation somewhere? What wouldn't surprise him? She was thoroughly lost, and then he was talking again, blessedly changing the subject so she could catch back up.

"You heard about Candler County? They found another boy. Folks are saying it's connected." He stirred his soup with the spoon as if he were mixing thoughts.

"Folks say a lot, mostly about things they know nothing about."

But a small, icy knot tightened in her chest, the kind that didn't belong to surprise but to exhaustion. The memory of the earlier killings—of Brad's family and the way the town had folded inward after the truth came out—still echoed, ghosts that left dents in people's lives. It was Mia's dreams that had pointed them toward the killer, though people mostly didn't hear that part of the story. Her nightmares would've seemed a little too fantastical, but they came with a price: Sarah, the woman who killed her husband's previous wife and child, attacked Mia and left her in the hospital. The memory of that assault lingered, tender still like a bruise.

Add to that the more recent murders, and Alexis had watched her town grieve and rage enough to last a lifetime.

"We've had enough," Alan said, his voice echoing her private thoughts. "People don't need more horror. Especially not involving kids."

"I know," Alexis said. "It's like everything that should be simple gets complicated."

She pinched the bridge of her nose, feeling the fatigue under her skin, and suddenly this day was too much.

"You look peaky, girl," Alan said.

The days of inventory and running the shop and talking nonstop to people all day; the nights of trying to coax words out of a story that refused to congeal into anything she trusted. Yeah, she was a little peaky.

"I'm trying to get back to work, to finish this damn book, but it's slow. I keep feeling like I'm waiting for something to happen, like I'm bracing for a wave of inspiration. But it's not coming."

Alan leaned back and considered her. "You're doing what you can. The shop's been doing well and you've been holding down the fort. Sometimes the work you can't see, the slow, invisible kind, is the most important."

"Not as fun, though."

"No, it's not," Alan laughed.

They talked a while longer about community, the people who'd shown up to help after the worst of it, and how fragile the ordinary felt. When the conversation looped back to the bookstore, Alexis admitted she'd been thinking about hosting an event.

"Mia's not ready to run the book club again, let alone the shop every day, but she wants to do something," Alexis explained. "She said she wants to reach out to the community in a smaller way. Maybe readings, a small author night. Something that isn't a book club but brings people in. Keeps the shop alive without adjusting everything around her."

"Which she'd hate," Alan supplied.

Alexis grinned. "You know her well, too."

Alan smiled. "Not as much as I'd like, but I'm sure she'll be back around more soon. Recovery like that takes time. Maybe you two could host impromptu read-ins? People come and bring whatever it is they're reading and do it together. Brings some life back to the place... and maybe wander next door to peruse some antiques from yours truly."

"You're shameless," she laughed, but his idea was good. She liked the image. An event that was soft at the edges, easy to plan, a gentle reintroduction to public life for people who'd been holding their breath. It sounded like something Mia could realistically sink her teeth into.

WHICH WAS EXACTLY what Mia said when Alexis told her about the plan later that night.

The two of them sat at the back table of the shop with a scrawled notebook between them and mugs of tea gone cold.

Mia looked thinner in the way that late nights and trauma made you thin. Her laugh came slower, but when she gave it, it held a joy that Alexis would never again take for granted.

They brainstormed potential event names and themes. "Stories & Stitching," inspired by Harper's audiobooks and crochet nights, was the current favorite.

"I don't want to force it," Mia said, tracing a finger along the page. "But I want people to have a place to gather."

"Then this is perfect. It's small. You can be as involved as you want. We'll do the heavy lifting."

They paused and laughed at their own seriousness, and for a moment the bookstore felt like the safe, stubborn heart of everything ordinary.

Everything was falling into its rightful place again. Everything, that is, except the writing. Alexis's private slow-burn project still slipped away from her when she tried to pin it down. Words that had once come easily now felt like uninvited strangers at a party she no longer remembered hosting.

"It's Sidney," Mia said when the topic came up in conversation.

Alexis snorted, then sighed. "No, it's not. I mean... okay, maybe." She searched for an answer she wasn't sure she believed. "He's part of it. But it's more than that. I don't know how to explain."

Mia looked at her with a steady look that was both an inventory and a kindness. "Sidney brought things into your world you don't get to choose. He's like danger and charm, secrets and sex all wrapped in one. Now he's not, and I don't think you've decided if you want him to again. That kind of indecision can clog a pen."

"Maybe," Alexis said, letting the idea sit like a tea bag steeping in hot water.

28

A hot flush crept up her neck as she finally acknowledged the hollow ache where Sidney's presence used to be. It shamed her to admit that it had taken months of absence and, more selfishly, her own writer's block to see it. Her therapist would say this is what happened when she disconnected from her feelings, and she was probably right.

Alexis stood in her kitchen, staring at the empty calendar and at the quiet of the house that had grown less Sidney-shaped over the months. She missed him in so many ways, big and small. Her nights were quieter, her weekends spent alone. There was no mug of his in the sink, no too-large shoes by the door. She missed the conversations they shared after a long day at work, the easy slide of their bodies together in the dark.

Most of all, she missed his voice.

She told herself that a phone call couldn't hurt. In her mind, she dialed Sidney's number and rehearsed small, practical sentences in her head.

Do you want to talk? Can I see you? I miss you.

She went over the scenario so many times in her mind that it almost felt as if she'd lived it. After a few more minutes of rehearsing and procrastination, she finally decided to just do it.

She took a deep breath, pressed call, and promptly forgot everything she wanted to say. The phone rang once, twice, and he didn't answer. Her heart raced. Voicemail. The sound was a small, fossilized thing that told her nothing.

She sat down hard at the kitchen table and let the silence fill the apartment like a guest who refused to leave. All that worry for nothing.

He'd been distant the last time she'd asked for space at the hospital, and he'd promised to be around, but a part of her had wanted to hear that reassurance with less edge and more softness. "Being around" wasn't exactly a scientific statement. But maybe tonight she could ask for that.

Maybe tonight she could say—come over?

And he would come.

Her finger hovered over the phone a dozen times before she finally pushed his contact and hit call once more. This time, his voice answered on the third ring, tired and threadbare in a way that made Alexis sit up straighter.

"Hey," he said.

"Hey," she said. "Are you busy tonight?"

There was a pause, as if he were considering why she'd be asking. And what he wanted to do about it.

"No, I'm not."

It wasn't as warm as she had hoped, but then again, she couldn't blame him. She hadn't gone silent, but neither had she been overly communicative. "I was hoping maybe we could talk. Get out. Or stay in. Whatever."

There was another pause, and she had the surreal sensation of hearing him weigh a dozen practicalities in a breath. "Yeah. I'm free tonight. I'll see you in an hour?"

"An hour is perfect," she said, relief and anxiety blooming in the same place in her belly.

As promised, he arrived an hour later, the familiar rumble of his approach announcing him before she saw him at the doorstep. He stood framed in her doorway in the slant of evening light, shoulders broad, hair a little mussed, a navy jacket zipped up half-way. He looked like a man who'd stepped out of the lines of an ordinary life and walked straight into hers.

His face didn't have that easy going look on it, and a look as hesitant as it was hungry had replaced the charming half-smile he often wore. Her stomach clenched with guilt at the sight of him, and a hot lump formed in her throat.

She had missed him so much more than she realized.

Alexis stepped back to let him in, and his scent filled her nose as he brushed past her, the places where their bodies barely touched sizzling with heat. She reached a hand out toward him, her expression filled with hunger now, too. Sidney looked down at it, and then their gazes met. They needed no words, only each other's touch. Their bodies met, the air pulsing with desperation.

Small, furtive touches became more urgent. Clothes littered the living room floor, breathy moans and low moans falling into the spaces between kisses. Their bodies were familiar maps they navigated without tenderness, only a clawing need, a conversation without words.

Before she knew it, Sidney was lifting her into the air, his arms grabbing her from under her thighs. He told her to hold on to his shoulders, and she gripped with all her strength, though not much was needed, she found. The man was deceptively strong.

Then he buried himself inside her, filling her as if she were made just for him, and she lost the ability to think or talk or do anything but feel. It had been far too long.

Her nails dug into the skin at his shoulders, blood welling around some of them, and she felt his teeth clamp onto the skin at the side of her neck. He drove into her again and again, the skin of her ass slapping against his pelvis and thighs.

Her orgasm ripped through her body without warning, and she cried out, her pussy clenching around him, as if to milk his cock with her pulsing wet heat. He growled into her neck and came with such force she was sure she'd felt the warmth of it.

He staggered toward the couch, and they collapsed together —her half seated and half sprawled across the cushions, him kneeling on the floor between her thighs. It was close and intimate, sexy and real. There were like two humans who had just survived a small apocalypse.

In a voice muffled by the flesh of her thigh, Sidney said, "So you wanted to talk?"

29

Sidney pulled himself onto the cushions and gathered Alexis against him. They lay there in the aftermath, in that thin, private silence that comes when two people have given one another something both urgent and tender. Sidney's heart thrummed under Alexis' palm, proof that this was real. He was real and warm and here. The lamp on the side table threw a pool of gold across the room, the clock in the kitchen keeping time with faint ticks.

"I don't want to talk yet," she said, answering his question.

"Okay," he said and pulled her closer.

She kept her hand on his chest until the rhythm steadied her own pulse. Her still-loose muscles content to hold on to the shape of him. For a while she did nothing but count their breaths and take in the little things she'd missed: the feel of his chest hair against her face, the little creases at the sides of his mouth when he slept, the way half his mouth would lift in a grin that made his eyes twinkle. She didn't care about anything else, nothing that had led to this moment. Only this.

"Hi," Sidney said, looking down at her with that grin.

"Hi," she replied somewhat sheepishly.

"Are you good?" His voice was careful, as if whatever he said next might crack this fragile peace like a glass snow globe dropped on the floor.

Alexis' cheek rubbed against his chest, the hair scratchy against her skin, when she nodded. "All green."

He made a sound as if he were pleased she remembered. She let her fingers rest still and breathed in the slight scent of winter and rain on his jacket. "I needed that," she said truthfully. The words came like a small exhale she hadn't known she'd been holding. "I've needed you."

"I'm glad you filled me in on that." His voice was teasing, but there was an undertone of hurt. She'd taken the space she needed, but it hadn't come without a cost. "I missed you, too."

It wasn't exactly what she'd said, but it wasn't untrue. She missed him. She tipped her face up to his, hoping he'd take the hint and kiss her, and to her pleasure, he did. Gone was the desperation, replaced by a soft wanting and unspoken words yet to be shared.

"I'm sorry for what I said, or how I said it. At the hospital," she clarified. Her voice was quiet. She didn't regret it, but she was sorry it hurt him, and she said as much.

"You needed space. You don't have to apologize for that."

Her heart constricted, but she didn't know why. Rarely did she feel apologetic for any of her choices. They were simply the choices she made, static no matter her future opinions of them. But sitting with him like this, feeling this way? Well, not apologizing just didn't feel right.

"I do. I also need my choices, my limits, and my decisions respected."

Sidney trailed his fingers in slow circles over her shoulder. She expected him to stiffen, maybe even to become defensive.

Instead, he sat with her in that quiet space, tracing patterns over her skin with fingers roughened at the tips.

"Of course," he said finally. "I'm sorry if I made you feel pushed. About your visions. About us. I can promise to try not to push, but I don't think I can promise to stop wanting more of you."

She wasn't ready to talk about their relationship yet. Honestly, she didn't think she had the answers he would want. But it didn't seem like she had much choice.

"That scares you," he said. It was somewhere between a statement and a question. It was both and neither at the same time.

"Does that worry you?"

"Yes."

"Why didn't you and Amanda work? Did it have something to do with that? Feeling pushed?"

He'd never asked her about that relationship whose breakup was the catalyst to their entire relationship, and she didn't want him asking now. She didn't want to revisit those memories, nor did she want to think about how stupid it probably was that she and her rebound were even together. Or getting back together? Is that what was happening? Her brain was still so clouded by sex and the aftermath of her pleasure that thinking straight was impossible.

But she turned her face up to his, and all her frustration dissipated. He looked scared, though he was trying to hide it. She suspected that underneath the charming exterior was someone as sensitive as she felt now. He deserved to know the truth, whether or not she wanted to talk about it.

"There were a lot of reasons we..." She stopped, took a breath, and corrected herself. "She ended things, but it was because of me. And no, before you go making assumptions, I have no delusions that I'm not a wonderful partner. But I need time and space, maybe more than most people. I needed more than she wanted to give, that's for sure."

"It happens. It's painful, but sometimes who we love and what they want isn't compatible," Sidney said.

"I don't avoid commitment. Not in the way people think. I just want to be free to embrace today, to live a life where we can grow wild and unplanned. I don't want my wings clipped. It doesn't mean I don't want to fly with someone." He kissed the top of her head and leaned his cheek on it, and she asked, "What about you? Why haven't you settled down yet?"

His chest rose with the deep breath he drew in. "I suppose I've always been married to the job. It's not easy meeting someone when you're like that."

"So you're saying you don't have drunk women every weekend throwing themselves at you after driving them home?" Alexis said, turning and looking up at him with a teasing glint in her eyes.

He chuckled and pressed a quick kiss on her lips. "No, doll. Just you."

"How do you do it?"

"Do what?" he asked.

"Your job. I'm sure there's a lot of it that's paperwork and talking to people, but you see the worst things on the worst days of people's lives. How do you stay married to that kind of job?"

"I guess I enjoy putting things in order. Some people call me a control freak, but when things are chaotic and people are falling apart, it helps them. I don't know. I just put my head down and get it done," he finished with a shrug.

"You sound like my dad," she laughed. "He was always in control. Of himself, of me, of my momma."

Alexis looked out the window across the room, wondering if the forecasted snow would fall. Even if it did, it wouldn't stick.

Likely it would leave a thin film over everything, turn to slush, and freeze into ice for the morning commuters.

"I don't want to end up like her," she blurted out. Her voice was so low it was almost a whisper, and she kept her eyes trained on the ground outside.

"What's she like?" he asked.

Alexis thought about the mother she'd grown up with versus the woman who stood in her driveway just months ago. "I don't know. Prim, proper, loving. The perfect mom."

"Except..."

"Except for everything else," she said with a humorless laugh. "Mostly how I've never been good enough for her, and how much she changed herself to be good enough for my father."

Sidney made a noise in the back of his throat.

"I don't want to give up everything I love, everything I am, to be under the thumb of an overbearing control freak." She looked back at him and winced. "No offense."

"None taken," he assured her.

Then Sidney stood, pulling Alexis up with him as he did so. He grabbed a blanket from the back of the couch and wrapped it around them, leading them to the front window.

"Look out there," he whispered. "Do you see how your snowdrops are popping up? Right now, they're small and green, and they'll only bloom when they're ready. No one can control the weather or force them early."

She leaned her head back against his chest and looked at the tiny hopeful shapes, letting his arms come around her. The moment pulsed between them—small, intimate, and yet momentous. The conflict inside her hadn't disappeared, but for tonight at least, it was a quieter voice.

30

December faded into January in a blur of too many holidays crushed into too little space on the calendar. The town had glittered and then boxed away when the flurry of holiday cheer died out, taped shut by resolutions no one would keep. The promised snow hadn't come, but Alexis hadn't expected it to. Not really. A white Christmas sounded beautiful on paper, but in the south, the real biting cold didn't arrive until after the new year.

Alexis met Nick at Sweet Bea's, the little cafe radiator there doing its best against the cold outside. He arrived with a stack of papers and a patient, sympathetic demeanor, which suited him well as a mentor—reviewing queries, flagging clauses, and helping Alexis navigate the small cruelties of publishing her work.

"Thank you for this," Alexis said. She sipped a steaming cup of hot chocolate, blowing on the top before she gingerly put her lips to the rim. Marshmallows and white foam danced on the surface as she set the mug down on the table.

"Like I told you the last time you said it, and the time before that, you don't have to thank me. I'm happy to help."

"Okay, okay." Then, with a cheeky grin, she said, "Thank you."

He laughed and pushed the stack of papers—a printed version of her manuscript clipped at the top corner—toward her.

"You need a stronger hook," Nick said, pointing to the first paragraph. "This opening's charming, but readers want a promise. You're dropping them in the middle of the action, but you've got to tell them why they should care."

She made a few notes in the notebook to her right, taking the comment with the practiced ear of an editor and the facial expressions of anyone but. "Noted."

"It gets easier," he reassured her.

She looked at him, a line creased in the skin between her brows. "What does?"

"Taking feedback instead of giving it." Nick laughed at her baffled look. "Your face is very loud."

"Oh." She smiled at that. She supposed it would be a change moving to this side of the writing process, but she of all people knew that editing was going to really make her book shine.

Conversation slid from plot mechanics and character arcs to lighter gossip—who'd been seen with whom, which shop had a new display, a mutual friend's upcoming wedding, the expected demise of Ben and Harper's short-lived romance—so that when Alexis finally arrived back home, she had manuscript feedback and enough gossip to inspire another three books.

She'd barely dropped her bag and the stack of papers on her desk when a knock on the door startled her. She turned with a jolt, pressing a hand to her heart as if to slow it, and opened the door. Sidney stood on the other side, his hands jammed into his pockets. He looked like a man who'd been pacing, a caged tiger prowling the perimeter of its cell.

"What are you doing here?" she asked.

Sidney stepped through the doorway, and she instinctively took a step back. His gaze darkened with hunger, and her mouth went dry, her stomach fluttering.

"I missed you," he said.

She gulped, taking another step back. "I see that."

He closed the distance between them and swung her up into his arms. She gasped and hung onto his shoulders as he walked them straight into the bedroom. She only had a moment to register being dropped, the soft bed at her back, before the weight of him pressed over her and he captured her mouth in his.

There was nothing but the meeting of mouths, of heat matching heat and bodies moving against one another. Sitting back on his heels, Sidney grinned at her as he peeled the clothing from her body. Then his mouth replaced the fabric, and he was dragging his lips and teeth up her legs, across her belly, clamping them on her breasts. Alexis moaned, arching against him even as her hands busily divested him of his clothing as well.

"Get the lube and your toy out," he said, nipping at her nipple and rolling to her side.

"Which one?" she asked, propping herself on her elbows.

"A vibrator."

Alexis opened the drawer of her nightstand and held up two vibrators. Sidney pointed to the petite one.

"That one is fine."

"Just fine?" she asked coyly. When he only nodded, she crinkled her nose and stuck out the tip of her tongue.

"Feeling a little sassy tonight, are we?"

"Always."

"I'm not afraid of a little sass," he said. Grabbing hold of her ankles, he yanked her closer to him so that he was neatly kneeling between her thighs. "Now let me show you what I do about it."

He leaned forward and captured her mouth with his as his hand worked to push a dollop of lube onto his fingers from the container beside her. His body towered over hers, power and certainly radiating from him with a visceral hum. She lost herself in his lips, her body turning to putty beneath him. Her hips rose to rub herself against his cock, and her breath quickened. His mouth moved across her cheek, down the side of her neck, over the tip of her shoulder. He kissed the skin softly, then nipped not so gently at her flesh.

He sat back, and his gaze bore into hers as his fingers found her asshole and massaged the entrance. Her eyes flew from his fingers to his eyes and back again. For a moment she was unsure, paralyzed by the uncertainty of it. It wasn't as if she hadn't already disclosed her enjoyment of this activity—their texting was frequently filled with fantasies to explore and sexual adventures to go on together—but it was one thing to speak of taking his cock in her ass in the hypothetical and another altogether to watch him prepare her for it.

Especially knowing the dimensions of that part of his anatomy as well as she did now.

He seemed to sense her body tensing as he slid his fingers gently in and out of her ass, because he grabbed her hand and moved it over pussy.

"Use your toy," he instructed.

Alexis nodded, her eyes wide and pupils dilated. She pressed a small button, and a quiet buzzing sound filled the room. She rubbed the tip over her clit, sucking in a breath when the vibrating silicone met her sensitive flesh. Her body relaxed into his ministrations, and soon he replaced his fingers with the tip of his cock. He was hard, the head of him pulsing as he oh-so-slowly stretched her open. He was patient for what seemed an eternity, and then he was embedded to the hilt, and she was gasping at the fullness of it.

He reached down and pressed the button on her vibrator, increasing the speed. He withdrew and slowly pushed back into her. She groaned, pushing up against him as if she could take any more of his length into her.

"That's it, take it, baby," he said. "That's a good girl."

Alexis' mouth opened on a moan and stayed open, her breath coming in sharp gasps as he pumped his cock in and out of her, her vibrator pressed onto her clit. She was dripping with wet, her legs shaking with pleasure so intense it bordered on pain.

"Fuck, harder. Please. Harder," she begged. Everything was fast and hot, and their bodies slicked with sweat. All she could think was that she wanted more and more and more.

"You want me to fuck your ass harder?" he asked, and she whimpered in response. His pace quickened, and he grabbed her knee and bent it up to allow him even deeper access. "I'm going to fill that pretty little ass, baby girl."

Alexis nearly screamed as his cock slammed into her, and then without warning, she bucked and everything exploded. The orgasm ripped through her with such ferocity that she dropped her vibrator and clung to Sidney's body, her fingernails digging into his skin hard enough to draw blood. He clamped his teeth hard at the base of her neck and growled as his own orgasm took him, plunging as deep as possible. His cock throbbed as he filled her, his breathing ragged.

They lay like that until their heartbeats had slowed. Sidney rubbed his lips against her collarbone. He eased himself from her and rose, padding to the bathroom. Alexis heard her water run and cabinets open and close. There were a few moments of splashing, and then Sidney returned holding a wet washcloth in one hand and a dry cloth in the other.

He cleaned her body, throwing the washcloths in a pile across the room when he was finished, and pulled the comforter out from underneath her. Before her brain could compute what was happening, Alexis found herself freshened, tucked in, snuggled against him. She took a deep breath and let herself relax into it. There would be plenty of time to think later. All she wanted now was to enjoy this moment... and maybe grab a snack.

ALEXIS WALKED TO THE KITCHEN, a little sore but satisfied. She grabbed a glass from the cabinet and filled it with water from the sink. She was in the middle of taking a sip when she spied movement outside the kitchen window. Leaning up on her tiptoes, she spied Harper crouched in the flower bed at the back of her house with her arms stretched out in front of her.

Alexis couldn't make out what she was saying, but she was too concerned—and curious for that matter—not to figure out what was happening. She opened the back door and peeked her head outside.

"What are you doing?" she whispered somewhat forcefully.

Harper jumped and looked as if she wanted to squeal. "Oh my god, Lex! You scared the bejesus out of me!"

"You're the one sneaking around in my backyard," she pointed out.

Harper considered that. "Fair point, but I have a good excuse." She pointed to the large terracotta flowerpot next to the back door. "That little disaster."

Alexis looked down at the pot, amused and wholly invested

now. It was empty except for potting soil and the gnarled brown stalk left from the mums she'd killed last fall. Seeing nothing, she stepped through the doorway to get a closer look. Sure enough, a tiny grey head and two bright eyes peered back at her, the body of the kitten it belonged to wedged in the gap between the pot and the house.

"How old is it?"

"Um, almost three months, I think."

"Where did you get a kitten?" she asked.

"Remember when my cat got herself knocked up?" Harper said with a sigh, and Alexis nodded. Then Harper gestured to the kitten. "This is the grandchild she gave me. Well, one of them. I got the other three adopted."

Alexis crouched down, and the cold ground seeped through her thick sweatpants like icy water. "What's your cat's name again?"

"Lucy," Harper said. "Short for Lucifer. Fitting, considering she gave birth to this demon."

"Well, that's unfortunate."

"Why?"

"We can't blame the man for this."

Harper laughed, cheeks pink. "No, unfortunately, she comes by it honestly. I just want to get the little gremlin inside. I can't find anyone who'll take her. People want the sweet ones. She's a terror."

"Aw, maybe she just doesn't want to be told what to do," she laughed. "Give me a sec."

Alexis stood abruptly and skipped into the house. She returned moments later with a handful of torn bits of ham. She folded her legs beneath her and offered some to the kitten. The tiny thing stayed right where it was for more minutes than she cared to count, and she cursed herself for not grabbing a sweat-shirt or socks before impulsively deciding to play "capture the kitty."

Finally, the kitten's nose flared, and it slowly inched closer to Alexis' outstretched hand. Alexis was careful to keep her glances slow and indirect, to blink slowly, and every other trick she could remember from the cat documentary she'd watched some time last year. The kitten nibbled at a piece of ham, and Alexis slowly petted her with her free hand.

It wasn't long before the kitten was happily purring, arching her back beneath Alexis' hand, and finishing the ham with a satisfying lip lick. Then it launched itself at Alexis's knee and wound in and out of her crossed legs like a ribbon. Its tiny purr vibrated through the air, making Alexis laugh and Harper sigh with relief.

Harper watched the exchange with an odd look on her face. "Do you want her?" Harper asked, half-joking.

The question surprised Alexis, and yet nothing had felt more right in her life. Shivering from the cold, she felt the decision fall into place like two gears locking together in perfect unison. A kitten around the house would be pleasant company, and if Mia was open to it, they could even have a bookshop cat. The customers would love it!

It was a commitment, a little life to take care of, but it would also be a friend—someone to sit on manuscripts, to curl in a sunbeam, to make the bookstore even warmer and more welcoming.

"Yes, I do," she said before she could talk herself out of it. She scooped the kitten into her arms and nuzzled her nose. The kitten squirmed and meowed, and Alexis tucked her head into the tiny ball of fuzz and wiggled her way up to a stand. "Let's go inside before we freeze to death."

Shivering, she said goodbye to Harper, who admitted it was a bittersweet moment, only spoiled slightly by how cold they all were. She also promised to drop off some cat food and a litter box within the hour. Alexis crooned nonsense into the kitten's ear as they walked inside. She padded to the bedroom, trying out various names under her breath.

"Luna. Delilah. Bambi. Sophie. Jewel. Fluffy."

None sounded right.

"Edgar," she said with a laugh. It was ridiculous, a gendered name that sounded more like that of an old man wearing a grey suit than a little grey girl cat. But the kitten blinked as if that were the only name in the world, and just like agreeing to adopt the kitten, it felt right.

"Who's Edgar?"

Alexis looked up, having nearly forgotten Sidney was there. She held up the kitten with a triumphant smile. "Meet Edgar. She's my new roommate."

"She? Edgar?" Sidney asked. He sat up in bed, rubbing his eyes and looking like he'd fallen asleep, however briefly, while she was gone.

Alexis nodded and set the kitten on the bed. She wasn't sure what she expected, but it wasn't a ball of fluff hopping around the bed. Edgar was fearless, pouncing on lumps in the blanket and nearly running off the bed.

"She's perfect," he said, offering his hand to the kitten. Edgar sniffed, then promptly head-butted his hand and rubbed her body down his arm. The sight—Sidney with a sleepy, lop-sided grin on his face and a kitten in his hand—was simple and oddly domestic.

Exhausted from the day, Alexis snuggled into the blankets next to Sidney. Edgar curled its little body into the dip between them, and before long they were all drifting to sleep.

31

A pale winter morning greeted them, a morning so still that it seemed the cold had scrubbed all life from it. For a moment they lay together—Sidney's arm thrown across Alexis's waist, her head pillowed against his forearm—and the little house held them like a small, private harbor. Edgar was a warm knot at the back of her knees, already purring before her grey eyes were even open.

Alexis blinked against the light. The memory of the night was a warm ribbon wrapping itself around her body. The way their mouths had sought each other, the way they'd pushed her body to its limits, the relief that had washed over her when she submitted to the will of someone else. She let herself lie without stirring, listening to Sidney's steady breath and to the kitten's small engine.

"Breakfast?" Sidney whispered, noticing she was already awake.

His voice, a low thing in the space between awake and asleep. She smiled up at him, and he shifted carefully to look at her, eyes warm and glittering.

"Please," Alexis said, and surprised herself by how eager she sounded. The idea of him in her kitchen making her a meal as simple as scrambled eggs and toast while her new kitten danced around his feet made her heart do a little dance.

And for a change, that dance didn't terrify her.

Sidney rose with the competence he'd always worn like a tool belt—quiet, efficient, somehow gentle. "Coming up," he said with a wink.

He padded into the kitchen, bare feet whispering over the floor with every step, and started what could very well be a morning ritual: a pan on the stove, butter melting with that small, bright hiss, the crack and snap of eggshells breaking open. Alexis followed him into the kitchen more slowly, wrapped in a robe, and watched him from the end of the hallway where the wall ended and the kitchen opened.

Edgar tumbled into the kitchen from behind her and stalked the perimeter of his feet, tail up like a flag of ownership. With a little butt wiggle, Edgar jumped from the floor to the counter, and when Sidney swirled the egg into the pan, the kitten swatted a tentative paw at the rim. Alexis laughed.

"You're not serious," she said when he spooned a bit of scrambled egg onto the counter.

He grinned, the sort of grin that was mostly mischief. "She's a carnivore in training."

Edgar nosed the morsel and then devoured it with the desperation of someone who'd just been offered a steak after weeks of starving in the desert. The sight—Sidney standing shirtless in her kitchen as he scrambled eggs and fed bits to the kitten with zero regard that she was watching—made Alexis' heart feel full. It was an intimacy of small things, not the dangerous kind that demanded she be less herself, but the domestic kind that said life could be careful and funny and shared.

"Do you want to come with me to the pet store?" Alexis asked after they'd eaten, the question fluttering out of her like an experiment. She felt a trace of giddiness, ridiculous and bright, at the idea of shopping for a creature that was now her responsibility, her family.

Sidney's eyes lit up. "I'd love to."

"Okay, we should get the basics. Litter, food, a carrier. Oh, and toys! Little bell balls. She needs a name tag, too, especially if we let her roam the shop."

"You're going to bring her to the shop?"

"Yes," Alexis said, picking up the kitten from its place prowling the kitchen table and hugging it to her chest. "She's going to be quite the connoisseur of books when she grows up."

"She'll be the perfect bookshop kitty."

Her chest tightened with a pleasant, private joy. The thought of doing ordinary errands with him felt like a small, safe future she could step into. When she was ready, of course.

"I want her to come so she can see things with me. Maybe it's silly, but I want this to be ours, not just mine."

He nodded and kissed the top of her head. "She's coming, and so am I."

It was a promise, even if he didn't use the words.

The car ride was a chorus of vocal protest from the tiny kitten on Alexis' lap. Edgar, cradled in a soft blanket she had found in a drawer, mewed as if cataloging the misdeeds of every human in the world. Alexis cooed at her the way people do to make animals feel safe, petting her soft fur and shushing her softly as Sidney drove.

The kitten's ears perked up when the bell over the door of the pet shop jangled its welcome. The air smelled of dry pet food, rawhide dog chews, and plastic. Sidney pushed a small cart while Alexis followed alongside, Edgar in her arms. They both looked around with wide eyes, taking in all the products, toys, and treats. Sidney pointed out sensible brands with a practicality she found adorable, though that didn't stop her from loading the cart with things she didn't need. In she threw a plush bed, more toys than Edgar could play with in a lifetime, a window hammock she imagined the kitten claiming like a small throne, and more.

"You're going to ruin me," Alexis admitted, holding up a fuzzy mouse toy with a feather tail.

"And you won't regret a second of it." Sidney laughed, that crooked tooth flashing.

She thought of the small ironies as she teetered between impulse and prudence. Her father had been a man who moved them according to orders and schedules outside of her control. He was a tidy soul and had always kept things tidy in a way that left no room for the small chaos of a child... or a girl growing into a woman for that matter.

They'd lived in barracks and bases and hotels for stretches of time, her mother smoothing edges to keep the peace. Pets, Alexis remembered, had been practical impossibilities in that life: too much responsibility when everything might need to be boxed up in a year or two. Her mother was never one for mess and hadn't been the type to argue when her father drew the lines.

"You know," she said to Sidney as he compared brands of litter with an almost anthropological zeal, "we never had pets when I was a kid. Dad moved us around, and my momma... well, she didn't want the dirt or the fuss of them. It was easier that way. Clean and efficient, I guess. But I think I always wanted one. I remember asking for a dog once, and my dad said we didn't have time to train another member of the household, like I was something that needed to be trained, too."

Sidney leaned over and kissed her on the top of her head. "All training should be consensual," he said, his eyes glittering.

A dusky flush bloomed across Alexis' cheeks, and she batted a hand at his chest. "Get your mind out of the gutter." Her eyes darted around. Their actions didn't embarrass her. Not exactly. She just didn't want Susie Homemaker in the next aisle over to know just how much she was learning about and enjoying playing with power dynamics in the bedroom.

Sidney smiled and mimed closing his lips like a zipper. "Just love her exactly the way you want to. That's all you've got to do."

She looked at him, surprised by how fierce and right that sounded. "I will," she said. "I'm going to love her so much she won't know what hit her."

They moved through the aisles like conspirators. Alexis picked up two identical bowls for food and water because symmetry soothed her, and a tiny brush for grooming because the idea of pampering the kitten felt like art. Sidney ensured the carrier had soft sides and clicked a seatbelt through its handle like a man who thought of safety as a kindness. They argued gently about the color of the litter box. She wanted a pale teal; he thought gray was nobler. In the end, they compromised on gray with a teal mat.

At the register, Alexis unloaded her choices onto the conveyor belt and paid with giddy pleasure. Buying so many things for such a tiny creature who could probably happily live off trash and birds outside felt absurd and sanctifying at once. The clerk, charmed by Edgar's demand to be petted, slipped in a sample pack of treats.

On the drive home, the kitten's protests dwindled to intermittent chirps, less alarm and more dignified protest. She finally settled into the blanket as if to say she had decided in favor of these strange humans. Sidney glanced at Alexis and smiled, the kind of smile that meant everything with no need for explanation. She felt unexpectedly and deliciously as if they'd done something together that mattered.

Even if adopting the kitten was hers and hers alone, they had adopted some small amount of this responsibility together, choosing a tiny life to fold into their own. However unintentionally. The toothbrush incident, the night she'd panicked over Sidney's leaving things at her apartment, felt like a different person's story now, an old draft revised.

As they pulled into the driveway, Alexis looked over at Sidney. The kitten in her lap, the morning sun bathed his skin in gold, and something inside her shifted.

"I love you," she said, though it admittedly sounded more like a question than a statement.

Sidney looked at her, his brows drawn together, his expression a mix of confusion and joy. "I love you." He seemed surprised, and his tone held the same question in it.

Then they laughed, low chuckles that filled the space between them with warm astonishment.

"You do?" Alexis couldn't help but ask.

Sidney grinned. "Yeah, I do."

Alexis watched his face with a depth of feeling she'd been careful to keep private, as if she were letting herself open a part of herself she didn't want to admit existed.

"Okay." She let out a breath that was both giddiness and relief.

"Okay," he answered.

"We did a good thing."

He nodded and reached for her hand, looking down to where their fingers intertwined and then back up to her. "We did."

32

Sidney sat cross-legged on the living room rug with a stack of case files fanned out around him like a paper moat, and he was the castle. The television had long ago been turned off, and the only sound in the apartment was the refrigerator's low hum and the occasional sharp chirp of his phone when it vibrated against the coffee table. Here, in his own quiet, the paper felt almost sacramental—exhibit photos, call logs, witness statements, sketches drawn and notes taken in hurried pen. He spread county maps across the floor, the locations of the victims' bodies marked with colored tabs. Beside it all was a legal pad full of observations, theories, and half-thoughts he'd scribbled in the margins of his day.

Three more children were dead, though the latest murders were all in neighboring counties. Three more towns with mothers and fathers staring at shoes by the front door that would never be walked in again.

There was a pattern here, he was sure of it, but so far it eluded him. Instead of connecting dots, he stared at a jagged trail of events with very little connecting them. Until recently, that is. He'd read the reports until the edges of the pages blurred, until words like "organized" and "ligature" floated like smoke across his eyes. He'd hoped for chaos, an erratic killer that left behind evidence he could actually use, but what he saw instead was the opposite: evolution.

Escalation.

The earlier murders had been brutal, yes, but of course, they were brutal. The victims were children. Different locations, victims of opportunity, no signature. An unorganized killer. In cases like that, the killer would leave some trace evidence behind, but months went by with little to nothing. It was chilling to know that the perpetrator responsible was still walking free.

The recent three murders, though, chilled Sidney in a novel way. They were cleaner in the worst possible sense. The killer strangled each child with a ligature, some type of cord, before any assault. The killer had inflicted nearly all the injuries post-mortem, as if killing was simply a necessary evil and not the goal. If the children were to be so abused, he thought with a shiver and a small measure of gratitude, at least it was when the victims could no longer feel.

From an investigative standpoint, it also hinted at someone with physical limitations, or perhaps a person who preferred control, who relished the power of domination at a distance. The thought turned his stomach.

He picked up a photo from the pile scattered around him. His fingers left grease smudges on the corner. Staring back at him was the face of a little boy in a red hoodie, frozen mid-laugh in a candid photograph his mother had posted to a neighborhood page the week before he disappeared. He'd been found face down in a yard, the snow softening the horror for a neighbor who'd screamed before they'd even known what it was they were seeing. That neighbor had called the police to report a body in the snow while the parents were still at work. These were the details that would keep him awake for nights on end.

That was how they were all found now. Snow didn't fall often here, but when it did, he'd come to expect the call. The call of a town that had found another child before the family even had time to register the loss.

Along with the predictability of the killer's emerging pattern were inconsistencies, too. Witness testimony from a convenience store a block away offered a shadow of a man slipping by on the day of one killing, and a woman who walked her dog claimed she'd seen someone acting oddly by the park near another body. But the witness descriptions didn't match, not exactly. One described a man who was tall, broad-shouldered. Another spoke of someone hunched and small. Some statements contradicted others on everything from jacket color to hair length. Witnesses were either unreliable, or there was more than one offender. The possibility of two killers operating in the same region, preying on children in different but overlapping patterns, felt like a fever dream. Experience taught him it was thankfully unlikely.

Sidney was close to calling the FBI's Behavioral Analysis Unit—close enough that he'd nearly filed a formal request through his local field office just an hour earlier. He didn't enjoy asking for help. He was a cop who believed in his work and in the ability to find the missing pieces, connect the threads that others missed, but this was bigger than his pride. The BAU would offer a view he could not: pattern analysis across jurisdictions, experience with ritualistic evolution, a psychological profile shaped by years of facing this kind of thing head-on. But involving the feds meant ceding control of the case's narrative. It meant admitting he didn't have a handle on it. For every hour he stalled, another child might be at risk.

For every file he set down, the guilt pressed down on him like a weight held to his sternum.

Another photograph caught his eye: a single snowdrop flower placed on a child's chest. He couldn't explain why, but it appeared deliberate. He traced its petals on the glossy paper with the tip of his finger. Snowdrops, an interesting choice for a flower.

Alexis had planted them at her mailbox months ago. They were symbols of innocence, of hope. Someone had left one on a body as if to send a message. He'd initially dismissed the floral detail as a coincidence, something the child could've collected. Now, with the three more recent victims and the consistent ligature, the flower felt less incidental and more intentional, a token left by someone who wanted the ritual, who wanted to send a message.

The paper of a local newspaper lay folded beside him, its headline screaming *The Snowman Strikes Again* in heavy black letters. Sidney had never liked nicknames for killers. They humanized a brutality that should remain clinical, but the nickname emphasized what he was already discovering about his killer's evolution: the symbolism of the snow, that the killer had left all the bodies in plain sight, always on the stark white snow as if staging trophies on a blank canvas. He preferred to think of the victims not as elements in a sensationalist story but as people: children with small rooms and favorite cartoons and parents who could not yet know that their worlds were forever reshaped.

Sidney's phone buzzed on the carpeted floor next to him, and he flinched as if the buzz was as loud as a gunshot echoing through the quiet room. He checked the screen: Alexis. He'd called her earlier in the morning, a check-in disguised as a casual question about calendars and coffee. She hadn't answered then either; he had assumed she was at the bookstore or buried in revisions.

He let it go to voicemail.

Tipping his head back, Sidney rubbed his eyes until they burned.

He needed a break.

SIDNEY

Coffee?

ALEXIS

Are you asking me out for coffee or offering to bring me some?

SIDNEY

Either.

He looked down at the files and photographs, his official notes, as well as his casual scribbles. They stared back at him like accusations, silent yet deafening. Sidney shook his head.

ALEXIS

I'm holding down the fort at the bookshop for Mia. She's home with a cold. You can grab some coffee and come hang with me here if you'd like?

SIDNEY

Sure. I'll stop by Sweet Bea's.

ALEXIS

You're the best.

He wasn't. He just needed her, even if he couldn't describe how or why. Maybe he simply needed people in general, but it didn't matter. She was the one he wanted to be with right now. Sidney considered telling her he was at a standstill with this investigation and wanted a semblance of normalcy. He thought about telling her just that, that he needed the face-to-face. He needed her.

Instead, he sent a simple text.

SIDNEY

See you in thirty.

Sweet Bea's was quiet when he strolled in to pick up his coffees to go. He noted a few familiar faces but no one he was really interested in talking to, not in his current mood at least. Gabby sat across the table from Mike, the air between them sizzling with tension, and Sidney wondered where Amy was. It seemed odd that Amy wouldn't be with them, but then again, he knew Gabby's reputation.

No doubt Mia and Alexis, probably Harper too, knew all the details. Those three always had their ears to the ground for the latest gossip, and they could spot a traitor in their midst from a mile away. "Not a girl's girl," he'd overheard. The girl could fix her teeth, cake her face with makeup, and glue on fake eyelashes that better resembled caterpillars, and it still wouldn't hide the ugliness inside.

Poor idiot, he thought as he pushed open the door, coffee successfully procured. Sidney hoped Mike hadn't screwed up with Amy. He didn't know the pair well, but he'd met them here and there. They seemed good together, happy. That was all anyone could wish for, after all.

Driving again was a blur of gray and white, the heater cutting and sputtering against the cold, the windshield streaked from using his windshield wipers to de-ice his car. His mind wandered back to the case, to the parents of the murder victims. There was a mother who'd posted the family photograph on Facebook and waited for her child to come home, parents like Lance and Danielle Davis who would never see their child again. He held their faces in his mind like an inventory of owed things: apologies, explanations, interviews.

No arrests. No leads. No evidence.

When he parked outside the bookshop, snow softened under his shoes, and the doorway's light lit a small rectangle on the sidewalk. Through the glowing shop windows, Sidney saw stacks of books emanating the kind of ordinary warmth that felt how the pages of books smelled. He carried the coffee cups inside, the bell chiming above the door with a small jingle.

Alexis emerged from between the shelves, cheeks flushed from whatever it was she'd been doing, hair tucked into a bun at the crown of her head. Edgar trotted behind her and came to greet him, too, her whiskers twitching at the scent of coffee when he squatted down to pet her.

"You're here," Alexis said with a wide smile, standing on her toes to peck him on the lips.

Sidney handed her the coffee without thinking and braced himself to resist the urge to unload the entire case on her right then and there. Instead, he found a moment of reprieve. Even if the weight of his work came careening back into his mind as soon as she asked how it was going, this moment existed. This quiet oasis held only them, the books that sheltered them from the world, and the scent of what could most literally be described as roasted bean water filling the air between them.

33

Alexis stepped out from the stacks with a bounce in her step and welcomed Sidney. She was excited for the surprise visit and grateful for the coffee. All they had was tea left in the shop, and she was already tired of whatever herbal blend Mia was stocking at the moment. He flashed her a tired smile that didn't reach his eyes; his cheeks were pink with cold.

"It doesn't look like we'll have any more snow, but you'd think they could at least plan for a little ice," Alexis teased as he approached. "We know we're always going to get that."

"More snow this year than I can ever remember, though."

"Not enough to change the fact that we're amateurs at winter."

He managed a humorless half-laugh. "You'd be surprised what we can mess up." He glanced at the sidewalk outside, noting where his shoes had made cracks in the slush.

They moved further into the shop, leaving behind the few people outside who moved like they were in a secret club—

urgent and bundled against the winter as they carried out their errands and counted down until they were inside again.

Sidney dropped into the chair beside her, his shoulders holding tension like a coat he couldn't shrug out of. It pulled his jaw tight and made the lines around his mouth hard. "How's business today?"

"Slow, but I figured it would be," she said. "We've got an event coming up in two weeks, though, which should liven things up. Mia's leading the charge there. Edgar's on a rampage, so beware. Little imp chewed through the corners of every copy of Wuthering Heights we have."

Sidney's lips twitched. "Maybe she's trying to tell you something about that book."

"Yeah, keep them away from her," Alexis said, slumping back in the chair with a grin. She might complain, but she loved the kitten's antics. Even if they were exhausting.

He tried to laugh, but it dissolved into something raw. He wiped a hand down his face as if to wipe away the anxiety that lived there. "Lex—there's something I need to ask."

Her breath hitched at the familiar tone, the way the words hung heavy in the air. "Okay," she said, eyeing him warily. These small, familiar silences never held good news. Leave it to a man to ruin a perfectly pleasant day. And after he'd brought her coffee and everything!

His voice was low with an undertone of shame, and the words landed like stones. "I need you to help with the case. Properly. I need you to call up what you see. Anything. Dates, places, names. Whatever you can give me."

She stopped breathing and closed her eyes. Rage sent ropes of heat coursing through her body. She knew it was an overreaction, that the sheer amount of anger she felt was disproportionate to the situation, but she couldn't help herself. She thought they were past this. They'd talked, set boundaries, and come to agreements. She wasn't a sideshow monkey to be asked to perform on a whim. He saw her visions as a gift, or worse, a tool. She knew they were a curse, waves of useless images that did nothing but disrupt her day and put her and others in actual danger. Didn't he remember the car wreck she'd almost had? The glass she'd shattered and then walked over? The countless other stories she'd shared?

The light from the surrounding lamps suddenly felt too bright, too hot. She opened her eyes and met his gaze, noting the hollowness in his eyes and the way he clenched his hands at his sides. Compassion was a bucket of icy water over the heat of anger boiling up inside her. She took a breath, imagining letting it out like steam through her nose.

"Sidney," she said slowly, measured. "I told you I can't. You say that I won't, but I can't. It's dangerous for others and for me. I won't be someone's oracle."

His face shifted as if drawing a curtain of black down over it. "You've helped before."

"No," she said sharply. "You recognized pieces of a crime scene after I talked about a nightmare. Not before. Not when it would matter. Nothing I saw would've prevented that kid dying."

He exhaled a sound like resentment. "But it could if you tried. You block them out, but what if you accepted them? There are kids dying, Lex, and it's getting worse. You know that. You can see the things that matter. You can—"

"I said no," she cut in, her voice low and threatening. "Is this why you came today? To bribe me with coffee and company?"

His jaw worked. "Of course not," he said, but he stopped himself as if he didn't want to admit that was all or part of why he'd come.

Alexis' eyes narrowed to slits. "I think you should go."

She wanted him gone as much as she wanted to say yes. Because despite her protests, she wasn't a monster. She didn't want children dying, and she wanted to be the kind of person who would step into the fire and torch her own edges to save them. But the way the visions swallowed her whole when she let them was a truth she had learned the hard way. Let the visions come, and maybe she'd see a street sign or feel the cold of the ground at her back.

Or maybe she'd fall into a vision while driving and hit a person crossing the street.

One option might give them helpful information, even if it was too late. Another could get someone hurt. It didn't feel like rocket science to stand her ground.

Sidney's face dropped. His body sagged. "Lex," he began, but the syllable cracked under the strain of his feelings, and he paused. He leaned forward until his elbows were on his knees, his head held in his hands. His chest filled with a deep breath. "I'm sorry. I should have—I shouldn't have come like this. I shouldn't have... asked."

His words had a clumsy to them in the way of a man unused to being wrong. Alexis watched him shaping an apology like a tool he didn't know how to use: tentative, honest, and awkward. Part of her still loved the fact that even in confession he tried to fix the thing by saying the right sequence of words; it was one of those tiny truths about him that made him human.

"No, you shouldn't have," she agreed. Her voice was quieter now, not because the anger had vanished, but because it had burned off some of its edges on her temper. She was tired, the kind of deep-seated tired of a soldier trudging home from battle. "I'm done going back and forth on this, Sidney. Either respect me or leave me alone."

He flinched at her words. It hurt her how much he looked

like a man who would give anything to take it back, but she couldn't allow her compassion for him to make herself smaller.

"I'm sorry," he said. "I was wrong."

He could've said more. Maybe he wanted to, Alexis wondered, but she was grateful he didn't. She watched the little changes in his face, how his brow lowered, the way his shoulders eased a fraction. He wasn't performative; he was ashamed. Still, her policy was to trust deeds over words. Words could be beautiful, and apologies sounded nice, but she needed consistent, irrefutable proof that someone meant what they said.

Sidney's next words were small and the sort of thing she'd wanted to hear for months. "If you ask me for boundaries, I'll keep them. Tell me to stay out, and I'll stay out. If you tell me to be present, I'll be present in the ways you need. I promise." He looked at her, eyes raw with hope.

Alexis tested the sound of the promise inside her head. It did not ring false, and she wanted, more than anything in that moment, to be spared argument. Peace felt like an increasingly rare commodity, something that stood at the edge of her life, sometimes just out of reach. She wanted it, that peace, right now, even if she didn't know if she trusted the path to it.

"Okay," she said finally, as if her reply surprised herself. It was not fully trust nor acquiescence. It was an exhausted truce. "Apology accepted. For now."

Sidney's exhale was a small, relieved sound, the stiffness dissipating from his shoulders like steam. Then he said softly, "Can I... stay with you tonight? I don't want to be alone."

Her immediate, guarded response was to say no. But she could see his need—feel it as if it were a tangible string pulling at her heart—and she understood how heavy it must be for a man such as him.

She looked at him, taking in the shadows under his eyes,

the slight tremor in his voice, the honest fatigue that made him less a force of authority and more someone who'd been worn thin. Sympathy rose in her like a tide. Her heart hitched at the thought of him dealing with that loneliness on his own.

"Yes," she said, surprising them both. "You can stay... on one condition. No shop talk. You're invited, but your work is not."

Sidney's face softened into a small grin. "I can do that."

They arranged their night in the small, practical ways that made life just a little easier, a little less emotionally fraught. Alexis was grateful she could focus on logistics. She would make them dinner; he would do the dishes. They would choose the movie together; he would rub her feet. The act of bargaining in quiet made the reconciliation feel less like a risk and more real.

They closed up the shop together, and Alexis moved among the stacks with the calm of someone folding the world into order. She hadn't realized until that moment just how lonely she was. Running her hand along spines, shutting the light on displays, checking the till, all tasks she typically did with Mia or after a day filled with the hum of customers. Between the slow season and Mia being out sick, she'd been on her own a lot lately.

Sidney helped with the practical tasks he'd promised, but he was also a steady companion in those last hours. His purposeful, competent motions were strangely comforting. He wasted no movement. When he took the dusty broom to sweep the front step of the shop, she watched his shoulders work and thought about how lovely it was to build something out of the small moments together, how much more she valued them than grand gestures.

Outside, the winter gave the street a bare outline, like the lines of a coloring book waiting to be filled in. Alexis watched it from the warmth of the shop as she grabbed her bag and prepared to brave the biting wind. Beside her, Sidney placed a hand on her back and ushered her to the door. She breathed in deeply and smiled to herself, grateful for the fragile truce that folded around them like a warm blanket.

She only hoped it would protect her from the cold.

34

Sidney woke with a start to the gentle thrashing and strangled mews of the woman next time him. He rubbed a hand over his face with a series of rough swipes as he turned to Alexis. The sun was barely dawning, the softest morning light drifting through the blinds, and he blinked to focus his eyes in the dark.

Suddenly, Alexis sat up with a sharp, startled gasp, like someone surfacing after being held underwater. Her eyes were wild and raw, and they flicked around the room with frantic speed. Sidney propped himself on an elbow and reached out to comfort her, rubbing her arm and making soft shushing sounds.

"Shhh, Lex. It's just a bad dream," he said.

Her gaze locked on his, her eyes unfocused as if she didn't recognize him. "Why did you—" she began, her voice small, boneless.

He wrapped his arms around her, but she resisted, pushing him away and scrambling up and huddling into her body. Her hand went to her throat as if she were still gasping for air. "Lex, wake up. Baby, you're still dreaming."

But her eyes were wide open, frantic.

Sidney sat up fully and held out an arm to her, gesturing with his hand for her to come closer again. His heart broke for her, for the sheer terror in her expression. "Shhh, it's okay. Lex, it's me. It's okay."

The seconds stretched into minutes that felt like hours, and the morning light slowly began filling the room, chasing away the shadows of the night. Finally, Alexis relaxed, her pupils constricted, and she inched over the bed and into Sidney's arms. He kept shushing her, wrapping his arms around her tightly and stroking her hair back from her forehead.

"I'm sorry. I... I don't know..." her voice trailed off.

"Shhh, it's okay. It was just a bad dream."

Alexis shook her head against his chest. "I still feel him chasing me. Like I was being hunted."

Sidney's ears perked up, and his eyes sharpened. "What do you mean?"

"I don't know," she said, pausing. Sleep still slurred her words and slowed them, as if her thoughts had not yet joined together. "The hair on the back of my neck... like being watched... and then a cloth on my face... so much blood..."

He knew he shouldn't say anything. He should let her breathe against him and come back to reality in the bubble of safety he was providing, but he knew her dreams were never really dreams. "Where did you see the blood?"

"On the white... no?" she said with a questioning tone, her brows drawing together. "No, not blood. Letters. And dark and fire in my chest. I couldn't breathe."

Alexis' breathing quickened, and she shifted restlessly against him.

He didn't notice.

"The letters, Lex. Tell me what letters you saw," he pushed, his mind already miles away.

"B, and an A," she said, then she was blinking and rubbing her eyes. She sat up and pushed a hand against the fluff of her hair, the curls frizzy and loose from sleep. "I need a sec."

Sidney was already up, moving through the small motions that were less efficiency or habit and more preoccupied. His eyes looked at the bedroom, then the surrounding kitchen, but he saw none of it. Not really. Instead, he was mentally sifting through his case notes, combing through evidence lists and photographs, looking for pieces of white fabric. It had to be a clue. He refused to believe anything else. His hands touched his shirt, the kettle, a knob on the stove. In a blur, he was half-dressed and making tea, walking back into the bedroom twenty minutes later carrying two mugs he didn't quite remember preparing.

Alexis watched him warily, her emotions unreadable. He handed her a steaming mug, the tag from the tea bag swinging against its side as she took it. She swallowed and took a tiny sip.

"Are you okay?" he asked.

She nodded. "I'm fine." Her voice still held the gravely roughness of sleep.

Sidney set his mug down on the nightstand next to him, missing the coaster completely, though neither of them noticed. His stomach was a hard knot, and his body was flushed and hot all over, but he ignored the sensations. He didn't have the time or the desire to dissect what this feeling meant, why this heaviness was threatening to drape over him like a weighted blanket. The case was hot and raw in him, and he found himself leaning closer to Alexis, unaware that she withdrew in response. "You said you saw something. White fabric and letters," he said. "Do you remember anything else about the cloth? Was it small, thick, thin? Anything?"

Alexis shook her head. "No—"

"Anything at all, Lex," Sidney pressed. His heart pounded, and his chest heaved with his breath. Possibilities, plausible and far-fetched, raced through his mind. "Was it like a towel or a washcloth?"

She shook her head again, and she rubbed a hand over her face, her movements becoming more agitated. "I don't know. I—"

"Could it have been something like a handkerchief? Something with someone's initials?" Sidney cut her off, his voice suddenly harsher, his fingers curling into fists in the blankets pooled around their bodies. He knew he was close, so close to the answers he so desperately needed. He had it: a breadcrumb. Enough to chase. He felt that quick, dangerous surge—the same sick thrill that makes some men flirt with danger as if the energy itself were a drug. For months he'd been starving for something that cut the fuzz off the edges of the case. Someone who hung initials on a kerchief had handed them an identity if he could only find the thread.

Alexis held up a hand and sat up straighter. "Sidney, I'm still waking up." She set her mug to the side with trembling hands. "I don't even..." She faltered and shook her head again as if to banish the last of the fog of sleep, her gaze dropping to where her hands rested in her lap. "Wait..."

He leaned closer. "Did you get anything else? A place, a scent, a voice—"

"Stop," she interrupted him forcefully.

Sidney's voice was strained, a band around his chest tightening. "We're so close, Lex. Just tell me what else you saw."

Her hands clasped together, her fingers curled into themselves so tightly that her knuckles went white. "Stop," she repeated. "I'm not good. I'm barely awake, and my body doesn't even feel like my body. Please don't push me like this."

Sidney felt a small, ugly click of annoyance that he hated in himself. Time was his enemy, and it already had a jump on him. It wasn't her fault, and yet he wanted to blame her. She, who was willing to withhold the gift that could help him find the killer, could save more children. Yet, still she stayed silent, or in denial. It didn't matter which. He was still left with near-nothingness.

"Lex, we can't wait," he said. "If you saw something that could help, we have to figure it out."

"Can you hear what you're doing to me? Do you even hear what you sound like?" Alexis asked, her voice rising in time with the angry flush that crept up her cheeks. "You're a cop! What cop really believes in psychics and visions and all this crap?! You're supposed to follow the evidence, not listen to some crackpot with bad dreams."

"You're not a crackpot, and they aren't just bad dreams," he said, his voice carrying something low and dangerous in its tone.

"They are. You're so hell-bent on pushing me for information that you don't care what it does to me. You don't care that it'll make you a laughingstock or ruin your career. I can't even convince you that having these fucking visions is dangerous for me. You're so caught up in this psychic theory that you can't even see how stupid you're being.

"Don't call me stupid."

"Don't milk me for information," she quipped.

He bristled, stung by the ugliness of it and the kernel of truth he didn't want to admit. "I'm trying to help."

"I know I wasn't awake," Alexis said. "I know you kept talking and asking and pushing while I was only half here."

His voice was clumsy and defensive, but there was an edge to it. "I'm trying to keep more kids from dying."

She flinched, and he worried he'd gone too far. "You turned me into a tool. You didn't care what it could do to me."

He felt the heat of guilt prick the back of his neck, and defensiveness snapped at him. "We don't have time for delicacy," he said.

"You used me," she said, her voice trembling as much as the arms she wrapped herself with.

"Kids are dying. If what you saw leads us anywhere, we have to move."

"You don't get to do that," she said. "You don't get to make me the bad guy here. Believe whatever you want, Sidney. Do whatever you want, but you can't make me believe I can do anything to help. You can't make me risk hurting myself or someone else."

He thought he saw a tear drip down her cheek, but he didn't care. He couldn't. His own anger bubbled up inside him with blinding rage. "How can you be so selfish?!" he yelled.

She recoiled as if slapped, and he immediately regretted his words. She froze, and for what must have been an eternity, they stared at one another. Then she slowly slid off the bed and backed away until her back was to the window. Silent tears poured down her face, her jaw clenched, arms wrapped tighter around her midsection. Dark wet dots bloomed across the chest of the white t-shirt she'd slept in as her tears fell.

The anger inside him subsided, the fog of aggression and desperation lifting, and he was left feeling empty and heavy. Sidney realized the weight he'd felt hanging over him, the knot in his stomach that wouldn't go away, was shame. He'd pushed again, he realized, and he regretted everything about this morning. He'd betrayed her, hurt her.

Correction: he was hurting her.

He reached for her, an automatic reflex to close the

distance, to comfort himself as much as her. "Lex, I didn't mean it like that."

It was a lie. They both knew he meant it exactly like that.

She shook her head, and he saw then how wide the space was between them. Her eyes were bright, and though he'd always liked that brightness—it had drawn him in from the moment he first saw her—it now shone with a harsh clarity.

"Leave," she said. "And don't come back. Don't call me. Don't text. Just go away."

The words stung. For a moment he wanted to bargain, to explain. He could have told her about the families waiting for answers, or how he was just trying to protect future victims. He wanted to drop to his knees in front of her and plead for forgiveness, but she's granted him too much already, and still they'd ended up here. Sidney knew there would be no forgiveness to be found after this, and he didn't deserve it anyway.

His shoulders drooped, and he nodded. "Okay," he said, but his voice cracked, and the sound was barely audible.

Alexis watched him as he dressed and collected his things. He considered trying to talk to her, to at least apologize or say something. Anything. But he felt her eyes on him as he moved through the room, felt the weight of his betrayal in them, so in the end, he simply left.

Not another word.

Not a glance back.

Nothing.

Gone.

Just as she'd asked.

35

Alexis didn't know how long she'd walked; time stopped when your brain went numb. She was barely bundled against the cold, but it didn't matter. She didn't feel it. The tears that streamed down her face had dried by the time she reached what was apparently her destination. She looked up at the sign, realizing she'd walked from her home to downtown St. John's and was standing in front of the bookshop.

Now all she wanted was Mia. Alexis thought about her in the way one thinks about their mother in times of distress, and her fingers were already pulling at the handle of the shop's door as if safety itself waited inside. The bell jingled to announce her arrival, and the smell of the shop, paper and candlelight, filled her nostrils.

But it was empty.

No Mia.

No comforting embrace.

No customers.

No predictable chaos.

She tried the back rooms and the office, but she was truly alone. Logic briefly broke through the fog in her mind. She pulled out her phone and shot off a text to Mia, telling her she had left the store unlocked. Alexis said she was sad to have missed Mia and promised to lock up behind her when she left.

Well, she thought, that was her good deed for the day done.

She left the shop with no real direction in mind, locking the door behind her as promised. Instead of going home, though, she found herself in front of the small antique shop next door. A Tiffany lamp bathed mismatched pieces of china warm golden light, and in the open area behind it she could see Mr. Baker—or rather, Alan, as he'd corrected her the last time she'd tried calling him that—arranging a set of small tins. He looked up in surprise, as if her thoughts had reached out to him and grabbed his attention. His face softened when he saw her.

"Alexis?" he said, hurrying to the door. "Are you all right?"

She tried to answer, but the sound came out as a ragged thing that was only half-intelligible and half-sob. The numbness she'd been clinging to dissolved in the doorway like sugar in warm tea.

"No," she said, and that single word let loose the deluge.

She stepped forward, and the tears poured out in a full, ugly wave. Alan, who had the quiet patience of someone who handled fragile things for a living, shut the door gently and guided her inside. His hand was stiff and icy against her back, but it was comforting nonetheless. He settled her into a chair at a small round table beside a window. He grabbed a small paper cup and filled it at the water dispenser by the front counter, setting it beside her without fanfare.

"Breathe," he said in his soft, steady voice. "Nice and slow. There you go." His hands were careful, competent, every move-ment measured and precise. Alexis found his surety and patience encouraging, though it did nothing to ease the outpouring of her heart.

She sobbed until she had no more sound nor an ounce of tears left in her eyes, her fingers wrapped around the chilly cup like a tether. Alan simply sat with her, a calm presence in a room of old things with no rush or need to hurry at all. He didn't ask questions, and she was grateful for it. She wasn't ready to give him the answers. He simply kept silent vigil with her until the wave subsided. When her breath had settled into smaller, raw inlets, she looked up and met his steady, kind eyes.

"Thank you," she said at last.

"There's no need for that," he tutted, sitting back in the matching chair across from her. The faded red fabric should've clashed with the bright red of the vest he wore, the differently aged shades in a fight for supremacy, but it didn't. She couldn't quite explain why.

Alan smiled, his eyes holding hers with gentle warmth. "Sometimes people need to be let down gently," he said. "Or held while they crumble."

Alexis let out a laugh that was more a hiccup and less a sound of amusement. "I think nothing about that was gentle," she said.

"No," Alan agreed. "But it will be gentler the next time it happens. It usually is."

Alexis sat for a few more minutes and sipped from her cup. The water was crisp on her tongue and soothed the hot stone lodged in her throat. She closed her eyes for a moment, opening them and taking a breath so deep her chest rose and fell with it.

"You want to know what happened, I'm sure," she said.

"Naturally, I'm a little curious."

"Just a little?" she laughed.

"Well," he said, his eyes twinkling as he propped an ankle on his knee, "maybe more than a little."

"Sidney, the guy I've been seeing, and I had a fight. It wasn't good. In fact, it was about as bad as it could get."

"Another woman?"

"No, nothing like that. I almost wish it were. It would be easier than this." Alexis huffed out a breath.

"What was it then?"

She stood suddenly, her hands coming up to gesture wildly in the air as she talked. "He's a cop, right? And he has this insane notion that I'm some kind of psychic. He's been stuck on this case—you know, the one about all the kids going missing and murdered. He's getting nowhere fast, and he thinks I'm his ticket to the fast lane."

Alan nodded and sipped his water, the small white cup out of place in his hands. They looked like hands that should hold vintage teacups, not cheap waxed paper.

She continued. "He just keeps pushing and pushing at me. Then this morning it all kind of exploded."

"Why?"

She paused. "A dream?" She said it like a question, as if simplifying it down to that felt silly.

"Over a dream?"

Alexis paced back and forth, telling him about the dream and the way Sidney had pulled bits and pieces out of her before she'd even been aware of herself. She talked about her visions of dirt and death, of how terrifying it felt as all the air left her body, of seeing the blood or letters in red against white, whatever it was she'd seen. "They're always so confusing and disorienting, and no matter what I say, he pushes. So I told him to leave."

Alan nodded. "It doesn't seem like you had much choice, dear."

Alexis threw her hands into the air. "I don't feel like I did."

"Why does it make you so sad, then?"

"Because what if I'm wrong?" she sank back into the chair. "Have you ever wondered about that? How do you live so long and not feel crushed by it?"

Alan chuckled and said, "Sometimes you learn to carry it. Sometimes you learn from it. Other times you leave it behind."

"That sounds awful."

He shrugged and raised his brows. "Life's not easy, my girl, but it's yours. You choose what you'll do with it, and it's all got weight. You've got to decide how much you're willing to carry."

When she left the shop some time later, night had descended on the downtown square, but life had lost some of its jagged edges. Alexis held a small tin of chamomile tea close to her chest, a parting gift from Alan with orders to brew a cup the moment she got home. She stepped out from the little antique shop and briefly considered calling a car to take her home, then decided against it. She wanted the walk and the cold. Anything to find some blessed numbness.

There would be plenty of time to think later.

36

Sidney walked into the temporary command trailer to see people moving like parts in an engine. The trailer smelled of stale coffee and printer toner. Maps with red and yellow pins flapped against the walls littered with photographs of victims, all children, and a row of monitors glowed with grainy CCTV stills. He shoved his hands into the front pockets of his jeans and rocked back on his heels out of habit, but mostly he was trying to hold himself together. The argument with Alexis replayed under everything—her voice, the slap of her words that had landed like a verdict. He'd left it behind and told himself he'd come back through it later, but it kept sneaking into his mind. Work would be the a perfect place to shove the ache aside. It had to be. Nothing else was working.

Agent Cleary arrived with the confident swagger of someone who had earned the right to cut through noise and didn't need to brag about it for everyone to know. She moved with the quiet efficiency of someone who'd shepherded chaos into order before. Her team was set up, including herself and another profiler, two analysts, and a tech with a sleeve full of cables. Others from her department and his milled about. Cleary looked at him with an assessing gaze that made him feel like an amoeba under the microscope.

"Neal," she said. "We spoke on the phone. Thanks for reaching out."

He gave a quick nod. "You have everything we've got so far," he said. "Three more victims recently, more organized this time, besides the earlier unorganized ones. Ligatures, postmortem injuries, and a flower left at each of the last three scenes, though some of those also appear in earlier murders. Witness statements are thin. No solid forensics."

The profiler, a woman with a stack of hair pinned up and eyes that looked like they'd learned to read a person's habits from a footprint, flipped the packet open and scanned the photos. She looked up at Sidney without rushing. "Does anything else stand out to you?"

Sidney walked to the map and pointed at the pins of the first murders. "The first were more opportunistic it seems," he said. "Since then, he's started leaving bodies in plain sight, often after it snows, like displays."

"I don't suppose you get much snow down here."

"Hardly ever. Maybe once or twice a year."

The profiler hummed. "A lifelong local. And evolving," she said. "An unorganized killer can become organized with time and reinforcement. They develop their rituals, hone their methods, develop a signature. Do we know if anything was taken from any of the victims? A trophy of some sort."

"Not that we know of."

"Bodies left in the snow, a flower laid on each. Maybe he's communicating something."

Sidney felt his jaw move like someone rearranging a puzzle. Communication. The word lodged. Whoever did this wanted a reaction. They wanted to be seen. He could hear the soft, dangerous thrill in that, someone testing the edges of detection and liking the way the press licked it up. Especially in a small town like St. John's. The residents could talk of little else, and he didn't even want to get started on the terror of all the parents.

Agent Cleary tapped a tablet and pulled up overlays—the map with timelines, victim information, behavior nodes. "We'll do a behavioral analysis," she said. "It will give us his playbook and how to find him."

"Hopefully," Sidney said, though he hated how wary he sounded.

"Yes, detective. Hopefully."

Sidney's chest tightened. He found himself talking, despite not knowing what to do, where he was needed, or what information they might actually need. "We have disagreements in witness statements about descriptions of the perpetrator, and sometimes I question if we're looking at one or two killers."

"Unlikely," she said without looking up.

An officer approached, and Agent Cleary leaned to the side to speak to him. Sidney pulled at the collar of his shirt, a hot flush creeping up his neck. He squeezed his eyes closed, the light from the fluorescent bulbs above suddenly too bright, their buzzing too loud. His pulse quickened, and his heart pounded. He mind raced, but he couldn't settle on a single thought. All he knew was that he couldn't breathe. He had to get out of this trailer or he'd suffocate.

Sidney made some excuse to whoever may be listening and made a hasty retreat. Hoping he'd been able to hold it together inside, he stumbled out the door and around the side of the trailer, his feet tripping over the tips of his shoes. With heaving breaths, he rested his weight against the wall. The building's shadow blanketed him and offered blessed peace. He closed his eyes and focused on his breathing.

In.

Out.

In.

And out.

When his heartbeat slowed, he found his feet moving. He wasn't sure where he was walking to, but he had to walk. Something inside him was pulling him... somewhere. The only thing he could think to do was not think at all, so he jammed his hands in his coat pocket and followed his feet.

Sidney hugged his coat tighter and watched the ocean chew at the fading light. His feet had led him all the way to the pier. He wasn't sure why, but his mind was too busy to care, so here he stood as if waiting for some greater purpose to appear before him. The wind cornered him in its mouth, sharp and accusatory, and he let it take whatever confession he hadn't yet been brave enough to name. When he realized where he'd ended up, he'd expected the ocean's waves to calm his thoughts. Instead, he found them multiplying—the faces of the children on the walls of that trailer, Alexis's face when she'd told him to leave, the way his words sounded, the way she'd folded in on herself like someone drawing a curtain.

"You look like you lost something," Ben said, dropping onto the rail beside him with the easy irreverence that was the backbone of their long friendship. He shoved a work-roughened hand into a pocket next to a crumpled half-empty pack of cigarettes. "Everything okay?"

Sidney exhaled and let the steam of his breath make a small cloud. "I messed up," he said. Saying it aloud made it more real somehow.

"What do you mean?"

"With Alexis. I messed up bad."

Ben's brows drew together, and his eyes searched his friend's face. "How bad?"

"Bad." Sidney blew out a breath looking out over the water. "I pushed her. I thought I was doing the right thing... no, that's not true. I knew it was wrong, and I did it anyway."

Ben watched him, not rushing in with solutions. That steadiness was exactly what Sidney needed. "What did you mean by 'pushed'?" Ben asked, as if coaxing a story out of someone who didn't want to tell it.

Sidney rubbed the stubble at his jaw. "Has she ever told you about anything weird happening to her?" Ben shook his head, and Sidney was tempted to tell him about the visions and his personal theories about what she could see. In the end, though, he'd betrayed her enough already. If she hadn't shared this secret—and it seemed everyone in this god forsaken small town had them—he would not do it for her. "Never mind. We had a fight, I crossed a major boundary, and then I called her selfish for having it."

"That's pretty bad," Ben agreed.

Sidney looked down and kicked the toe of his boot against the wooden pier, the dry sand making a grating, rough sound. "She deserved better."

Ben made a small noise in the back of his throat, the sound as much sympathy as curiosity. "That's a given, asshole, but was this fight the "end everything" kind of bad?"

The question landed with a weight Sidney wasn't sure he was ready to carry. "She wants freedom," he said slowly. "Not the kind of freedom that means she's never going to be there for people, but the kind where she gets to choose when and how. She doesn't want to feel pushed into anything. She wants to walk together, be invited, led even."

Ben nodded. "That sounds like her. You two have always been...different speeds, huh? There's a problem, you fix it. You have a goal, you go for it."

"Yes," Sidney said, his voice slow and his eyes watchful. He wasn't sure where Ben was going with this.

"She's more of a gardener, right? Plants things. Waits for seasons. Wants to go with the flow and not try to plan everything out?"

"Yeah." Sidney gave a humorless chuckle. "She plants snowdrops and thinks in paragraphs. I think in deadlines and checklists. I never realized I was treating her like a box to be checked."

Sidney knew there was more to the way he'd treated Alexis, more that betrayed how he'd fixated on his desires and made her feel used, but he could only say so much to Ben. Alexis would need to hear all of it, he realized. Whatever it meant for their future, she needed to hear it. He knew he couldn't salvage their relationship; he was sure of that. But maybe he could salvage a friendship. They'd shared too much to abandon that.

"You've always been a charmer with the ladies," Ben said, eyes glittering, "But you don't really understand them. You can't lead anyone anywhere if you're staring at your checklist and yanking on the damn lead."

A hot flush of defensiveness raced over his skin, but Ben was right, and shame knotted his stomach. Sidney shifted as if the act of standing itself was uncomfortable. Something prickled just beneath his skin, something that wasn't shame or anger.

Fear.

It was fear.

Because deep down Sidney didn't want to just be friends with Alexis. He didn't want to lose her at all, but he didn't want to just be friends. He wanted everything. The relationship, the life together, the big plans, the boring everyday moments. That's what he wanted, and he was terrified to admit it because what if he'd really lost it? What if there was no coming back from this?

Ben watched him carefully, seeing the play of emotions on Sidney's face, and prodded with the patience of a man who'd seen him bristle and fall apart and recompose a thousand times. "So... what are you going to do about it?"

Sidney chewed on the question. It widened. He thought about everything that had led him to this point, everything that had happened both good and bad. He imagined Alexis back in her little house going through her day with her small careful rituals, all the innocuous choices she made on her terms. What could it look like to do that together? How could they build what he wanted to build without losing themselves? Was it even possible? "I'm not sure, but I've got some time to figure it out. Give me a lift?"

Ben gave a slow, pleased smile. "Sure."

Sidney followed Ben to his car, the icy wind blowing off the water at their backs.

"What if she won't see me?" he blurted out. The question was raw and immediate, and it tumbled from his mouth like a tangled ball of yarn. "What if I blew it?"

"Then you did what you could," Ben said. "And if she wants space, you take it like a man who knows what he broke. If she wants to talk, you listen." Ben's voice held the rough tenderness of years of barstool wisdom. "Just go, Sidney. Don't make it about you. This is about her."

Sidney felt something inside him shift. Maybe it was hope. Maybe it was delusion. But it settled into him with a strange sense of warmth as the sound of lapping waves and brisk wind buffeting off the water faded behind him.

37

Alexis waved at the paperboy as he rode past the bookshop. He stood up on the pedals of his bike with paper cards clipped to the spokes. Morning light slanted through the front windows and made dust motes dance like tiny pixies over the shelves. Edgar slept in a sun puddle on the chair by the window, one hind leg splayed the way kittens do when they are entirely uncaring about where they sleep. She stretched, her soft soft, contented meow ending on a purr, and Alexis found herself smiling before she remembered she'd been trying not to smile at anything at all.

Apparently kittens were the solution to heartbreak.

She set water to boiling in the electric kettle and prepared a small mug of instant hot chocolate because she needed the small kindness for herself. Mia turned her nose up at the stuff, but she kept a small stash among the fancy teas and coffee grounds just for Alexis. She stirred it with the kind of ritual that required no thinking: rip, pour, stir. The metal spoon clinked against the sides of the mug like music.

The bell above the door jingled and Nick walked in like

Santa himself, only instead of a giant red bag of presents he held up a plastic bag as if it were a hunting trophy. He set it down like a gift. "Figured you could use some rock salt," he said. "For out front."

"What if I wanted to put it out back instead?" she teased, but she was grateful.

"Very funny," he said with a grin, wiping his hands.

"Want hot chocolate? I've got—well, only the instant stuff."

Nick peered at the coffee-and-tea bar with interest. "Instant? Do you have milk?"

"No milk." She shrugged. "Just water."

Nick made a face of mock horror. "Water? That's a crime against hot cocoa."

She grinned. "Hardly. There's probably already powdered milk in the packet."

"I don't want to think about that," he said with a shiver.

"Does that mean you don't want any?" she asked, pausing with her finger on the kettle's switch.

"I'll let you enjoy that delicacy on your own."

Alexis shrugged. "Suit yourself." She picked up her mug and walked over to a group of chairs, folding herself into one and beckoning Nick to join her.

They settled into comfortable conversation, first arguing the merits of milk versus water before Nick was catching her up on everything Mia hadn't, the book he was working on, and their plans for spring. It was deliciously trivial, like a small stitch in the day, blessedly normal and surprisingly healing.

But when he finally left, and she was alone again, she sat in the quiet of the bookstore and wondered why she still felt so hollow. She spread the rock salt out front and tended to the few customers that dropped into the store. Edgar followed like a shadow, occasionally winding around her ankles until she stroked her fur. For a while the world dwindled to the rhythm of that: the loop of a kitten's purr, the soft jingle of the door, the sound of books sliding off and on shelves.

Her thoughts, of course, found the fault line quickly enough.

Sidney.

She couldn't keep herself busy enough to stop thinking about him for long. She saw him standing at her door, the way he grinned at her face flushed after their bedroom adventures, remembered the feel of his warmth wrapped around her and his fingers stroking her hair back from her forehead. She thought about their last fight and the cruel, clumsy word he'd used—selfish—how it had landed in the space between them like a boulder heaved into a pond. It played like a repeating clip in her head.

It was easy to let her mind tell the comfortable story, that if he'd left her alone, respected her boundaries, she could have shut the visions off. She could have locked them away and kept a tidy life. A peaceful life. It would be safer, simpler. She imagined evenings uninterrupted by visions or dreams and no nosy relentless cop to push her about them. In that daydream, her visions were only background noise she could ignore rather than chasms she fell into and couldn't climb out of.

And then an inconvenient truth nudged its way into the tidy tale. What if she'd been wrong? What if the very thing she'd been resisting—accepting the whole of herself, even the parts that terrified her—was the wrong thing to turn away from? Sidney was adamant that was the correct (the only correct) path forward, that being loved didn't have to mean being contained. She'd dismissed the idea then, but now it ate at her mind like a worm chewing into a fruit. If she tried to pretend the visions weren't real, did that make them harder to bear when they came? Was shutting part of herself away doing more harm than good?

It had always seemed like the better solution. In fact, she'd always maintained that her self-control was the reason her secret was still a secret. But what if she was wrong?

The thought made her chest tighten. She told herself she was only being reasonable; she'd been hurt before. She'd learned to build walls, and walls had protected her. And the more she let them down, the most she considered maybe Sidney was right, the more a different ache crept in.

She missed him.

Not the things they did or the exploits they enjoyed together but the way his presence had become an anchor on nights when everything spun. She almost reached for her phone then. She didn't want to call him, she assured herself. All she wanted to do was send a stupid text about the hot chocolate debate. It would be an olive branch, but she stopped before she could finish typing the words. Tears pricked at the corners of her eyes, and she pressed the heel of her hand against them until stars exploded across her closed eyes.

She told herself she wouldn't be the first to call. She had more pride than that, even if it made her stubborn to be that way. Yet under the pride, doubt prickled... because maybe Sidney was right... But maybe the story she'd written where he was the villain wasn't the whole truth either. Maybe acceptance, as terrifying and messy as it was sure to be, was part of the answer. The possibility was both untenable and not entirely unbearable.

She set the empty cup down and let her fingers trace the rim for a moment, listening to the quiet. Edgar hopped into her lap, her tiny paws feeling like miniature daggers digging into Alexis' thighs.

"You're judging me," she said to the cat.

The creature simply settled into a seat and stared at her with steady insistence. Alexis stared back through slitted eyes, her mouth pressed into a firm line, but she didn't have the opportunity to say more. The vision slammed into her with the force of a speeding train. This was not the fuzzy, remote glimpse she'd sometimes get, an impression or a smell that could be shrugged off. No, this was cinematic, intimate, and horrifying in its engulfing.

Reality melted away and there was only her own body.

She stared down at her own hands. They were the first and only thing she could see, and they were pale, shaking, and reaching. Reaching for something. For what? Then she saw it: her phone. Black against her tan palms. She was both inside and outside her body, watching and being watched at once. She smelled old wood and dust, but when she looked around there were shadows everywhere. A few thin streaks of light speared through her vision, each one filled with thick clouds of dancing specks.

She smelled the sweet chemical scent before she saw the shadow coming down over her face. It was huge and loomed over her like some monster hovering over a child's bed. Her mouth filled with something sour and metallic, and her throat tightened. She tried to scream, to pull away, to draw in a breath that didn't make her head spin, but it was no use. She could only make a wet, choked noise. She sank down with a heavy thud, a tea set falling to the floor beside her and shattering. A thin cord came around her neck, there was a sharp pain as it was pulled tight, and then there was nothing but pain and fear.

This was it. She knew it. This was her last moment on this earth. This was how she died.

She gasped and ripped her eyes open, finding herself bent over on all fours on the bookshop floor. Her fingers dug into the thin carpet as if she might find some stability there. Objects around her came back into focus in small, merciful bursts.

Instinct had her standing and orienting herself as soon as she was steady enough. If Sidney was, in fact, right about her visions, then this one meant something. She shivered at the thought. If it was real, she worried she'd been witness to her own death. She grabbed at her phone, fingers fumbling but determined. Her thumb found Sidney's name, but for a moment she felt ridiculous. Perhaps she was overreacting.

She lowered the phone, wondering if she should just slip it back into her pocket when a sound like fabric on wood, a soft displacement of air, whispered in the air behind her. Before she could react, a rag was pressed against her mouth and nose.

It smelled the same as the vision: sickly sweet and clinical. Her jaw clamped down on nothing, and she tasted the copper of her own panic. She tried to fight, but the strength was gone from her limbs, and the darkness folded in around her. Her phone, once clenched in her hand, slipped and bounced against the floor with a series of hollow thuds. Edgar's yowl shredded the air, sharp and panicked, but the sound was thin and tinny in her ears.

Then the darkness closed around her completely, and everything folded into the quiet of nothingness.

38

___

"You okay?" Ben asked, glancing over at Sidney in the passenger seat as the trees blinked past. He had the easy cadence of someone who'd known Sidney long enough to read the man's silence.

"I've got a bad feeling," Sidney said without turning his head. He didn't want to name it. He didn't want to logic it away with some intellectual explanation. There was an icy knot in his gut, and every moment spent in the truck felt like one moment too long.

Ben's jaw tightened in a way that replaced curiosity with worry. He'd known Sidney too long not to take his gut feelings seriously. He pushed the truck forward, and the town blurred into a string of buildings and cars and people. The silence between them was its own pressure, a witness to the turmoil of a man who could think of nothing but how to save the greatest thing that had ever come into his life.

Only he wasn't sure she also wanted to save it.

He certainly didn't believe he was the best thing that had come into her life, but that was an insecurity to address at another time. As they drove, Sidney tried to pin the anxiety down to something reasonable: nerves from the argument, the immediate need to repair the break he'd made with Alexis, the guilt about the way things had fallen apart, fear that he couldn't fix it this time. He wanted to rehearse what he would say to her, but he knew he needed to give her the space to talk and feel and decide. He wanted to make wild promises, to offer her the moon if only she'd give him another chance. He wanted to beg her to let him try, to show her they could balance this push and pull dance they were in, to dance together instead of letting it destroy them.

And he told himself that it would be enough if she only gave him enough time to hear her out and never speak to her again. If that's what she truly wanted. He hoped for more. He hoped for friendship at the bare minimum, but he wanted more, and he would not be ashamed of that.

Still, no matter how he tried to cast blame on his thoughts and anxieties, the knot in his stomach grew. It pulsed like a second heartbeat. He could feel it as Ben turned into Alexis's driveway. A hollow tightening, a wrongness that defied logic and sense. The house sat small and quiet under the gray light of winter. The mailbox wore its ring of white snowdrops like a crown at its feet. Sidney caught his breath at the sight of those blooms, stubborn signs of life standing proud while the earth slept around them.

He looked at the house, and his brows drew together. "Something's wrong," he said, throwing the door of the truck open. His boots thudded against the concrete as he jumped out of the truck and ran up the walk.

He pounded on the front door with a fist in a series of rapid bangs. "Alexis!" He shouted the name the way you throw a rope to someone drifting out to sea.

No answer. The house gave back only its own hush. Sidney

pressed his shoulder to the wood, but the lock was solid. The door didn't budge. He peered through the nearest window and found only dark interiors and the furniture's silhouettes. He stepped back, and the quiet of the night enveloped the house. It had a wrongness to it, as if the place had all the life sucked out of it.

Ben's voice echoed through the open window of the truck behind him, clipped with worry. "Sidney... what is it?"

Then Sidney flung open the door, and he all but leaped back into the seat. "Drive to the bookshop. Now."

The truck's engine kicked, and Ben's hands were steady as they cut across town, tires kicking up thin sheets of ice that had settled into the dips and cracks of the road from the rain the night before. Sidney's thumb danced across the screen of his phone and found Alexis' number on its own, but she didn't answer. Again he tried to call. Again, there was no answer. Over and over, the calls piled up into silence. He tried calling the shop's main number. It should have been open, but again there was no answer.

"Anything?" Ben asked, but Sidney shook his head. "Mia didn't pick up either."

No sooner had he said it than Ben's phone started ringing. He answered it before the second ring, holding the phone to his ear as he navigated the half-frozen streets of downtown St. John's.

"Is Alexis with you?" Ben said into the phone. "No, nothing to worry about yet. Sidney couldn't get in touch with her, is all. I'll call you back soon. Promise."

Sidney looked at Ben expectantly, hoping against all hope that he would hear what he wanted to hear, but Ben shook his head. So that was that, then. Alexis wasn't at home. She wasn't with Mia, and she wasn't answering her phone. Where was she?

They slid to a stop outside the bookstore, and Sidney told Ben to keep the engine running. "Stay," he said, his voice flat. It was not a request. He moved with the same suppressed calm he used on scene: method, not panic.

The air felt wrong the moment he stepped out of the truck. Instinct had him drawing his gun from the holster inside his waistband. He peered through the glass at the front of the shop. Lights burned inside, illuminating a stack of books still sitting on the counter and mugs sitting lonely on a table at the center, as if someone had left in a hurry.

He tried the door. Locked. He looked across the room and saw—impossible in itself—Alexis' phone lying face down in the middle of the floor, a small rectangle of abandonment. No bag, no jacket. A chair overturned.

Edgar pawed the glass and howled louder than he imagined a small kitten could, and the sound set his skin to prickling with its thin, brittle edge. It was as if the cat knew something. Why else would it be here all alone? Alexis would never leave it by itself here. The kitten's cry made Sidney's chest tighten, and he promised her he would find Alexis. Not that the cat could hear or even understand him, but it felt important to say it aloud.

Adjusting his grip on his weapon, Sidney stepped back from the locked door and surveyed his surroundings. The truck rumbled behind him, and there were distant sounds of people moving from place to place, but he took a deep breath and closed it all out. His training narrowed into a sequence of steps, and he followed them. He scanned the shop's windows, the alley between the buildings, the concrete walkway in front of the shop.

It appeared someone, perhaps Alexis, had spread rock salt on the ground just outside the shop. The application wasn't what he would call even—haphazard or rushed, he'd say—but it was more sparse in one direction. Sidney followed the disturbance, noting that it led toward the antique shop next door. He inched closer and saw that its door was not quite shut. The deadbolt protruded, but the frame wasn't flush with the door. It was strange, and he didn't believe in coincidences.

He edged toward it, gun held in front of him, breath counted. He leaned into the door with his shoulder, careful to ease his weight into it slowly. It resisted only a moment, then it moved without a soft sigh.

Inside, the smell of old enveloped his senses—old paper, linseed oil, leather, and wood. On the counter, half-hidden under a pile of dust rags and a spread of catalog cards, lay a white kerchief, crumpled and used. He cocked his head to the side, his eyes checking the room before he allowed himself to focus his attention on it. There, in a flourish of red embroidered initials, appeared the letters A.B. More connections.

His throat went dry. A noise from the back, a quiet thud and shuffling, caught his attention. He stared through the dim light, one hand releasing the gun and pulling his phone from his back pocket.

"It's Neal. I'm at Baker's Antiques. Suspected abduction and potential hostage situation. Request immediate backup." He kept his voice flat and focused. Panic wouldn't serve him.

When he moved, gun up, each step was soft on the worn floorboards. He wound his way through the aisles until he reached a door at the back of the shop. A narrow sliver of light leaked from under that door, thin and sharp as the blade of a knife. Sidney's years in uniform, all of his training, and every instinct in his body bristled at the edge of readiness. He eased into the room, hoping to take stock of the situation with a calculated eye. Instead, the sight slammed into him like a blast of heat straight to the face, so immediate and overwhelming that it robbed him of breath.

A man hunched over a body. He was not young, nor was he the creature of madness Sidney had sometimes pictured in his nightmares. He was Alan Baker, the owner of Baker's Antiques, and he was leaning over Alexis, hands fixed on a thin metal wire around her throat. Alexis sagged in a heap on the floor, breaths sharp and rasping. She pushed at the man with all the fading strength she could muster, her feet barely kicking. And yet, she still fought. With everything she still had, she fought.

"Police!" Sidney's command was sharp and loud, a punch in the air.

Alan spun around at the sound. His face was white with exertion, and his eyes flashed and darted around the room. His movements were like those of a frantic prey animal cornered by its fiercest predator. The cord around Alexis' neck loosened, and Sidney heard her drag in a gasping breath cut short when Alan yanked on the cord again. The air between them filled with deadly tension. Only one of them was leaving this room alive, and they both knew it. Alan dragged Alexis back against him, using her body as a makeshift shield, and the cord's lines pressed red into her skin.

"Let her go," Sidney said, voice pure and precise.

Alan's face split into a thing that had no softness left. "No," he said, his breathing labored. "She is mine. My escape." The words were jagged, desperate, and small. He yanked at the garrote, pulling it tighter until she was gasping once again. "Move out of my way, or I will strangle her."

Sidney calculated how long Alexis could survive, how long until she was unconscious. It wasn't long. There was no time for negotiation, and he did not lower his weapon. "I can't do that, Alan. You've hurt a lot of people."

Alan's humorless laugh was an ugly sound, airless and brittle. He held Alexis closer as if her body could steady both of them, but Sidney could see that the weight of her was too much for the old man.

"You have nothing. You'll connect me to nothing." There was no pleading, no measure of remorse, only the arrogance of cold conviction.

Sidney thought of the handkerchief, of Alexis' visions. He wasn't sure what he had other than the feeling deep in his gut that this was his guy. This was the man who'd ended so many innocent lives. It wasn't up to him to figure out exactly how it all connected yet. Right now, getting Alexis out alive was his only prerogative.

"You're making a mistake," Sidney said. "You don't have to do this. Let her go, and you'll walk out of here. Do it now, or I take the offer off the table."

Alan's knuckles whitened around the handle attached to either end of the garrote. Alexis clawed weakly at the cord around her neck, fingers dragging desperately at her skin as she slipped into darkness. Her eyes rolled as she fought to stay connected to air, and she sagged against the old man's fraying grip.

Sidney had no interest in theatrics. He was running out of time. Alexis was running out of time. "Last chance, Baker," he said.

Alan's eyes flicked to Sidney's gun and then to Alexis, and for the briefest moment a flash of fear washed over him, and the mask of arrogance dropped. Then his jaw hardened, and he heaved Alexis against him again, dragging her along as he inched around the wall of the room. Alan's hands shook as he struggled to maintain pressure around her throat, and then Alexis's body slackened, and his hold failed. She crumpled in his arms like a rag doll, and the old man couldn't support the sudden weight of her. Her body slid to the floor, leaving Alan open and stunned. The garrote slipped from his fingers and went slack around her neck.

Sidney did not hesitate. The decision closed around him with the thick finality of heavy theater curtains dropping upon a hollow stage. He squeezed the trigger and fired one shot, a single explosion ripping through the air between them. The bullet punched into Alan's chest and red bloomed across his shirt. Alan staggered into the desk behind him, a ragged sound tearing from his throat. His eyes were wide as his legs crumpled beneath him.

Sidney grabbed Alexis under the arm and dragged her to the room, his eyes trained on Alan as his chest shuddered with his final breaths. Sidney pressed his fingertips to the side of Alexis' next, searching for a pulse that would prove she was still alive. It fluttered under his fingers like a small bird in danger. He shouted her name, slapping the sides of her face until he could see her breath coming in small gasps once again. They were fragile, but they were there. He braced his hands under her shoulders and lifted her body to adjust her position against him.

He did not celebrate nor relax. He simply held her to his body and closed his eyes against the horrors of it all, the end brought on not by trial or justice but by simple necessity and the bitter math of choices. Sidney stared at Alan, at the man who had killed countless children and almost Alexis. Tomorrow he would finish putting the pieces together, figure out how to put this in front of the court without putting a psychic on trial. Today, he was simply glad it was over.

Sidney heard the door of the shop open and a rush of offi-cers flooded in. "Back here. Suspect is down. Victim alive but thready," he yelled. He could barely think straight.

He held Alexis as if presence could steady what force had

broken. His chest became raw with each breath. He felt responsible for her, for this. He had crossed lines, putting her in harm's way. This was his fault. Somehow, someway, he'd put her in the crossfire, but he would keep her safe. Forever safe. It was his sworn duty, the least he owed her after all this. He repeated it over and over in his head, his silent promise to her.

39

Her first awareness was of sound—the slap of a heavy body against the floor, a single gunshot ringing through the air, a far-away yell—fragments without context or meaning. She pried open her heavy eyelids, and even the dim light was an assault on her senses. Then the world slowly stitched itself back together, and Alexis looked around, trying to focus. The edges of her vision burned like an overexposed photograph. Every breath felt wrong, a burning sensation from her lips to her throat.

She didn't know where she was, and she had no memory of how she'd gotten here. Frowning, she tried to remember. There was Nick's face, Edgar meowing incessantly, the feel of the kitten winding around her legs, cold wind and salt. Then there was nothing. Darkness and a sickly sweet smell and a burning that filled her lungs.

A warm hand was steady on her shoulder. "Alexis," someone said. She turned and realized it was Sidney's voice pulling her from her spotty memories. He leaned in, his face pulled tight with worry. "Can you hear me? Look at me."

She tried. Sharp gravel packed her throat. She tried to answer, but the sound that came out was a raw, hoarse whistle that burned as it left her. She wanted to say his name, to ask him what had happened, but the effort turned to splinters in her throat. The world around her rearranged into the shape of people in uniform moving like slow machinery. A light flashed across her vision as someone measured her pupil response, and another person fussed with a collar around her neck. Her body was moved and manipulated, but it didn't feel like her own.

Sidney's hand was under her neck, fingers steady and purposeful. "You're going to be okay," he said low, as if repeating the sentence could make it true.

Voices orbited them—calls for a stretcher, a paramedic asking for an Ambu bag—words and objects that were alien to her mind and aching body. Her hands trembled. Her vision blurred and her eyes rolled from face to the ground. She spotted the cord that lay in a dark coil on the floor next to her. Even in the blur it looked obscene, a thick wire with wooden handles at each end scored with age and stained with dirt and oils from the hands that used it.

Her eyes widened and flew from the metal cord to Sidney and back again. She tried to ask him about it. She needed to know, needed to hear that the thing that had nearly killed her was the same that had ended so many other lives. The question came out in a tiny, broken thread. "Did he use that—" Her voice failed, and she couldn't find the end of the sentence. She didn't know whether that was because of her injuries, or if she simply couldn't bear to finish the question.

Sidney grabbed her hand, squeezing it in his, and his eyes went hard with the answer neither one of them wanted to be true. "Yes, I think so."

His words landed in her chest like a stone, and her stomach rolled. She stared at the garrote, at the wire and the handles, at the wood worn smooth over years. Nausea rose like a tide. Her stomach wrenched, and she vomited, her body convulsing with horror and revulsion.

Sidney turned her head gently, hand steady at the base of her skull, and she retched until she was empty. His touch was calm and efficient, with practiced movements, and it steadied her. A napkin was wiped across her mouth, and then she was moved carefully onto a stretcher. A medic clipped an oxygen mask in place over her face, and there was a hiss of cold air suddenly pushing into her nose.

She looked around, but the room wavered as dizziness swept over her. Sidney's face hovered near her with an intensity that made her feel both guarded and seen. There was a possessive way that he watched now—less ownership than a desperate protectiveness—and it made the surrounding chaos bearable for a sliver of a second.

The back doors of the ambulance opened to the chill air, and the winter wind hit her face as they lifted her out onto the sidewalk. People gathered behind a line of yellow tape, their gazes morbidly curious and concerned at once. Her gaze traveled over them, and then she saw, like an accusation, a pot of snowdrops in front of the antique shop. She realized she was being wheeled out of that very shop, and for the briefest moment he wondered where Alan was, if he was alright.

Realization came flooding over her with horror as she remembered the way he'd looked at him, the way his hands had pulled tight the metal around her neck. Her eyes fixed on a pot outside the door, and she saw them: tiny white cups bobbing on thin stems, small and stubbornly blooming in a season that didn't seem for them, brave and absurd.

Snowdrops.

Then a flash from the vision tore her mind open: the same tiny white flowers, placed on a child's chest with the same hands she'd seen so close to her neck. Horror took her all at once. She could feel the chemical burning her nose, smell its sickly sweet scent, see the pale handkerchief. The pieces came together with a small, savage clarity. A.B., Alan Baker. She'd been working beside him, dropping in to check up on him, sharing lunch with him... all while he was doing... that to all those children. Children! The knowledge was a knife in her side.

If Sidney had pressed her for visions, she thought in a jagged rush, he'd had good cause. Maybe if she'd been less stubborn, if she had allowed her gift to be used like one, maybe she could have pointed them to this man sooner. Maybe she could have stopped him. Guilt, so hot and sharp, swept over her, and she felt nauseous all over again. She had denied that her visions were real for so long to protect herself. Yet now that denial was an active wound, her peace bought with the lives and suffering of innocent children. Panic surged with bright terror.

Sidney saw the change in her before she could make coherent words. His hand tightened on her shoulder. "Are you all right?" he asked.

She tried to answer, but her vision blurred, and the image of snowdrops swam at the edges of her sight, an accusation bathed in white. Her world narrowed, and then everything tightened and slackened. The world folded away as a uniformed woman draped a thermal blanket over her body, and the hum of Sidney's voice faded into the background. When the blackness finally came, it was heavy and total.

40

Home. Finally.

Alexis pushed open her front door and almost cried with relief. She was home. Her throat still ached every time she swallowed, a raw ribbon of pain and tenderness where the cord had bitten, and a pale red crescent of laid over bruises of purple and black. She moved slower than usual, each small motion careful as if she were teaching her body how to be a body again.

She smiled when she spied her couch. On it, folded precisely and impossibly neat, was a crocheted blanket in colors that someone's grandmother might have chosen—apricot, sea glass, and mossy green. Atop it sat a paper flower, a ridiculously happy little yellow thing, and a Get Well Soon card, no envelope. Alexis picked up the card and read the familiar looping handwriting inside, Harper's familiar, earnest script. Alexis smiled through happy tears as she read the note. Harper spoke of cleaning the house and making her the blanket. She even apologized for the hideous colors (it was apparently the only yarn the craft had in stock in the amount she needed) but assured her what it lacked in beauty it made up for in softness. Harper had also taken care of Edgar and sang the kitten's praises.

The note was signed:

Call me if you need anything at all. —H.

Speak of the devil, Alexis thought as a meow erupted across the house, the sound so furious in its intensity that she couldn't help but laugh, the sound breaking like a brittle bell. Edgar launched herself into her lap as if the world had been on hold and now allowed, pushing at her face and neck ferociously and emitting a frenzied purr that vibrated through her ribs. Alexis buried her face in Edgar's fur and let the smell of her wrap itself around her. Her laugh was as much a laugh as it was a sob, and she felt ridiculous and grateful in equal measure. She was alive. She was home. Edgar was here. All was right in the world.

Well, nearly.

She shrugged out of her coat one arm at a time so as not to put down the cat, letting it drop where she stood, the weight oddly freeing. She stepped out of her shoes easily enough, walking across her tiny house with a building surety, as if she reclaimed that safe, small, private feeling of home.

Alexis moved toward the bathroom with the single-mindedness of someone who wanted hot water to remap a hurt body and bring the mind back to sanity. The shower was an endless small mercy, and the heat washed the hospital smell from her skin, loosened the ache in her muscles. Steam filled the room, and for a handful of moments, she let herself float on the steam until there was no more hot water.

Stepping from the shower, she wrapped a towel around her body and was squeezing the last of the water from her curls when there was a short, deliberate knock at the door. The sound made her heart stutter. Her fingers paused, and the edge of the towel she'd been holding beneath her arm slipped. She scrambled to grab it, tucking it into the top of itself, and stood there for a breath too long, listening. Her body hadn't been able to relax since the incident, and she saw being startled as a new reflex, albeit hopefully a temporary one.

The knock came again—firm, not furtive.

She pulled the towel up and moved to the door, each step hesitant but measured. Her throat rasped when she swallowed, and she looked out the window facing her front porch before moving to the door. Sidney stood on the other side, his body held patiently still. Letting out a sigh of relief, she opened the door, and there he was—Sidney—holding a small bouquet. Sprays of violets, yellow daisies, some ranunculus, all papery and peach. He held them with both hands as if the flowers had weight beyond their stems.

Her face must have given something away because Sidney smiled that crooked half-grin. "Mia said you were back," he said.

"Were you checking up on me?" She tried for light and landed on guarded. It wasn't exactly what she wanted to say, but she was so tired. It was the best she could do. She cleared her throat. It hurt. The ache reminded her she'd been very close to not coming back at all.

Sidney shrugged clumsily. "Of course," he said. He was trying to be smooth, easy, to embody the suave side of him that was ever so charming. Instead, he was almost stiff and awkward. He looked at her as if he wished he knew what to do to make things right.

Alexis wished she knew what to tell him, but she hadn't figured it out herself either. Still, she didn't want to be rude. She stepped back and let him come in. For a moment they simply stood inside the door, the two of them in a world full of unspoken words and unshared feelings. In the middle of it all, the bouquet was bright and absurd.

"Do you want soup?" she asked because the question felt domestically mundane enough to bridge the bitter gap. Her voice was hoarse; he flinched at the sound of it.

He opened his mouth and then closed it. "I brought flowers," he said, a little sheepishly.

"Yes," she said slowly, gesturing to the kitchen behind her. "But do you want soup?"

"Oh, uh, well," Sidney stuttered and cleared his throat. "That is to say, no, thank you. I already ate."

Alexis shrugged and said, "Suit yourself. Why are you here?"

"To see you."

She took a deep breath, her chest rising as it filled. "Look, I just got home, and I'm beyond exhausted, so unless you're going to put me to bed, can we please do this later?"

Sidney paused for a moment, taking in the hoarse rasp of her voice, the dark circles beneath her eyes. Then a mischievous sparkle lit his eyes, and he stepped toward her. "Your wish is my command," he said.

Her brows drew together, but a smile tugged at her lips. The flowers dropped to the floor, and suddenly Sidney was hoisting her into his arms. "Wait, what about my flowers?" Alexis said, muffling a giggle and looking over his shoulder at the bouquet abandoned on the floor.

Sidney just kept walking toward the bedroom. "I'll buy you more."

His breath warmed the bruise at her throat, and for a moment she forgot to keep her guard up. She let herself rest her head on his shoulder, the small, dangerous pleasure of being physically held after horror. "I suppose I'll let you," she heard herself say, the words slipping out from some vulnerable place that only wanted to be held like this.

He laid her gently on the bed and tucked the surrounding covers with a tenderness she hadn't expected from a man used to sirens and flashlights and adrenaline. There was always a roughness between them—tangled blankets, breathless arrangements, pushing the limits of their bodies and minds—but tonight his touch was careful, reverent almost. He sat at the edge of the bed and fussed with the edge of the blanket.

"Can we talk?" he asked, tentative in a way that made her heart fold.

"You can," she replied, and the joke was in the tone. She pointed to her throat. It didn't take a rocket scientist to figure out that she would be less loquacious than usual.

He nodded, and after a small silence, he exhaled, the confession pouring out faster than he probably intended. "This is my fault, all of this. I'm sorry. I had more to say, but now you're staring at me, and I don't have the right words anymore. Maybe I never did. I don't know how to fix this, but I want to, and I'm sorry."

She watched the shape of his mouth as he spoke, the way his face changed and his body sank into itself. He looked brittle and real, vulnerable and human. There was a rawness emanating from him, and it made something in her ease. Maybe because she felt raw, too.

She reached for his hand. The skin was warm and calloused, and his fingers closed around hers like a promise. She wanted to trust in that, though she wasn't sure how. They sat like that for a while, hands laced, watching the small motes of dust spin in the dim light of her bedroom.

When Sidney's voice came again, it was quieter. "I don't expect forgiveness. I was afraid, and I felt helpless, and I nearly sacrificed you for it. I was wrong."

"Did he really do it?" she asked, because she had to.

Sidney nodded. "Yes. We found more evidence connecting him to the murders."

The knowledge landed with its own kind of ugly relief. The man who had haunted her visions, who haunted her nightmares now, was gone. Guilty, dead, gone. Relief threaded with horror at what had been done, the lives ended, and Alexis felt tears prick at the corners of her eyes.

"Then it was worth it," she said after a breath, the words strange in her mouth. "Not that I would do it that way again, but maybe... maybe you were right about the things I see."

Sidney watched her carefully. "I understand," he said softly, but she shook her head.

"No. I don't think you do. Not yet." She lifted her fingers and traced the back of his hand with a slow touch. "I want to forgive you. I want to mean it. But I need you to move slowly. I need slow. I like slow."

He closed his fingers over hers and understood what she was asking for under the words. She needed more than pretty apologies. She needed him to show that he could be safe, constant.

"I can do slow," he said, and she wanted to believe there was a steadiness in his voice. He squeezed her hand, then picked it up, kissed her palm, and pressed it to his cheek reverently. "You smell delicious," he added, the ridiculousness of the comment making them both laugh.

"Be grateful you got here after my shower then," she quipped, the dry humor a stitch in the seam of her heart.

He grinned—crooked tooth flashing—and with a boyish flourish he dived into the bed beside her. For a moment they wrestled with blankets and bodies until they were comfortably cuddled up together. Laughter eased something taut in her, like a muscle loosening after a knot teases free, and they settled into the quiet.

Eventually, Sidney asked, "Are you hungry?"

She nodded, but when he swung his legs off the bed to head to the kitchen, she grabbed his wrist and tugged him back with a pointed look. "Not that kind of hungry," she said, lips quirked.

His brow creased, searching. He leaned in, eyes asking a better question than words could manage. She closed the space between them and kissed him long and hard. When they parted, his eyes were shining wet with emotion.

"I love you." He said it without pretense or ornament while cupping her cheek with hands that could've just as easily been holding the world's greatest treasure, and it wouldn't have felt any different to him. "I love all of you. Every part. Always."

She let the weight of his words settle within her. He was offering her a love that was not conditional, not a performance or a grade, a love that would not demand the parts of her she feared to show, a love that promised choice and respect.

"I love you," she said finally, her response simple and fierce. "Every part. Always."

EPILOGUE

"Are you ready?" Sidney asked as he leaned around the door frame and peered into the back room. Alexis was just stepping out of the shower, and he wiggled his eyebrows at her with a grin.

"Clearly, I'm not. Now get on outta here. You're letting all the steam out," she said, though she couldn't help but grin. Over a year since he'd moved in, and the man could still make her giggle and blush.

Sidney was in the kitchen by the time she finished—jawline dusted with the shadow of a beard, hair mussed in a way that was, she knew, deliberately careless. He was rummaging through the drawer when he noticed her standing there in the dress she'd worn the first night they met, the one that clung to every curve and had him salivating just as it had from the start. He glanced up and smiled, the small, crooked thing she had loved from the start. Whatever task he'd been doing was quickly forgotten, the drawer abandoned and left open.

"Hi," he said.

"Hi yourself. Are you ready?" she asked.

Sidney moved to her slow and smooth, his hand gliding over the curve of her hip as he pulled her in close. "We could just stay in, you know."

She smiled and leaned her head to the side, opening her neck for him and letting his mouth trace the line of her jaw and down her neck. "Mmm, and miss the fun we've got planned tonight?"

"That's the thing," Sidney said in a voice husky with arousal. "We've already had this fun once."

His lips found the sensitive hollow of her neck, and then his teeth were nipping at her flesh. Alexis gasped, her pulse quickening and the flesh between her thighs throbbing in response. "True, but you promised me a roleplay night, and we've already roped Ben into our plan."

Sidney groaned playfully and stepped back. "When I said roleplay, I was thinking more like Slave Leia," he said with a laugh.

"Yup, but you got suckered into recreating the night we met instead. Sucks for you." Alexis punctuated her sentence by standing on her tiptoes and licking the tip of his nose before dancing off to find her shoes.

Sidney shook his head, amused by her antics and more than willing to join in on the fun tonight. "Maybe I'll get lucky this time."

"You could've then, too, if you weren't such a gentleman," she sang, slipping her feet into her heels and lifting each in turn to adjust the strap.

"Officer Do-Good, I believe you called me," he said as if he didn't remember exactly what she'd called him.

Alexis stood, now properly shod, and shimmied her hips to readjust her dress. "Indeed," she said, remembering the nickname as well.

"Speaking of—don't forget to write what you dreamed

about the other night for the case," he said, half-joking, half professional.

She laughed, picking a cat hair off the fabric at her breast. "I got it. I thought you'd be less of a workaholic as a PI, you know."

He gave her the half-stern, half-amused look she expected. It was a conversation they had often, and though she poked at him about his work habits, he knew she didn't really mind. Not nowadays, that is.

"Yeah, yeah, yeah. But even so, better work-life balance," he said. "I'm going now. Don't be late."

She watched him pretend to walk around her and leave with a raised brow, laughing when he did just as she expected and ducked back to kiss the corner of her mouth.

"See you later," he said.

"Mmm, see you."

The door clicked shut behind her, and excitement fizzed in her limbs. They had fussed and planned this for weeks. Ben was in on it as the obliging bartender, and they'd both agreed to reprise their roles as a drunken woman at the bar and off-duty cop helping the little lady get home safe.

When she strode into the bar, it was already warm with bodies and light, and the music created an atmosphere that welcomed you in. Ben moved behind the bar, sleeves rolled up, his movements the same ritual he'd been doing that night so very long ago and every working night since. He caught her eye and tipped an imaginary hat to her with a grin. She slid onto the stool and let the noise fold around her. She ordered the same drink: a glass of the house white wine.

Sidney arrived a few minutes later, looking every bit the man who could fill a room without trying—handsome and slightly undone in a way that made her heart break open with fondness—but she pretended not to notice, and he didn't acknowledge her. They all had their part to play.

Butterflies danced in her stomach, and she sipped her wine as naturally as she could, watching the people come and go, leaning into the conversations around her as she saw fit.

When she had nearly finished her glass, Ben walked over to her seat at the bar and said, "Now, darlin.' I'm going to have to cut you off now."

Alexis gave a mock sigh and grinned, propping her chin in her hand. "And why's that?"

"Well, because you've had one too many, and it just wouldn't be right for me to give you more," he said.

Alexis smiled. "Call me a cab?"

"I'll do you one better." Ben leaned toward the far end of the bar and asked, "Hey, Sid, do me a favor?"

"I thought I told her never to call me that," Sidney said, the corner of his mouth lifting in amusement.

Ben gestured at Alexis with his head. "Will you make sure this one gets home?"

"Sure, I'm leaving anyway." He stood and moved toward her, and Alexis swore he'd never looked so dark, so dangerous.

Or so sexy.

Ben turned back to Alexis. "Lex, this is Sidney Neal, a detective over in Candler County. He'll get you home tonight," he said with a wink.

Alexis stood, and Sidney took her elbow as if it would stabilize her. In truth, she wasn't unsteady from alcohol. She'd barely had any. Rather, her head was swimming with desire.

"So you're Officer Do-Good, huh?"

"Yes, ma'am. Alright if I take you home?"

"No, you'll do."

Sidney grinned as if he were also remembering how the night had gone. They walked to his car, and he held the door for her. Alexis slid into the passenger side and relaxed into the seat. The drive was the same route, of course. They rounded the same corner, drove beneath the same streetlights, rolled over the same small cracked paving stones. This time, though, there was no drunken talk of exes and relationships ending. There was only them and their entire future of possibilities ahead.

Alexis watched Sidney in the passenger seat as the lights they passed danced over his face. His profile was a study in calmness, and she cherished the peace and consistency he brought to her life. When they were finally home, the butterflies had evolved into ravenous dragons clawing their way out of her insides. It was the only way to describe the nerves racing through her body. He walked her to the door just as he'd done before, and Alexis unlocked the door.

Then she turned, sank back against it, and pulled Sidney against her, placing his hand on her hip and looking up at him from under her lashes. His fingers tightened their grip on her, and his pulse hammered at his throat. She pushed her hips seductively against his.

"Thanks for tonight," she said, her lips so close to his that she could feel his hot breath on hers.

"Aren't you forgetting something?" he asked.

Alexis cocked her head and scrunched her lips to the side, a mischievous look on her face. "No, I don't think so."

"Don't you want me to stay with you tonight? Scare away the nightmares?" he teased.

"Oh, you're right..." and her voice trailed off as her hand dipped into the neckline of her dress.

Sidney blinked, caught between performance and disbelief, when she drew from her bra two gold bands. They were smooth, unadorned circles, honest and beautiful in their simplicity. He laughed a breathless little sound that was more shock than humor, and she held the rings out, palms open.

"Will you stay with me tonight?" she asked.

Sidney took the ring with trembling fingers and slipped it on his hand, looking at the simple gold against his skin as if it were the most precious metal ever to have been mined from this earth. He took the other ring and slid it onto her finger. "Always."

Sidney pulled her into his arms, and Alexis breathed a sigh of relief. Relief from what, she wasn't sure, but as the anxiety left her body, a warmth grew and made her feel as if she were glowing. His cheek rested on the top of her head, his arms wrapped around her. A few moments later, he pulled back a small distance and grinned in the crooked, boyish way that could make her laugh even on their worst nights.

"Does this mean we're going to the courthouse tomorrow?" he asked, half-teasing, half-hopeful.

"You better believe it," she said. "You're stuck with me."

And she finally felt, with a clarity that had nothing to do with mystical powers or psychic visions, that there was nowhere else she'd rather be stuck than right here, with him, in the warm center of a life chosen together.

BONUS CONTENT

For a bonus threesome scene and a playlist inspired by the
book, visit SelenaCollins.com/snow/#bonus

ALSO BY SELENA COLLINS

St. John's Secrets

Small town romance, big secrets.

Book 1: Dream of Me

Book 2: When the Snow Falls

Book 3: To Catch a Curse

SelenaCollins.com/secrets

TO CATCH A CURSE

Read Harper's story in Book Three!

Harper Abernathy is a simple woman who loves her cat, cooking, and crochet... she's also a witch.

And cursed.

When she's recruited to show the mysterious new guy around town, sparks fly, and a long-buried secret awakens.

Read Harper's story at SelenaCollins.com/curse

ABOUT THE AUTHOR

Selena Collins is an author of contemporary romance who likes her characters strong and her happily ever afters spicy. Her work is often sprinkled with suspense, fantasy, and paranormal elements, making for sensual stories with a dash of "other."

Selena is a widow living outside of Atlanta, Georgia with her children and their zoo of pets.

In her spare time, she makes silly videos on the internet, shares behind the scenes on her website, finds new hobbies constantly, and is terrible at texting people back.

To learn more, read other books by Selena, or stalk her social media (in a non-creepy way, please and thank you), visit SelenaCollins.com.